FORBIDDEN
CONFESSIONS

VOLUME 1

SHAYLA BLACK

FORBIDDEN Confessions
Volume 1

New York Times
Bestselling Author

SHAYLA BLACK

Steamy. Emotional. Forever.

CONTENTS

More Than Want You
Wicked as Sin
About Shayla Black
Other Books by Shayla Black

FORBIDDEN CONFESSIONS, VOLUME 1
Written by Shayla Black

SEDUCING THE INNOCENT © 2019 by Shelley Bradley LLC
SEDUCING THE BRIDE © 2020 by Shelley Bradley LLC
SEDUCING THE STRANGER © 2020 by Shelley Bradley LLC
SEDUCING THE ENEMY © 2020 by Shelley Bradley LLC

This book is an original publication by Shayla Black.

Copyright 2020 Shelley Bradley LLC

Cover Design by: Rachel Connolly
Edited by: Amy Knupp of Blue Otter
Proofread by: Fedora Chen

Excerpt from *More Than Want You* © 2017 by Shelley Bradley LLC

Excerpt from *Wicked as Sin* © 2020 by Shelley Bradley LLC

ISBN: 978-1-936596-70-6

SEDUCING THE *Innocent*

A Forbidden Confession

SHAYLA BLACK

Steamy. Emotional. Forever.

ABOUT SEDUCING THE INNOCENT

Is she willing to give her secret crush everything to make him stay?

I'm Kayla.

I'm twenty one.

I'm afraid because ever since a sudden, terrible tragedy, I'm alone in the world—except for my brother's best friend. But now Oliver intends to move back to London.

I'm in love with him. And I have to persuade him to stay...somehow.

Maybe if I tell him I'm a virgin and show him just how far I'm willing to go to keep him, he'll give in.

Of course, I never expected that he'd be keeping a shocking secret of his own...

Enjoy this Forbidden Confession. HEA guaranteed!

CHAPTER ONE

Connecticut
Friday, March 13

Kayla

"I'm leaving," Oliver Ryan says as I plod out of my bedroom and start a zombie-walk toward the coffeemaker for a much-needed caffeine boost.

"Where to?" It's too early in the morning for him to head to work. I know he's not jogging or hitting the gym in that tight gray T-shirt and the faded jeans that cling in all the right places and make me sigh. Is he going to the coffeehouse? The grocery store?

"Back to London. I'm moving. I leave tonight."

I whirl around to face him, suddenly wide-awake. Did I hear that right? Oliver is leaving me for good?

His solemn gray eyes, like a London morning, stare back at me, unblinking.

My heart falls. "What? Why?"

"Shane's gone." He pulls at the back of his neck and looks away. "And it would be best if I didn't stay."

Best for whom?

Tomorrow, I'll resume my last semester of college after a much-needed spring break, and I look forward to graduating in May. But if Oliver goes, I'll be utterly alone. Yes, I'm a grown woman. I'm capable of making my own decisions. I've been doing that since I turned eighteen and my mother decided to follow her heart—and her latest fling—to Italy. Of course I can live alone.

But I don't want to.

"You'll do great," Oliver murmurs before he turns away.

I'm somewhere between shocked and numb as I brew my coffee. Is there anything I can say or do to change his mind? A hundred ideas run through my brain. They all sound ridiculous.

Without his best friend here, why would Oliver stay?

As the brew finishes dripping into my cup, he whisks by, carrying a pair of suitcases, shoulders and arms bulging, and heads toward the front door. I chew my lip, fighting panic. He's already packed? Yes, and he has one foot out the door.

God, my life is falling apart.

For the past three years, I've had two anchors: my brother, Shane, and his best friend, Oliver. They took me under their wing after my mother skipped the continent. They were both protective and supportive, in some ways more nurturing than Mom. Most special, they were always there for me. Vice versa, too.

Then, nearly four weeks ago, Shane fell asleep at the wheel after pulling double shifts at the hospital and hit an embankment. He died instantly, just shy of his twenty-ninth birthday. Since then, Oliver and I have been dealing with his funeral, his estate…and the never-ending nightmare of grief. I still can't believe it. The three of us enjoyed such a wonderful Valentine's Day together. None of us had anyone special in our romantic lives, so we watched goofy movies and gorged on candy. Of course, I had to pretend I wasn't ogling Oliver…

Two days later, my brother died.

I've thanked God every day that Shane didn't suffer and that Oliver has been my shoulder to cry on, my hand to hold, my rock. I haven't completely fallen apart because I've had the stiff-upper-lip Brit beside me.

And now he's leaving. Shock still pings through my system.

I want to beg him to stay. But if returning home will make him happy, how can I be selfish? He's more than done his duty after Shane's death. Staying in the house where we all lived as a mismatched family of sorts must hurt Oliver the same way it pains me. Shane's absence often feels like a black hole sucking me under when I least expect it.

I have to let Oliver move on and be happy…even if that's without me.

Shane bequeathed me his house, which was paid off in the event of his death. I also inherited my brother's life insurance money, which will help me finish school debt free. I have a roof over my head and I never have to worry where my next meal is coming from. I'm smart and I've maintained most of the household responsibilities for years. I'll certainly survive.

But somehow, I know my life will never be right again without Oliver Ryan.

"You're really going tonight?" My voice trembles as I leave my coffee untouched and follow him to the door. "And you're not coming back?"

He thrusts long fingers through his short brown waves, then

flicks his gray eyes in my direction. After a quick glance at my face and a discreet peek lower, he looks away. "I am."

I glance down at myself. Crap, I'm still wearing exactly what I slept in: tiny pink boy shorts and the matching pale tank top, almost transparent from years of washing. I wince. Oliver can probably see my nipples. And with the morning chill, the hard peaks poke the cotton. I've had these pajamas since I was a kid. They're too tight, and I should trash them, but I love their softness.

I cross my arms over my chest for modesty. After all, inadvertently flashing Oliver is obviously making him uncomfortable. No surprise since he probably sees me as a sister. He's behaved like my second big brother for years.

I've always had a secret crush on him. But he doesn't know —or care. And this morning, he's so distant I worry he'll leave without a word if I disappear long enough to find a robe.

Why is he going all the way to London? It's where he grew up, but it's also very far away. Did he fall for another woman when he flew back to see his parents for the holidays? If he did, he never said a word. Then again, he doesn't confide in me about his sex life. I know he has one. Women talk, and I've heard the sound bites. In bed, he's supposedly creative, talented, long-lasting…and kinky.

I'm jealous. I have no right to feel that way, but the hard knot in my stomach every time I think about him with someone else hurts.

"My flight is at five thirty this evening." He hazards a glance at me again, then curses under his breath. "Sorry."

With that clipped apology, he brushes past me and heads toward his bedroom once more, presumably to collect another of his suitcases.

As I watch him go, I squeeze my eyes shut and resist the

urge to cry. Once he boards that plane, will I see him again? Other than my friend Perrie, who's graduating with me before heading back to Phoenix, I'll have no one. Oliver is the person I've relied on most, the one I've always counted on. I know it's not fair, but it feels as if he's abandoning me.

Dejected, I slog to the bathroom to brush my teeth and hair. Selfish or not, I scour my head for a plan to make him stay. He's always been happy here. If I put my mind to it, maybe I can find a way for him to be again. Or I could offer to go with him. But something about the way he's behaving feels less like he's leaving to start a new future and more like he's running away from me.

Two minutes and sparkling white teeth later, I still have no idea what to do. After tearing out my sloppy bun, I quickly swipe a paddle brush through my long hair. The thick curls caress my shoulders, cutting dark swaths over my tank and ending at my waist.

Oliver said once that he liked it loose and down. Okay, it's a lame start, but until I can figure out how else to persuade him not to leave the house, job, and people he's enjoyed for the last three years, I can try small ways to make him happy.

Unfortunately, I only have a handful of hours to think of some big ways—or I'll lose him forever.

Oliver

Fuck.

I stomp my way back to the kitchen and scrub a hand down my face. My transport to the airport is supposed to pick me up in four hours. I've managed—somehow—to keep my hands off my best friend's little sister for the past three years. But if she keeps prancing around the house wearing next to nothing, with her bloody tempting nipples on display under that fucking transparent tank, I will tear it off her saucy little body, pluck those sweet berries in my mouth, and fuck her senseless.

But I can't. The day Shane introduced me to Kayla, he made me promise I would never touch her. I can't dishonor his wishes now.

With a curse, I reach for the coffeemaker and spot the steaming mug Kayla left behind. I hear her at the back of the house. I should be a friend and take it to her. But I don't think my self-control can handle the view of her half-naked anymore. Restraint only goes so far.

Since she hasn't doctored the brew with heaping teaspoons of sugar and that dreadful flavored creamer yet, I lift her MESSY HAIR, DON'T CARE mug and down a scalding swallow. Caffeine is good. The sting of the burn is better. It takes my mind off her —and the way she looked at me as if I'm ripping her heart out.

She's driving me utterly mad.

On the counter beside the coffeemaker, I hear a ding and glance down to see Kayla's phone. I don't intend to pry, but a message from her good friend Perrie pops up, asking if she's talked to Justin since last night.

Who the devil is Justin? Someone Kayla is dating? Someone she's now shagging? And what happened last night?

The phone dings again. Up pops a message from the afore-mentioned Justin that reads: You look so fucking hot. Feel like giving me a bite of those, baby?

A bite of what?

I shouldn't peek. I know that quite well. But if some dead-beat thinks he's going to hustle Kayla into bed...

Who will stop fuckwits like him when you're gone?

I have no answer, but I'm determined to deal with the situation while I'm still here.

Grinding my teeth together, I launch Kayla's messages. I've told her a hundred times to put a passcode on her phone. She never has, and now I'm using that to my advantage.

I don't bother reading her string of messages with Perrie. Her university friend is very sweet and would never intentionally lead Kayla into trouble. But whoever this Justin is, he sounds as if he needs a fist in his face. I'm convinced he does the moment I open his message.

The photo he sent doesn't merely make me mad. It makes me anxious. It makes me violent. And dear god, it makes me sweat.

I don't know what the devil Kayla has been up to or how Justin got this photo, but I intend to find the fuck out. I may nearly be out of strength to guard Kayla's body without defiling it, but no other man will put his hands on her as long as I'm still here.

And I intend to make that clear to Kayla—now.

CHAPTER TWO

Kayla

I'm arranging my hair around my shoulders when Oliver stomps down the hall and uses his body to block the doorway, trapping me inside the bathroom. He's seething as he clutches my phone, looking red-faced and infuriated.

"What's wrong?" I've never seen even-tempered Oliver this agitated.

"Your phone dinged, so I picked it up to bring it to you and got quite a shock." His expression turns hard. "What the bloody hell happened last night?"

"Nothing," I croak. "Since spring break is almost over, Perrie and I went to a party."

"A party, was it?"

"Yeah. Just a get-together with some friends and—" I frown, trying to remember what happened. I was a little tipsy, and I vaguely remember this game of—

"A mere get-together? What's *this,* then?" He shoves my phone in my face.

The image on my screen makes my eyes widen in shock and a wild flush of embarrassment heat up my face. *Shit.* "It's, um... a picture of my breasts."

"Indeed. Your *naked* breasts." Oliver doesn't seem merely disapproving or disappointed, like Shane would have been. Those two were always my watchdogs in the past, keeping players and losers alike at bay. Probably why I'm still a virgin. But Oliver's reaction now is totally different. He's beyond furious.

"So? I don't love that this picture is probably making the rounds on social media, but I wasn't the only one topless last night."

"Some wanker named Justin texted this to you. Who the fuck is he?"

A jackass I can barely tolerate. He keeps trying to hook up with me; I'm not interested. "No one."

"Clearly, he's someone since he's seen you half-naked and I haven't."

Is Oliver saying he wants to?

He rakes his stare over my tank. "Did he touch them?"

"No." I shake my head in emphasis. With his stare on my nipples, they're so sensitive that the caress of my hair across them nearly has me gasping.

He shoves my phone on the bathroom counter. "Did anyone touch them?"

"No. Why does it matter?"

Oliver ignores my question and clenches his jaw as he gathers my hair in his fists before pushing it behind my shoulders to hang down my back. His gaze fuses to my breasts once more, barely covered by my old tank. My nipples draw up even tighter. There's no way he doesn't notice.

I swallow. What is he thinking?

"Are you lying to me?" he demands.

I shake my head. "A group of us played strip poker. You know I'm terrible at cards. I had a little too much wine. I wasn't the only one who lost her clothes. Perrie got all the way down to a thong and..." I toss my hands in the air. "Justin must have snapped that picture when I wasn't looking."

My answer doesn't calm him at all.

"Take off your shirt. I intend to check you for bruising and whisker burn."

"What?" I rear back. Show Oliver my bare breasts?

"Take. Off. Your. Shirt," he growls. "Now."

"If someone touched me, why the hell do you care? I'm a big girl. And you're leaving."

"Do it, Kayla." He doesn't sound at all like my second big brother, but a jealous lover.

I wonder... Is he demanding to inspect me simply because he thinks someone else manhandled me, or because he wants to see my breasts for his own pleasure?

That notion has my pussy clenching.

Clandestinely, I walk my stare down Oliver's body—wide shoulders, a muscled chest, lean abs, narrow hips. A thick erection bulges between his legs.

Holy shit!

If I show him my breasts, will he stop seeing me as a sister and finally see me as a woman? If he likes it, is there any chance he'll be tempted enough to stay?

I'll never know if I don't try.

Heart pounding, I cross my arms over my middle and grab the hem of my tank top, sweeping it off my body.

Gaze glued to my breasts, Oliver lets out a rush of breath. "Kayla..."

"Yeah?" I pant.

He swallows, then seems to recover his wits and holds out his hand. "Give me your shirt."

With shaking fingers, I place my tank in his upturned palm. My mounds feel heavy under his stare.

"Come closer." His voice shudders.

I don't know what he wants, but the longer I keep him occupied, the less time he'll spend packing to leave.

I gather my courage and step closer to him—so close I can see every individual hair of the dark morning stubble covering his jaw and the rapid pulse at his neck. I glance down discreetly through my lashes. His cock is not only still erect but bigger than before. The sight of him all aroused makes me achy and wet.

Am I responsible for that?

Then he drops my tank top on the counter beside me and raises his hand. His warm palm cups my right breast. I suck in a breath at the shock of his hot touch.

Then the fingers of his other hand trace some of the delicate veins under my pale skin, drawing closer and closer to my nipple but never actually touching it. The ache between my legs grows unbearable and my heart races as he repeats the process with the other breast, but this time, his thumb slips over its hard crest.

I can't help it; I moan.

"You like that?"

"Yes." My voice is breathy.

He hesitates. "Justin didn't do this to you?"

"No."

"Did he fuck you?"

"No."

"You swear?"

I nod. "I don't want him."

"Good." He sounds relieved.

"Why? Do you want me to be alone?" I ask as he caresses my breasts again. "Despite what you and Shane always thought, I can't be a virgin forever."

Eventually, I'll find a man I can stomach having sex with. But I only want Oliver…

He swallows, then frowns. "Your brother and I taught you to save yourself for someone who loves you and will value your gift. You should be adored. Justin seems like a worthless wanker who won't care a whit about you the next day. When I'm gone, I have faith you'll make the right choices for your life and your body."

I bite my lip. Oliver knows me well. I won't go to bed with a guy just to say I finally had sex. Maybe I'm living in a fairy tale, but I really do want my first time to be special. I want to be with someone I love.

Like Oliver, who suddenly stares at me as if I fascinate him. He caresses my breasts so tenderly I nearly cry.

Why is he touching me this way if he's leaving? The question frustrates me and ignites my temper. "Well, now that you're packing up and heading out, you don't have to worry about me anymore. I'll find someone to take my V-card. I'm an adult, so it's not like saving it is a big deal anymore."

"It fucking is." Oliver grabs my shoulders, and his stare delves deep into me as if he's determined to make me understand. "Christ. For that remark, I should spank your ass so red you can't sit for a week."

I suck in a breath, wide-eyed. Three years ago, that threat would have sent me running for cover. Oliver is the sort of man who means what he says. If he threatens, he follows through. But today, I'm not scared. In fact, I like the idea of his hand on my ass. My pussy clenches again.

"What else do you want to do to me?" I say breathlessly.

He feathers his thumbs across my sensitive nipples in tandem. My knees buckle. I have to hold on to the counter to stay upright. And when he pinches both tips lightly, tingles zing through my body. Slowly melting, I suck in a breath and fight the urge to beg him to touch me more. I force myself to wait for Oliver's answer because, while I know he likes sex, I'm not convinced his erection means he desires *me*.

One of his warm hands leaves my breast and skates down my waist, settling over my hip to bring me closer. I can smell a hint of toothpaste and coffee on his breath.

"Have you let any of those tossers you've dated kiss you, Kayla?"

I swallow. What will he do if I tell him the truth? "A few."

He scowls as if my answer pains him. "Did you like it?"

I wanted to, but... "It was all right. No one has blown my panties off."

I suspect Oliver could.

His eyes soften. "Kissing can be wonderful. Someday, when you find a man you care about, one who knows what he's doing, you'll love it."

I have a man I very much care about standing right in front of me, and the thought of kissing Oliver makes my body throb in arousal. I sway closer, pressing my aching breasts against his chest. "What about you? I'll bet you know what you're doing."

The second the words leave my mouth, my heart careens out of control.

"I shouldn't kiss you, Kayla," Oliver practically groans.

"Please," I beg. "Just once." When he stares at my lips, they tingle. Everything in my body flushes hot. Even my skin feels too tight. And the ache between my legs coils relentlessly. "You've already touched my breasts."

"Are you bloody trying to kill me?" His voice sounds rough with need.

That excites me even more.

"Is one kiss asking so much?" I clasp his T-shirt in my fists and tilt my face under his.

He hesitates for a long moment, his eyes searching mine, nostrils flaring, jaw rigid.

"Kayla," he growls. "Goddamn it..."

Just when I'm sure he's going to walk away, Oliver grabs me by the nape, holding me immobile. His breathing turns hard and rough. I tremble. He's wrestling with himself. My heart revs. What is he thinking? Is there any chance he'll kiss me?

Suddenly, he jerks me against his body and seizes my lips.

His tongue invades, sliding against mine until I tingle, caressing until I moan. He teases me. He possesses me. He inhales me with his hunger. And oh, my god, I kiss him back with everything I feel because he's blowing my mind and igniting my body.

I feel utterly owned.

This is so much better than any lip-lock I've endured from the fumbling boys I've dated. This passion is everything I've wanted from Oliver.

He grips my waist, caresses his way down to the swells of my hips, then yanks me against him so he can knead the cheeks of my ass and notch his erection against my barely covered pussy. I cry out, but he swallows the sound with another ferocious kiss, nipping at my lips and sampling me with his tongue before delving back inside.

Helplessly, I throw my arms around his neck and drown in

sensations. His free hand captures my breast again, squeezing and roughing my nipple. I swelter at the possessive feel of his touch.

Suddenly, he jerks away and steps back, panting raggedly. "Do you like kissing now?"

"When you do it, I love it," I confess. "Will you do it again?"

He closes his eyes. "I shouldn't."

"But I want you to."

"Kayla...no. This needs to stop now. Push me away."

I don't. I won't. Instead, I ease closer, slide against him, and press my lips to his in invitation.

Oliver grabs me. He stiffens, breathing hard and fast.

And his resistance runs out.

With a groan, he takes my mouth again and reaches between us, cupping the swelling flesh between my legs. Through my thin underwear, he rubs me in beguiling circles. "Fuck, you're wet."

"It's your fault," I breathe as Oliver presses harder against my cunt.

"What the devil..." He frowns and pulls away.

Is something wrong with me? "What?"

Scowling, he grabs the waistband of my boy shorts, shoves them down to my thighs, and affixes his gaze *there*. His eyes bulge. My knees wobble. The air feels thick and heavy.

"You shave?" he croaks.

I tremble. "Yes."

"If you've never had a lover, why?"

I once overheard him and Shane talking about women. Oliver said he preferred them bare. He's still staring at my naked mound with a hungry gaze, looking as if he intends to eat me whole. More heat suffuses me, and the ache between my legs cranks up, tightening unmercifully.

The hand he stroked over my underwear clenches into a fist at his side. The lights of the bathroom are bright, and as I shift my weight from one leg to the other, I can feel how wet I am. There's no way Oliver can't see it.

"Do you like it?"

"Christ, you look so sweet," he chokes out as he eases his fingers toward me, then softly caresses my bare flesh. "So wet. So smooth and pretty."

I bite my lip—and decide to take a risk. If I want this to continue, I have to. "I did it for you."

His gaze bounces up to mine. "Did you? Oh, love…"

Before I can answer, his fingers part my slick folds. He finds my clit. I jolt at the contact.

He rubs slowly. Under his sure touch, I feel as if I'm coming undone, unraveling from the inside out. Unconsciously, I spread my legs wider.

"Fuck." He swallows and eases the tips of his fingers into my virginal opening. "I shouldn't do this, but you feel so silky and hot and… I've had so many fantasies about touching you. How am I supposed to stay away?"

As soon as his words make it past the pleasure reeling through my brain, I gasp and grab on to his arms. "You've wanted *me*?"

As if speaking the question brings him back to his senses, he jerks away. "Why do you bloody think I'm leaving? Shane would've had my balls for desiring you this way."

Oliver can't leave because he worries what my brother might have thought. I refuse to let him.

I reach out and grab his erection through his jeans. He groans long and low, head tossed back like he's in pain, but his expression fills with pleasure.

Oh, wow. His cock is so thick I can barely get my hand

around it. And as I start to stroke him like some of my sorority sisters have dished about doing to their boyfriends, I can feel how long and strong he is.

I panic a little. The times I've masturbated, I've had trouble getting more than one of my own fingers up there. How will he shove all of this inside me? Will it burn and sting as he batters his way deep?

I know my first time will hurt. That worries me, but if I can persuade him to say yes, Oliver will make it good. He cares about me, and I'm willing to do *anything* to make him stay.

Pressing my mouth to his and slipping my tongue inside, I unbuckle his belt and reach for his zipper.

He grabs my wrists. "Kayla."

"Please. You want me. I want you. We're adults. Shane is gone. Why shouldn't we have each other? And maybe you can stay. We could make it work, even be like…a new family."

Oliver

NOTHING KAYLA SAID COULD TEMPT me more.

Shane's little sister is idealistic; I know that. But when it comes to her, so am I. She can't possibly know that my fantasies about her aren't purely sexual—though there are plenty of hot, sweaty, forbidden notions about her running through my head and contributing to my spank bank. But the notion of creating a family with Kayla sends my desire ratcheting to another level.

My parents divorced when I was a teenager. Shitty situation. They were both assholes, wanting me to take sides. They argued over me, then tried to buy my loyalty. When that didn't work, they each tried to poison me against the other. As soon as I could, I moved to a flat with some friends. But that wasn't far enough to escape them.

So when I finally scraped enough money together, I bought a plane ticket and headed across the pond. I'd known Shane from an online gaming forum for years. He welcomed me with open arms and became the brother I never had. Though things are better with my parents now, I still consider Shane my real family because he was there for me when it counted. I miss the crazy bastard every day.

Kayla…is different. No matter how much I willed it, she never felt like a sister to me. The moment I set eyes on her, I wanted her. Because I was so much older and more experienced, Shane didn't approve. Yes, he's gone, but I still feel as if I owe him my allegiance.

How the hell can I make Kayla understand that and back away without hurting her feelings? Because if I kiss her again—big mistake—or put my hands on her once more—an even bigger mistake—I may not be able to stop what happens next.

"Oliver…" she murmurs, looking so soft and appealing, even under the bright bathroom lights. "Please."

"Your brother—"

"Would want us both to be happy. You know that's true."

I can't deny that, just like I can't deny that Kayla isn't underage and in high school anymore.

Damn her doe eyes. The way she's looking at me like she's aching and only I can cure her gets to me. I want to give in; I know I shouldn't. She's right in front of me, so close I can smell her musky-vanilla scent that often ruins my concentration and plagues my sleep.

"I need you."

Bloody hell. She's begging and basically naked. I want to be stronger…but a man has his limits.

Kayla just trampled all over mine.

I shut off my brain and close my eyes, then let out a damning curse before I lunge into her personal space. I grind my mouth over hers, tongue plunging in ravenous strokes. She softens and moans. And I drown in her taste.

I can't resist her hard nipples, either. They're mere inches from my fingers, inviting me.

When I pinch the hard peaks again, she sucks in a sharp breath. Her kiss turns frenzied, and she moans with these little sounds that make me itch to strip off her clothes.

It's ten times worse when she reaches for my zip again and works her fingers into my pants and breaches my briefs.

Just before she grabs my cock, I find the will to break our kiss and grab her shoulders, holding her at arm's length. I can't seem to catch my fucking breath.

"Stop there, Kayla. Before this goes too far. Before we do something you'll regret."

She blinks at me. The need and love in her eyes are unmistakable. "I would never regret you, Oliver. Ever."

I swallow. "You would. You don't understand how badly I ache for you. I've been fighting this, taking cold showers every morning, and jacking off every night. I feel wretched for wanting you so badly in every way. But I'm being brutally honest."

"Don't feel guilty. I've wanted you, too. You've been here for me for years, supported and cared for me. Let me give some of that love back to you."

I shake my head. "I'm no good for you. Experience life before someone like me ties you down."

She ignores my speech and starts tearing at my shirt. "Why? I'd rather experience life *with* you."

I brush her hands away. "When it comes to you, I'm already

too possessive. Gavin asked you out last month, and I wanted to crush him. I'd like to gouge Justin's eyes out simply for looking at your breasts."

A soft smile breaks across her face. "Really?"

"It's no cause for celebration," I snarl. "What do you think will happen between us if you give me your virginity?"

The question makes her frown and reminds me how innocent she is. "We'll be together."

"I'll consider you *mine*. I'll have you naked and flat on your back every chance I get. I'll be inside you constantly. And I won't let you go."

Rather than chasing her away, my words seem to arouse her. It's obvious in the blush that blooms in her cheeks and the hardening of her pretty, dark nipples. She presses a hand against her chest, where I see her heart beating hard at the base of her neck.

"You mean that?" Wonder laces her words.

I scowl. Why isn't anything I say bloody scaring her off? "Of course. And you should heed my warning."

"If I was yours, would you stay here, instead of going back to London?"

Doesn't Kayla understand? Maybe not. She's innocent. If I spell it out for her, hopefully she'll grasp the gravity of what she's asking and run shrieking in the other direction.

I grasp her chin and force her to look into my eyes. "If you let me fuck you—even once—you'll never be rid of me. Perhaps that sounds caveman to you. I don't care. I'll bury myself deep in your cunt every day. Several times a day. You'll want to go out with your friends, go to parties, have fun. Flirt with other men." I shake my head. "I'll throw you down, kiss you breathless, and fuck you until you're too exhausted to move. You'll miss everything you should be experiencing just out of university. Because I'm a selfish prick, guilt won't stop me from reaching for you in the middle of the night and working my cock into you. Then again, when you try to sleep late on weekends, I'll be waking you to take more of me. I'll be merciless. Nooners will be frequent. Dinners will be delayed. And I won't care because I'll be too insistent to make you remember who you belong to and too determined to have you scream my name."

With every word, her eyes grow wider. Her cheeks get redder. I try to resist a glance down at her untouched pussy... but I'm weak. It's wetter than before.

Oh, fuck. She's aroused by what I said?

"If you'll stay here with me..." she whispers, "then I don't need bars or parties or other guys. I want you. Yes. Yes to all of it."

I shake my head. "Damn it, don't you understand? You're a fever that makes me burn, and I'll ruin your life trying to put out the flame. I'll take everything you have to give and demand more."

"That's okay. I—"

"It's not. I'll shove my cock down your throat, Kayla, and make you learn to take me so deep, my load will never even hit your tongue. Before you've had time to catch your breath, I'll turn you around and bend you over to work my cock into that sweet backside. And make no mistake, I'll enjoy every squeal. Your pleading won't have any effect on me. I'll have you stripped and my cock filling one of your perfect little holes all the time. You'll beg me for mercy. But when it comes to you, I have none."

"Maybe you mean for all of that to sound terrible. But it doesn't. It only makes me want you more," she whispers. "I'm still saying yes, Oliver. I always will."

"I don't want to be that bastard who robs you of choices. I couldn't bear for you to hate me."

"Hate? I'm the one asking you for more. You've been half my world for the last three years. With Shane's passing, I realize just how important you are. How much I care. I'm not ready to lose you."

I scowl. "You consider me your brother."

"No. I tried to...but I've never thought of you that way." Kayla takes a deep breath like she's gathering her courage. "I love you."

Seriously? I rake a hand through my hair. Her admission undoes me completely.

I seize the back of her neck and drag her face to mine until our lips brush. "Fuck, I love you, too. That's been my dirty secret for years."

"Really? Oh, my god. Oliver!" Joy lightens her face. "Then you have to stay. We can move if this house reminds you of Shane too much, but we can be together—"

"Will you still love me if you're graduating college pregnant?" I challenge because I can't be less than honest about what I want.

"Pregnant? I graduate in seven weeks. I don't think that's possible."

"Care to bet? I'm almost thirty, Kayla. If you say yes, I'll want to start our future now. I want children immediately. Shane's death taught me there might not be a tomorrow. So if you let me in your bed today, I will do everything in my power to make certain you're accepting your degree and expecting our baby. I'll fuck you constantly to make it happen."

She looks stunned. She's totally silent. Have I finally frightened her away? If I have, I know I should be relieved.

But the thought of leaving Kayla is killing me. I've been in love with her for so long, the notion of a future that doesn't include her is wrenching. And knowing she'll eventually couple off with another man who will take all the sweetness I've wanted for myself?

It's enough to break me.

I cup her cheek. "Tell me what you're thinking, love."

"I-I'm...trying to work it out in my head."

Of course. "I'm demanding a lot. I'm aware of that. I fully expect you to say no. And I understand."

When she does, I'll go. I'll have no choice.

"This isn't what I originally planned..."

"I know." I kiss her forehead and step back. "I'm sorry."

"Wait! No. What I'm trying to say is yes. Twenty-one is sooner than I imagined having kids, but I'll have a degree in a handful of weeks. I can look for a work-at-home job, perfect for after I give birth."

My heart stops. "You're saying yes? You're certain? This is sudden. You're young and—"

"You know that my dad left when I was three. Other than Shane's funeral, I haven't seen my mother in years. Honestly, what I want most in life is roots. Real family. I thought I'd lost any chance of that when I lost my brother. But you're giving me new hope. I've always wanted a big, loving family. The idea of you and me starting a new circle of life together"—she smiles —"sounds perfect. In fact, that would make me the happiest woman on earth. Now is the perfect time to lose my virginity. You're the only man I want to give it to."

She's as certifiably insane as I am.

As if to prove that, she reaches into my pants and grabs my cock. "I want you to push every inch into my virgin pussy and make me yours. I want you to come inside me. Love me. Stay with me."

I seize her shoulders. "Last chance. Be very certain. I mean it; no condoms or pills. You'll take all of me deep inside of you, where I belong, every single time. There will be no going back."

"I know. And I'm agreeing. Like you said, no one is guaranteed tomorrow. I don't want to wait to get pregnant. And now that I've had a minute to warm to the idea, I love the thought of holding our son or daughter, feeding our baby from my breasts, then watching him or her sleep peacefully."

"You mean, before I lay you down and fuck you again?"

"I certainly hope you would." She gives me a coy smile and presses herself against me. "Please, Oliver. I'm saying yes."

"You won't be ashamed to be knocked up by your brother's best friend?"

"I'll feel blessed to have created a little miracle with the man I love. Can we start now?"

CHAPTER THREE

Kayla

H e hesitates a long moment, and I have no idea if he's finally going to cave in and give me what we both want.

Vicious need suddenly tightens his dark features as he yanks my boy shorts up, then tucks my hand in his. "If you're sure…"

"I am."

"Then I need to be inside you now."

His words make me ache and throb. "I need that, too."

"After I fuck you enough to take off the edge, we'll move into the master bedroom together. I'll apologize now. That might be hours."

A few steps down the hallway, we enter the room we'll soon share. He lifts me to the center of the bed, body taut, as if his self-control is strangling him. "Your first time should be in a bed."

And I like this bed. He obviously slept here last night. The sheets smell like him. They're rumpled and cozy and musky.

Oliver spends a long moment looking at me, and I grow self-conscious, covering my breasts with my hands.

He grabs my wrists and shoves them flat against the mattress. "Don't hide or keep yourself from me."

Innocently, I blink up at him.

"You'll make me crazy," he explains. "I'm already halfway there."

"All right."

"Fuck, you're a pretty thing." He sheds his shirt, revealing wide shoulders and a strong chest that's starred in many of my fantasies. He crawls across the bed, pressing his half-covered body to mine, then thumbs one of my nipples. "You're so soft, but your body makes me so hard. When you pranced through the house wearing that pajama top, I could see straight through it. It was all I could do not to press you against a wall and shag you."

His words make me tremble. Other guys have tried to talk dirty to me. I've always rolled my eyes because they sounded ridiculous. But Oliver makes me melt.

"Hurry." I start pulling off my boy shorts.

He helps me. The instant the thin cotton hits the floor, he fastens his hands on the insides of my thighs and shoves them wide apart, peering closely at me. I can feel his stare right *there*.

I hold my breath. My heart pounds in my ears.

He thumbs my clit. "Your pussy is lovely. You'll keep that shaved close for me, yes?"

It's a gentle but firm order. "Of course."

"Mmm…" He brushes up my body and opens his mouth over one of my sensitive nipples, pulling on it, scraping it with his teeth, licking it with his tongue. A bolt of electricity connects my stiff peaks to my clit, burning me. I want him everywhere. I want him now.

But he won't be rushed. As he moves to the other nipple, giving it the same treatment, every pass of his lips over them is a bit rougher and more demanding. The sucking, pinching, flicking, twisting, and scraping arouses me like crazy. I wriggle. Juices seep from my aching cunt, wetting the insides of my thighs, but still he keeps on, moaning, his mouth growing more urgent.

"Oliver…" I pant. "No more. Make me yours."

"I will. Soon." But he doesn't stray from my nipples.

Long minutes pass in a haze of pleasure. All the sensations in my body seem to come directly through the peaks of my breasts. Still he doesn't let up, even though they're swollen and chafed. He merely drags them into his mouth again and pulls. They sting so sweetly. I feel almost embarrassingly wet and try to roll away. "Oliver, no more. They're sore."

He pins me down, his face full of apology and agonized need. "I want your nipples raw, Kayla. I need you aching for me." He drops his hand between my thighs and groans. "Feels as if you like it, too. You're drenched. God, I've got to taste your virgin cunt. I want you on my tongue. I'm dying to make you come."

I nod eagerly and slowly spread my thighs wider. His nostrils flare; his eyes glitter with harsh lust. Then he buries his face in my pussy. Nothing slow or subtle. He eats me like a starving man, his tongue devouring every slick surface, savoring my clit. He moans, and his fingers tighten on my thighs, spreading them so wide my muscles burn. And he just keeps on nibbling, slurping, and sucking on me.

God, I've never imagined anything like this. Putting my own hands between my legs never felt this good. I arch and clench his hair in my hands, but it's not enough. Grabbing the short strands as best I can, I press his face deeper into my cunt. "Oliver!"

He comes up with a smile, licking his lips. "You taste perfect, love. I'll be spending a lot of time here."

As he draws my clit into his mouth again, I can feel the tide of heat rising. It claws and climbs up my body, until I'm thrashing. My thighs tremble violently. I cry out.

"That's my girl… Come for me!"

I do. The explosion burns, pounding and overtaking every part of me. I've never felt anything better in my life. The pleasure is intense. I scream. I swoon. As the climax crests, I nearly black out.

I'm still catching my breath when Oliver stands and rips off the rest of his clothes.

My eyes bulge. He felt huge, and I've seen other penises in pictures, but never in person. I know immediately that he's large, especially when he wraps a hand around his cock and strokes it.

"Kneel." Oliver points to the spot on the floor in front of him.

I scramble to my knees, and he grabs my hair in his fist and guides my face to his waiting erection. A drop of pearly fluid seeps from the slit at the head. The sight arouses both my curiosity and my pussy. I stick out my tongue and lick at the moisture.

Oliver groans and tightens his fist in my hair. "Oh, that's it, love. Suck me deep."

I do, reveling in the feel of such soft skin over his hard cock against my tongue. I feel sexy and my pussy burns as I lower my mouth, trying to take as much of him as I can. Then I suck my way back up.

He grits his teeth and shoves in deeper. "Look at me."

Through my lashes, I stare up at him, swirling my tongue around the head of his cock, then lapping up another drop of the salty fluid. I moan. His jaw clenches. He pulls harder on my hair. Pain prickles across my scalp, heightening my senses. Stark hunger prowls across his face. My empty cunt tightens.

"Those innocent eyes are making me harder. And that sweet fucking mouth. You haven't sucked any other man's cock, have you?" When I try to lift away to answer, he snarls and thrusts against my throat. "You don't need your mouth free to tell me."

Oliver is right. I shake my head.

"I love that I'll be the first—and only—man to come in your mouth, pussy, and ass." He sounds gratified by that prospect. "I promise to keep you so full and sated, you'll never want anyone else."

I try to smile up at him, but he eases his iron-hard dick to the back of my throat again. Involuntarily, I gag. It breaks my rhythm. I'm sure I'm doing it all wrong, and I don't want to disappoint Oliver. He's being patient with my inexperience. But I want this pleasure to be exactly what he needs. I force myself to inhale and exhale through my nose and relax, so I can suck him in completely.

"God, you're amazing. I don't know how I resisted you for so long. I want you every way I can have you."

I moan around his length, my taste buds saturated by his flavor.

"Faster."

When I hear the ache in his voice, I pick up the pace, dragging my lips up and down his thick shaft. My jaw hurts from opening so wide, and he shuttles his way between my lips ruthlessly. His groans of pleasure swell the folds of my slick pussy. I feel so desperate to please him.

His cock twitches in my mouth and swells. I suck him even

harder and lower my head as far down his shaft as I can, my nose nearly touching his dark mound of pubic hair. I can smell his musky, manly scent wafting from his testicles. I cup them with one hand and draw them up closer to my face.

"Fuck, yes." He stabs his way between my lips frantically now.

I try to let him slide deeper. My lips feel chafed, and the muscles of my jaw scream for relief. But I ignore all that because there's something so satisfying about undoing him.

"Take every inch of my cock past your lips, love."

He pushes all the way in, holding my face right against his ridged abdomen. He probes my mouth in short, rough strokes. I do my best to keep up. As if he knows I can, Oliver merely cups my face and thrusts deeper.

"That's pretty, your little rosebud lips stretched so wide around my cock." He withdraws a fraction, then thrusts right back in. "You look so sexy with me violating your mouth and those dark eyes pleading with me to fuck you. I will—as soon as I come down your virgin throat. You'll be a good girl and swallow everything I give you, won't you?"

I nod, then suck his dick so hard my cheeks hollow out. He groans, tightens his fists in my hair, then fucks my mouth wildly. Spurts of hot liquid splash against my throat, salty and unexpected. I swallow all I can.

When his thick crest hits my throat again, I nearly choke. I turn my head with a gasp. A drop of his semen oozes onto my lower lip.

As soon as I catch my breath, I glance up at him. He collects the stray drop on the tip of his finger. "Open up."

I part my lips for him.

"Stick out your tongue," he demands.

I do, and he swipes his finger and the salty fluid across the middle. I taste him all over again. God, I want him even more now.

"Close your mouth. Like that, yes. Swallow."

I do as instructed, then blink up at him for approval.

"Perfect." He curls a gentle finger under my chin before his thumb brushes my lips. He smiles faintly. "So swollen and red. Are they sore, like your nipples?"

"Yes."

"Excellent. Did you enjoy sucking me off?"

I nod, squirming to ease the ache in my pussy. Tasting him only made my desire rise. I need more.

"Stop fidgeting. I'll put out your fire soon." He caresses my cheek so gently. "But I need to know if you still want to be mine?"

"Yes." I close my eyes, ready to give him all of me, always. "Please."

"Did you save yourself for me? Is that why you never slept with someone like Justin?"

"For the past few years, I fantasized about you being my first," I admit into the hush. "You're the only man I've ever wanted, and it feels like I've waited forever."

"Fuck, I wanted you the second your brother introduced us. I knew he'd kill me if I touched you. If he were here now, he'd likely castrate me."

I shake my head. "He looked up to you. There was no one he trusted more. He'd insist on knowing for sure how you felt about me—"

"I love you, Kayla."

I smile at him, my heart bursting. "I love you, too. And Shane would be good with that. In fact, I think he'd be thrilled."

Oliver cranes his head to look upward. "You'll have to get used to this, you big bastard. You hear me? I'm going to debauch your sister." He leans down and nuzzles my neck. "I'm going to get inside of you, Kayla. Now. And make you mine always."

At his vow, my blood turns electric. My pussy cramps with desperate need.

He helps me flat on the bed again and immediately begins to fondle every tingling, aching part of me. My folds are swollen, my juices spilling onto his fingers.

When he rubs my clit in leisurely circles that make me wriggle and arch to increase the friction, I cry out. "Hurry."

He pulls away. "Believe me, I can't wait to bury myself inside you. I'll fuck you until you scream, then release deep inside you, love. I'll flood you with my seed every morning before we go about our day so I'll be inside you even when I'm not with you."

His words alone ramp me up. He's incredibly possessive, but that arouses me. Best of all, I have no doubt he means it.

"Spread your legs for me."

I race to comply, feeling his gaze all over my breasts and my flat stomach before settling onto my hairless mound. I show him my puffy, wet cunt. At the sight, his cock bobs, getting harder. The thick head turns purple. Oliver is big, and having him inside me will hurt at first, but I just know he'll eventually make me cry out in ecstasy.

"That's a love, with your legs all spread just for me." He takes his cock in hand and strokes it. "Now open up. Let me see."

I can't spread my legs any wider. Already the muscles of my thighs ache, and I look at him in confusion.

"Use your fingers to spread yourself open for me. I intend to see that untouched cunt so I can remember what it looked like before I shoved my cock deep and made you mine."

I shiver, melting at his demanding words. I do what he says, parting the lips of my pussy with trembling fingers. He studies me for a long moment, swiping his thumb over my clit lightly, back and forth. Just as I gasp with the rising heat of another orgasm, he fits the fat head of his cock against my small opening and starts working his way in.

My body resists, my folds swollen and tight. Oliver isn't having any of that. He grabs my thighs, lifting them around his hips so they hug his muscled body.

"Put your hands over your head," he insists.

I hesitate. Once I do, I'll be defenseless. His cock will invade every corner of my pussy. Now that the moment is here, I fear the pain a little. But I want this. I want him.

Finally, I do as he asks, and something primal tightens his face. "That's lovely. Perfect. Now be a sweet love and take my cock."

Before I can respond, he presses in, burrowing his way into my pussy. With the first thrust, he can't submerge every inch, so he withdraws and takes another plunge in. I cry out. The next thrust still stings, but not as badly. Finally, with a mighty shove, my body yields and takes him in completely, gripping him tightly. His balls slap against my ass.

He tilts his hips and presses in as deep as he can possibly go, then throws his head back with a guttural groan. "Fuck. That's it. I've got every inch inside you."

I whimper. "It still hurts."

"I'm sorry. The first few times will be uncomfortable, but that won't last. I promise."

He pinches my tender nipples, tweaking them hard again. As I gasp, he eases back, then pushes that big cock into me with slow, deep strokes that have me trembling. My pussy screams. Twinges of pain linger…but the pleasure is building fast. And above it all, I'm euphoric to be with Oliver, to be pleasing him, to be starting our future.

To hopefully be conceiving our first baby.

I move with him as he rocks into me, stroking deep and hitting a spot that has me digging my nails into his shoulders. "Oliver!"

"I'm finally fucking you. You feel like silk around me." He groans and palms my breasts, pulling on my nipples again. "I love you."

He picks up the pace, and lightning sparks inside me. My pussy starts to pulse as he fucks me faster, deeper, as if need is overcoming his self-control. My orgasm creeps up as desire pools and coils between my legs. He twists my nipples again. They're so chafed, and the pain hits me before mellowing into a warm burn that seeps right down to my clit.

"Oliver..." I gasp out, blinking at him.

How does he already understand my body so well?

He smiles. "You like that?"

"Yes," I pant.

When my body tenses and my pussy begins to flutter around him, he reaches between us and works my clit in slow, devastating strokes. "Come for me."

As if his permission frees all the sensations tightening and growing deep inside me, it explodes in a bright flare of ecstasy. He continues to work at my nub and grinds relentlessly into my pussy again and again. A moment later, his body shudders. "That's it. Take me. Take. Every. Drop. I. Give. You."

He drills into me harder with every stroke, hot jets of his seed spilling so deep in my unprotected depths. Oliver is right; if we keep this up, I'll soon be pregnant. The thought only brings me peace. I smile as the haze and glow of orgasm overtake me.

Yes, I originally planned to finish college before getting serious about a guy or starting a family. But Oliver will take care of me. I'll never love any man more. I know that deep in my heart.

Slowly, he withdraws and crouches over me. As the midmorning sun streams through the windows, I see blood. My virgin blood. Then he drops his gaze to my pussy. As hot semen oozes out, he gathers it with his finger and pushes it back inside me as deep as he can. He props a couple of pillows under my hips, tilting them up.

"Lie there for a bit, just like that, love. I'll be back."

"Will that help me get pregnant faster?"

"It can't hurt. Besides, you look beyond sexy that way." He winks.

I laugh and close my eyes. I can't remember the last time I was this sublimely happy.

He lies beside me, cuddling me against him and kissing my ear. "I love you."

"And I love you, Oliver."

CHAPTER FOUR

Oliver

Twenty minutes later, I hear a phone ding somewhere in the house. It doesn't take long to realize it's Kayla's phone. I wander from room to room until I find the device in her bathroom. Another message from Justin is waiting.

Come on, baby. You have the prettiest tits. I want to nibble them. And if you let me pop your cherry, I'll make you feel good.

I see a hundred shades of red. I want to reach through the phone and beat the piss out of him for daring to treat Kayla like an object and wanting the woman who's mine. But I could get angry...or I could get even.

Gnashing my teeth, I quickly type. Why don't you come over now?

He sends an emoji with a shocked face. Seriously?

Yes. I'm waiting. With a fist for him.

On my way. You won't regret it.

"No, I won't," I drawl as I set the device aside. "But you will."

Ten minutes later, he screeches into the drive with his ridiculously souped-up truck, pale hair spiked and bleached, muscle shirt showing off swanky new ink, and a smirk I want to smack off his mouth. I'm not letting him into the house with Kayla, not while she's naked in our bed, sated and smiling. That's for me alone.

I intend to make that clear to Justin.

With a shove of the front door, I slam my way out and glare him down as he exits his truck. He freezes when he sees me barreling toward him.

"Hey. Is, um…Kayla here?"

"Yes, my girlfriend is inside, and we both found the message that popped up on her phone a few hours ago quite disturbing. Out of respect for her, I suggest you delete the photo from your phone and ask anyone you sent it to to do the same."

He scowls. "I didn't send it to anyone. Look, I don't know who you are—"

"Oliver."

Recognition lights his eyes. Justin may not have met me, but he's clearly heard of me. "Yeah, well, she invited me over to"— he shrugs like he's the shit—"you know, fuck her. So maybe she's not your girlfriend anymore."

"She is. Delete the photo."

"I don't have to do shit."

"You do if you want to keep your face intact."

"Nah, man. That goes in my spank bank."

That's all I can tolerate. I grab Justin by the throat and shove him against his truck. "You will never again look at my girlfriend's breasts while you wank yourself. Delete the fucking photo."

"I want to talk to her first."

"She's asleep right now. In my bed, and she won't be leaving it."

"Did you fuck—"

I tighten my fingers around his neck until he chokes. "I don't recommend that you finish your sentence. Delete the photo, get in your truck, drive away, and *never* contact Kayla again. Or you will answer to me. Am I clear?"

When he pushes me away, I let him. Then he shrugs and acts like it's no big deal. "Whatever. Here." He reaches for his phone and deletes Kayla's topless picture from his camera roll. "It's gone. Now get out of my face. If she wants to fuck some older, uptight dude, there's plenty of pussy out there, happy to put out. I got no problems moving on."

He's a prick and a misogynist. How did Kayla ever meet him? "Excellent. Now get the fuck off her property."

With a scowl, he hops back in his truck and screeches his way out of the drive, turning toward me as he reverses out, middle finger extended.

If he thinks that bothers me, he's sorely mistaken. I got what I wanted; that photo should never trouble Kayla again. She's mine to protect, and I'll do it every day for the rest of our lives.

Pushing my way back into the house, I cock my head and listen, but it's still quiet. I delete Justin's contact from her device as I head toward the back of the house to check on Kayla.

She's sprawled across our bed, sleeping peacefully, hips still propped up on the soft mound of pillows I placed under them, legs gracefully spread.

The sight only makes me want her more.

I set her phone on her nightstand, then bend to leave a lingering kiss on her forehead before turning to the shower. Her body may not be ready for more sex yet, but I am. I'll give her a few more minutes to rest…and maybe let my seed take root.

In thirty minutes, I'll be waking her again to splash her unprotected womb with more.

Kayla

I HEAR THE WATER RUNNING. Oliver? There's no one else in the house, so it makes sense, but how am I hearing him shower from my bedroom?

With a frown, I shift to get comfortable and wince. I'm sore— right between the legs. My pussy feels like it's been battered. And why am I propped up on pillows?

Everything comes rushing back to me. Justin's photo. My tank top. Oliver's insistence that he examine my breasts. Oh, my god. He kissed me. And he fucked me without any shred of protection.

I could be pregnant even now.

And that's what he wants.

The memories are delicious, and I smile, stretch, and sigh. I never expected the rest of my life to start today. I'm so incredibly happy.

Nearby, my phone dings. It's the sound I've assigned to Perrie. She's one of my best friends. I'm going to miss her after graduation…

I crane my head around and see my phone on the night-stand, then grab it with an outstretched hand. She texted something, but I don't bother to read it, just dial her. Perrie and I have long shared a very similar secret. I *have* to tell her my amazing news.

I'm praying it will give her hope.

"Hey, girlie," she answers. "Did you get my messages about Justin? He's such a douche. I wanted to give you a heads-up—"

"Forget him. You're never going to guess what happened to me this morning."

"What?"

I fill her in, generally speaking. She doesn't need *all* the details. What she needs to know is that my secret crush finally gave in to me and we're going to live happily ever after.

When I finish my explanation, Perrie all but squees for me. "That's incredible."

"It was *amazing*. I'm so glad I waited for him."

"I'm thrilled for you, doll. And after everything you've been through, losing your brother and all, you deserve nothing but bliss."

"Thanks. But you deserve that, too."

"You're sweet." She speaks the words like someone who's sure she'll never have who she truly wants.

"Have you given any thought about what you're going to say to Hayden when you get back to Phoenix?"

"Of course."

"Let me rephrase that. I know you think about him all the time. Have you decided what you're going to do?"

"No," she admits with a glum sigh. "It's not like I can blurt out how I feel about him. I did that once. Disaster."

"Years have passed. You've both changed."

"Probably not enough for it to make a difference. He's my dad's best friend and business partner. There are so many obstacles between us…"

"Challenges," I correct. "And you excel at those. Use that crafty mind. Get creative."

"And embarrass myself again?" She sighs. "Maybe I should try dating someone else."

"Don't settle. Try Hayden one more time. Please. You deserve to be happy, too."

"I don't know how my dad would take it, anyway. I doubt he'd approve."

"There's a chance my brother wouldn't have approved of Oliver and me, but it's our lives. And we've decided to be happy together." I drop my voice as the shower cuts off. "He's trying to get me pregnant."

"Already?"

"Why wait? I'm about to graduate. We both know what we want. Neither of us has any interest in waiting for a tomorrow that may never come. We're grabbing the happiness we can now and making our own new family."

"You know, you're right. I'm so thrilled for you." She groans. "But I've got to go. Study group before a presentation on Monday. What kind of horrible professor makes students present a case study at nine a.m. after spring break?"

"An asshole." I laugh.

"Exactly. You going to spend the weekend in bed with Oliver?"

Just then, the bathroom door opens in a cloud of steam and he steps out wearing nothing but a towel and a smile. "Absolutely. Bye."

"Bye!" She ends the call with a giggle.

I laugh and set the phone aside. "Just Perrie."

He sends me an indulgent grin, then reaches onto the counter for a cold water bottle and hands it to me. "Feeling all right, love?"

I stretch like a happy cat, then gulp some of the cool liquid down. "Great."

Oliver watches, eyes darkening with hunger when I start to rise. He helps me to my feet.

Immediately, seed runs down my thighs. I look around help-lessly for a tissue or towel, but he shakes his head, then shoves a pair of panties on me. It only takes a few seconds before I realize that his sperm is oozing onto the fabric covering my pussy, keeping it damp and absorbing his scent.

"Get used to this." He rubs a pair of fingers over my cunt, working the wet cotton between my labia, onto my clit. "Now I'll be with you for the rest of the day."

My flesh leaps to life. I love that idea.

I wind my arms around him. "Oliver…"

"Let's get you moved into the master bedroom now. I've already brought my suitcases in."

"Later." I rub against him and whisper a soft little "Fuck me again" in his ear.

He smiles, and it looks suspiciously like gloating. "I'm trying to be thoughtful and let your body recover. You're tempting me like a naughty girl."

"I'd rather have you naked than thoughtful." I bat my lashes.

Oliver laughs. "God, you were made for me."

"Is that a yes?"

He sends me a stare full of mock censure. "Behave. I'm trying to tell you something important."

My smile freezes. *Please tell me he hasn't changed his mind…* "What?"

"I've called my parents and let them know I'm not returning to London after all. They're disappointed but they know how I feel about you. They've known for quite some time."

"Are you sorry you're not going home?"

"Are you mad? Home is here with you. I was dreading leaving you, Kayla. I've been in love with you for so long that I wasn't sure how I was going to live without you." He sighs in regret. "I wish now that I'd confessed ages ago. I worried Shane wouldn't approve. I worried I'd be too demanding and rough. I worried you'd resent me someday."

"Impossible. I'll only love you more."

He pulls at the back of his neck nervously. "I hope you still think that when I tell you I made Justin go away for good."

"You did?" I jump into his arms. "He's been a thorn in my side since one of my sorority sisters introduced him to me. If I never talk to him again, that would be great."

My acceptance makes him smile. "Done. Did you have any idea when you woke up this morning how this day would unfold?"

"None." I smile, even as he pulls at my sore nipples again. "I'm just bummed that I have to go back to school on Monday. Are you going back to work then?"

"I rang my boss while you napped. He's glad I've decided to stay. Apparently, he wasn't looking forward to replacing me…"

That doesn't surprise me. "You're smart. And a hard worker."

"Maybe you can skip a day or two of class? I can finagle a few days away from my desk. What do you say?"

I love the idea and wriggle against him. When he gets hard once more, I giggle.

He moans. "Are you trying to lead me around by my cock or kill me with sex?"

"Both," I venture.

"We'll see who's laughing in an hour," he warns with a sensual growl.

I giggle again.

"You think that's funny?"

"No. I'm just happy. I never expected you to make my dreams come true. I love you."

He strokes my pussy again and groans when he finds it even wetter than before. He tears off my panties, tosses me on my back, then sinks his entire length into me in one savage stroke. "We'll move your things into the bedroom later. Right now, I want to show you how much I love you, too."

EPILOGUE

Seven weeks later

Graduation day dawns like all the others recently. I wake to the feel of Oliver sucking my nipples and toying with my pussy. He wants inside me—again. Our bed smells like sex since he awakened me twice during the night. I'm deliciously sore all over, but my pussy still cramps with sharp need whenever he touches me. I spread my legs for him.

I'm surprised when he doesn't sink between them right away.

Eyeing him, half-dressed and rumpled and still so, so sexy to me, I lift onto my elbows. "Oliver?"

"Yes, I'm going to fuck you, love. But I've got two presents for you first." He prods me out of bed naked—I'm never allowed to wear anything to sleep except the wedding ring he slipped on my finger two weekends ago in Vegas—then hustles me to the garage. Inside sits a sleek new white convertible sedan with a big red bow. After I squeal and throw my arms around his neck, I slide in and rub my bare ass on the gorgeous leather seats.

Oliver promises I can test drive the car soon, so I kiss him, letting my hands roam his now familiar body as he leads me to the master bathroom. On the counter sits a bag from the local drugstore. I know what's inside before I even look at it.

"You think…" I turn to him, biting my lip. We've been hoping and trying, but I had a period last month, although abbreviated, so I'm not sure.

Oliver just smiles. "I'm almost certain. Go on."

I rifle through the sack and find a home pregnancy test. I tear into the box, follow the instructions, and what do you know? I'm pregnant!

He slides his arms around me, and I caress my flat stomach, amazed to think that we've already created life.

"It's happening. We're starting our new family, Oliver."

"I'm so proud of you. You graduated near the top of your class, got multiple job offers, and now you're going to make your devoted husband a father. I love you."

"I love you, too," I sigh.

"Yeah? Want to come back to bed and show me how much?"

I eagerly comply, crying out when he sinks his hard cock deep into me. I moan as he caresses my belly and pumps into me slowly, kissing my neck.

"You've made me so happy, Kayla."

Me, too. "I have you, so I have everything I could ever want."

He thrusts in again, giving me the most delicious friction. "Everything? Didn't you say you fancied a bit of bondage? I've got some restraints and a pair of nipple clamps with your name on them..."

I moan. Oliver always loves me well and thoroughly. "Please. I can't wait."

SEDUCING
THE
Bride

A Forbidden Confession

SHAYLA BLACK
Steamy. Emotional. Forever.

ABOUT SEDUCING THE BRIDE

Can he persuade his best friend's daughter that she belongs to him?

I'm Hayden.

I'm old enough to know better.

I can have any woman I want—except Perrie Atkins.

She's too young. Off limits. Innocent. Forbidden.

She's my best friend's daughter.

Once, she had a crush on me. Now that she's grown and engaged to another man, I can't just let her go. But how many bridges am I willing to burn to convince her that she's mine? Maybe if I tell her I'm in love with her, she'll choose me.

Then again, Perrie has shocked me for years—and now is no different…

Enjoy this Forbidden Confession. HEA guaranteed!

PROLOGUE

August
Phoenix

Hayden

I'm going to hell.

That's not news; I've known for a while. But as I fantasize—not for the first time—about my friend and business
partner's barely legal daughter, I have no doubt purgatory has
an engraved throne waiting for me.

"Come on, slowpoke!" Perrie Atkins grabs my hand and
flips her gaze my way, her dark, wet hair clinging to her pale,
so-soft skin.

She giggles as she drags me back into the simulated ocean to
wait for another wave, her dimples flashing with rosy-cheeked
excitement. I can't not notice that her pink bikini bottoms, which
are held up by little bows, reveal more of her ass than they
conceal.

"Again?" I pretend to grouse.

I secretly love spending time with her.

Eight years ago, when I was fresh out of college and had just bought half of a successful construction business, not so much. But at the time, my partner, Dan, was a newly single father. Business was booming, projects were at a critical point…and I was green. So I pulled a lot of babysitting duty. After watching teen angst movies, baking cookies, teaching Perrie pre-algebra, holding her while she'd cried over her first crush, and bringing her to this water park a lot, I got to know her. And I found myself enjoying the witty, intrepid kid.

Then…puberty hit. Things changed. It was fine at first. Perrie was still cute, going on about anime that confused me and K-pop music. I loved teasing her about her "favorite tunes." How could she possibly know which song she liked most when they were sung in Korean? She got a pixie cut before her sweet sixteen and sobbed afterward. But I managed to coax a smile out of her when I called her my brunette Tinker Bell.

Then she decided to become a cheerleader her senior year. With her eighteenth birthday looming, and the skirts suddenly skimpy, I couldn't deny that somewhere in the last few years of s'mores, arcade games, and bad B horror movies, she had grown up.

I didn't feel like a proud "uncle" at all. I felt like a perv for recognizing that Perrie was totally fuckable. Worse, I was dying to be the man who proved just how true that was. My fixation only seems more real because I haven't had sex in nearly a year. She's the only woman I want.

Yeah, I'm going to hell.

"What's the matter? Getting old?" she taunts. "Should I sign you up for AARP?"

I'm thirty—nowhere near retirement age. To her, I probably seem ancient. That's depressing as hell.

"What do you know? You're barely old enough to wipe your own ass."

"Ha! Age is just a number. Besides..." She crosses her arms over her chest. "I'm better and smarter than you."

I don't dare look at her beaded nipples poking her little bikini top. Well, not again. "Are you now?"

We play this game a lot, too. She's adorably competitive at everything—video games, sports, trivia, crosswords, driving records, reading lists—and I love that about her. She keeps me on my toes, encourages me, and makes me strive to be better.

I already feel guilty for this blistering torch I'm carrying for her. But it's worse this summer because it's become absolutely clear that I don't just want to peel off her clothes and pop her still-untouched cherry.

I'm in love with her.

Dan would crucify me if he had any idea what I was thinking about his baby girl. And I wouldn't blame him.

I absolutely, positively cannot cross the line with Perrie. Besides the risk of blowing up the business I share with the man I consider an older brother, there's the girl herself. She's got a big, bright future in front of her, starting with an Ivy League university back East—on a full scholarship. Yeah, she's that smart. She needs to leave Phoenix, see the world, meet people, experience life. And she needs to do that without me.

My head knows it. My cock hates that idea.

Even if Dan didn't bury me alive in quick-dry cement for touching his daughter, I doubt Perrie thinks of me that way. Sure, I've caught her looking once or twice. Curiosity about the opposite sex is normal, and because she's an only child, she spends her time with adults—mostly me. She's mature beyond her years and seriously hated the games high school boys played. But she's human; she has hormones. Hell, I peeked into her room last week, thinking she was in bed with a headache… but I swear I caught her masturbating. Seeing her panting, flushed, and shuddering under her covers has plagued my sex drive since.

I keep telling myself this is all moot. She's leaving to start her amazing new life tomorrow morning, and our outing to this water park we've visited together many times is our last. But the subversive part of my brain keeps insisting I still have a whole night to find a creative way—preferably without clothes—to change her mind.

God, I'm an idiot.

"When we walked in, I saw they still have that Tempest machine in the arcade," she remarked with a challenging smile. "Bet I can beat you again."

"You wish. This time will be different."

She raises that dark arch of a brow at me. "Because you've been practicing?"

"Because I'm determined," I lie.

I'm actually relieved she's found something else for us to do in public. As long as we're not alone, I can't be too reckless about putting my hands on her.

"Here it comes!" Her smile brightens as the man-made wave spouts from the edge of the pool and swells across the water before crashing over us.

The force of the water tugs at me and threatens to drag her under. Sputtering and gasping, she flings herself against me, wrapping her arms around my shoulders and her legs around my middle. She's petite, but her curves feel so fucking seductive and lush.

Our eyes meet. Her lips part. She blinks, water droplets

clinging to her long black lashes. She's mere inches away. All I'd have to do to kiss her is grab a fistful of her lush brown hair, pull her against me, and crush her lips under my own.

Could I talk her into my bed and out of her virginity?

Other than my conscience, every part of me salutes that idea, especially the overeager appendage between my legs. But if I let her near my cock, she'll realize how badly I want her.

To avert that crisis, I tickle her ribs and get the expected squeal in return before I carefully set her aside.

She sends me a little pout. "Pushing me away already? You'll be rid of me soon enough."

That softens my heart…if not the rest of my body. "I never want to be rid of you, sweet pea."

"It still doesn't seem real that I'm leaving. I've done all the paperwork and packed up everything, got my plane ticket …" She frowns. "Tell me I'm making the right decision."

"It's a great school. You're going to love it there and amazing things will happen for you." That's what I tell myself. "You'll learn new things, gain independence…" *Meet boys. Have sex.*

I try not to think about that. Sure, it would be better for her if she found some lucky guy who made her happy. But she doesn't even know him yet, and I already want to punch him.

"That's what Dad says."

"What do you think?"

She sighs. "It all sounded great…before I was hours away from leaving."

"You're just nervous, and it's totally understandable. Give it at least a semester. Then, if you hate it, talk to your dad. Dan will understand, and you two can come up with a plan."

"Can't I call you instead? You know he's not much for giving me advice."

I can't argue with her there. Dan is a great guy, just seemingly ill-equipped to handle a teenage daughter on his own.

"You can always call me," I tell her. "But once you get there and settled, you're not going to want to."

"Of course I will. I'll miss you."

Her whisper spreads sparks through my blood. It seems like she's saying so much with those three words. That's got to be my wishful thinking.

"I'll miss you, too, sweet pea."

After another few hours under the sweltering summer sun and a Tempest marathon in the arcade, I guide an exhausted Perrie through the dark parking lot.

As I start my truck, she smiles over at me, holding up one of the arcade's tokens. "One left over!"

"Save it for next time we're together. We'll play again then, okay?"

"Sure."

"Promise?"

"I promise. You know I never break those."

She doesn't. I can always count on Perrie.

Her little smile turns wistful. "Today was great. Thanks for everything."

"Always a pleasure. Ice cream?" I offer simply to prolong our last few minutes together. If she'd let me eat it off her body, I'd love it even more.

For the first time ever, she turns down her favorite dessert. "Would you mind just taking me home? I...need to talk to you about something."

"Sure."

I wrack my brain to figure out what's bothering her and why she hasn't already told me. It doesn't help that she's unusually silent or that the closer we get to her house, the more pensive she becomes.

When I pull into the driveway and park the truck, I turn to her with a frown. "Perrie?"

She looks toward the house. All the windows are dark. Dan still isn't home. Since he's a workaholic, it's no surprise.

"Can you come in? I might need help getting my suitcases down the stairs."

"No problem."

I jump out of my vehicle and usher her through the front door. Inside the house, lots of Perrie's things are already missing, like her ever-present Bluetooth speaker, her car keys, the random bottle of nail polish... Somehow, the place already seems emptier and she's not even gone.

Her leaving is going to be rough.

I drag in a deep breath as I follow her up the stairs, grateful that she's put on shorts. They're so tiny that the curve of her ass hangs out under the hem, but they cover more than her bikini bottoms. I've got to be grateful for small favors.

Inside her room, I spot two big suitcases near the door and reach for them. "Both of these?"

"Yeah. Wait." She wraps a tentative hand around my arm, looking downright nervous.

"You okay?"

She bites her lip again, seemingly hesitant and agitated. "You like me, right?"

As a person? Or as a woman?

"Sure. We've been friends for years," I say carefully.

She sighs. "What if I don't want to be friends?"

My heart stutters. "I don't understand."

But I think I do.

"I'm not making sense." She raises her chin and pins me

with an unblinking stare. "Hayden, I'm in love with you. I always have been. I want you to spend tonight with me. Please."

Perrie Atkins just propositioned me. *Holy shit.*

I swallow, struck mute. My mouth hangs open. My heart revs. My cock... Well, it's predictable.

Before I can say a word, she launches herself against me, winds her arms around my neck, and slants her lips over mine.

All thoughts freeze under an onslaught of *oh, hell yes.*

Her kiss is wholly unpracticed, but I'm aroused as fuck because I'm finally feeling Perrie.

My brain screams that I need to push her away...but the rest of me has a totally different scheme. It's irresponsible and will lead me straight to Hades, but I'm voting in favor of sin.

With a groan, I grip her ass in my hands, then turn to push her against the wall, plunging into her mouth and devouring her like I'm starved because I am.

Her little whimper as she wraps her legs around my hips goes straight to my dick. She clings to me with her whole body, parting her lips wider to accommodate the insistent stab of my tongue and spilling more of her candy flavor for me to consume.

As I recklessly inhale her, I shove aside every thought except this moment.

A million images of us together in her bed—me rooting through her virgin flesh and rutting on top of her without clothing or anything as practical as a condom between us— bombard my brain. My patience goes up in flames. After one kiss, I'm more aroused than I've ever been in my life.

Fuck, I have to stop. Now. If I don't, I won't be able to. Then every filthy fantasy swimming in my brain will become a reality.

And all of Perrie's grand plans for the future will come to a halt. Her life will be over.

I can't be responsible for that.

Heaving in a ragged breath, I shove her away from me. "No."

Still panting, she sends me a pleading stare. Tears swim in her big green eyes. Her lips look so goddamn red and lush from our rough kiss, it's all I can do not to grab her again.

"Hayden…"

Somewhere, I find the will to put more distance between us. "I said no, Perrie. I won't spend the night with you. I don't see you like that."

"Bullshit." She looks down at the hard length beneath the fly of my shorts. "You're lying."

No matter what my mouth says, my dick gives me away.

"I want a woman. You're just a kid."

"I'm not adult enough because I'm a virgin?" She looks hurt.

"Sexual experience has nothing to do with it." The last thing I want to do is encourage her to find the first hard prick to take her innocence. "But you've never paid a bill or spent a night under a roof you've had to earn. Hell, last month, you were still venting about high school." Since she's been running the household in her mom's absence for nearly eight years, accusing her of immaturity is a low blow. But I can't feel bad about saying whatever will put a stop to her ruination. "We're at different places in our lives, Perrie."

"You love me," she hurls. "I know it. The way you kissed me proved it."

Shit. "The way I kissed you proves I'm a guy who likes pussy. And if you weren't Dan's daughter, I'd probably take it. But you are, and I don't want to fuck up a friendship. So I'm going now."

I turn to leave her room before I do whatever it takes to wipe that crestfallen look off her face and replace it with a sated smile.

"Wait!" she calls out.

The desperate catch in her voice nearly does me in.

"Take this." She marches in front of me and slaps her last game token in my hand, then sends me a determined stare. "Save it. Every day I'm gone, I want you to look at it, feel it, and remember me. Know that I'll be saving myself for you. One day, Hayden Hughes, you'll want me. Not just my pussy. *Me.* When that day comes, return the token to me. Anytime, anywhere, I'll be yours for the night. Then I'll prove I'm all the woman you need."

The little metal disc burns my palm as she sidles past me, toward her adjoining bathroom.

As she slams the door, I shove the token in my pocket with a curse. Of course she wouldn't give up easily. Persistence is one of Perrie's qualities I usually admire. Tonight, it makes me fucking afraid that she really will wait until the memory of that blistering kiss breaks me down and I'm unable to resist her anymore.

"That day isn't coming," I yell through the door to her, but they're empty words. "I'll see you during Christmas break. And we won't talk about this then—or ever."

When I shove my way out of the house and drive off into the night, I'm not relieved. In fact, I can't help but wonder if I've just made the worst mistake of my life.

CHAPTER ONE

June, nearly four years later

Perrie didn't come home for Christmas that year. Or visit at all the following summer. There was always an amazing trip with a roommate, a really important internship she couldn't miss, or another class to take. I knew Dan talked to Perrie regularly. He even flew back East a few times to visit her. A couple months ago he attended her graduation. But she never returned to Phoenix. Worse, she never spoke to me in those long four years, even the time I broke down and called a few weeks after her departure.

I've missed her like hell and spent years second-guessing the way I acted that final, terrible night. A million times, I wondered what would have happened if I had taken her to bed, plucked her innocence, and made her promises for the future I wish we were planning together even now. I'll never know.

Tonight, she's finally coming home.

"Thanks for being here." Dan claps me on the shoulder with one hand while slipping me a cold beer with the other.

I tried to beg off this family reunion to save my sanity by pointing out that Perrie is his only child and they should spend this precious time together. He merely insisted that I'm like family and that he wants us all together.

"My pleasure." As lies go, it's a whopper.

"I'm excited Perrie is on her way home. I can't wait to hear her big announcement."

I've got a bad feeling about it. She was always the kind of girl who shouted good things from the rooftops. Her social media should be loaded with this stuff. So not even giving her father a hint makes me nervous as hell.

Forcing a smile, I clap him on the back. "She's probably landed an amazing job. No surprise, right? She went to a top-notch school, graduated summa cum laude, and has made a million connections, I'm sure."

"I'm really proud of her." His smile falters into something melancholy. "Sometimes, I look back and regret all the time I spent working instead of being with her, especially after her mother left. But she always had you. That meant the world to both of us."

"She's a special girl." It's one of the few things I can say that won't give away how horribly I've missed Perrie and how the hole she left in my heart has just about killed me.

From the family room, we both hear the slam of a car door. I drag in a breath and clutch my beer can so tightly it nearly crumples in my fist. I have no idea what I'll say to her.

Dan turns and marches for the front door. "That should be Perrie."

Fuck, I have to keep it together. I can't grab her, jerk her into my arms, and kiss her. I can't confess how fucking much I've missed her in my life. I especially don't dare whisper that she's still number one in my spank bank, which I frequent because real sex with random women is always a disappointment.

None of them is Perrie.

But if there's any hope for us, I won't find out how she feels by hiding out with my cold one in the next room, so I follow Dan.

When I walk into the foyer, it isn't Dan's daughter coming through the door, suitcase in hand. Instead, I see a man in his mid-twenties wearing a charcoal business suit that clearly costs a small fortune. His slight build, pale skin, and smooth, manicured hands tell me he's a well-paid desk jockey.

"Who are you?" He definitely doesn't resemble any rideshare driver I've ever had.

The guy sets a black suitcase aside and thrusts his hand in my direction. "Derek Kingston. You must be Hayden."

"Yeah." Should I know this guy? "Good to meet you."

As he shakes my hand, he smiles. "I've heard all about you."

His raised brow tells me not all of it is good.

I scowl. "I'm sorry. How do you know Perrie?"

"Are you her boyfriend?" a beaming Dan asks.

"She didn't tell you?"

An instant later, Perrie comes through the door and wraps her hand around Derek's arm. It's impossible to miss the giant teardrop-shaped diamond on the ring finger of her left hand.

She's *engaged?*

"We're getting married. I wanted to surprise everyone." She sends her father a too-cheery smile and presses a kiss to his cheek.

She hasn't once looked my way.

"I'm definitely surprised." Dan nods, seeming to take it all in.

Join the club. Less than sixty seconds ago, I was bracing to set eyes on Perrie again...and trying to figure out what to do about her stranglehold on my heart. This new development makes it obvious that worry is moot.

"I didn't know you were even dating anyone," Dan adds.

Perrie laughs too quickly. I know her sounds and expressions. She's a bundle of nerves. "Now you do. Honestly, it happened quickly. We met through mutual friends just before the holidays. One thing led to another, and we started dating about three months ago."

Three months ago?

"That seems fast," I remark.

She finally looks my way. "In my experience, when you wait on love, it usually passes you by."

Clearly, Perrie can still deliver a zinger.

She's also more beautiful—and fuckable—than ever. The pixie cut she once had is a long-distant memory, replaced by dark waves that flow to the middle of her back. The sheer pink shade on her full lips and the dusting of brown shadow on her eyes only accent her stunning features. Her cheeks still have a hint of girlish fullness that makes her look oh so sweet. But she's got this new air of confidence that's alluring as hell.

Lust seizes my breath. My blood courses. My skin feels tight and hot. It takes everything I've got not to grab her, hold her, kiss her, and remind her how close we were and how much closer we could be—if she weren't planning to marry someone else.

Derek wraps his arm around Perrie's waist possessively. "Well said, darling."

It takes all my restraint not to beat the shit out of him.

Dan smiles proudly. "Why don't you two come in and sit?

We'll have a drink and you can tell Hayden and me all about your wedding plans."

I'd rather have all my teeth ripped out with pliers, but as everyone adjourns to the living room, I maneuver myself between Perrie and her fiancé. "I didn't get to say hello."

I drop my hand on her shoulder. That single touch pings need through me as her soft gasp reaches my ears. Then she zips her stare to me, sharp and startled.

There's the awareness we shared four years ago. Perrie still feels it.

"Hi, Hayden." She backs away from me with a tight smile and sticks out her hand.

Oh, sweet pea. We're way past a handshake…

But I slide my palm against hers because I need to feel her out. Not up—though I'm dying to do that, too. But I've got to decide if I'm going to let Perrie be the one who got away…or if I'm going to fight to win her back.

I give her hand a tug, sending her tumbling against me. Our chests collide. I encircle her waist with an unyielding arm. When our gazes meet, she blinks, turns tense, holds her breath. Her nipples turn so hard they're impossible not to notice.

Yeah, she's not immune to me—not even a little.

Repressing a smile, I reach under her hair, wrap my fingers around her nape, and press my lips to the shell of her ear. "I've missed you."

She shivers and softens against me. "Missed you, too."

I hate to let Perrie go after her gratifying whisper, but I have to—at least for now. As much as I want her, I also want what's best for her. Is there *any* chance that's Derek?

"Come sit with me, darling." Her fiancé grabs her hand and leads her to the sofa, sitting her in the corner, as far from me as possible.

I can't fault his instincts…

When Dan sits in the recliner closest to them, I take the love seat on the other side of the room. From here, I can study Perrie's face, Derek's behavior, and their interaction.

She settles stiffly next to the man she intends to marry. They don't touch…until Derek grabs her hand.

"I wanted to meet you in person, Mr. Atkins, and officially ask you for Perrie's hand first." He gives us an aw-shucks smile. "But I just couldn't wait. This girl is one of a kind."

Dan looks pleased by Derek's praise. I'm not. He's only stating the obvious.

"I understand," my friend and business partner says. "Tell me more about you."

He's not going to grill this guy about why he's rushing Perrie to the altar?

"Well, I'm co-CEO of an environmental tech company. A buddy of mine and I started the firm, and we're moving our headquarters to Seattle next month…"

As Derek drones on, I get irritated. Not only does he sound like a self-important asshole, but I realize he intends to take Perrie far away again. Deep down, I'd held out hope that she'd come back to Phoenix after graduation…

"What do you think of Seattle?" I ask her.

She shrugs. "I haven't been yet. Derek says it's amazing…"

So he doesn't care if she likes where they'll live?

"What will you do there?"

"I'm sure she'll find a job," Derek answers for her. "She's so smart and charming. There are lots of great start-ups and little women-owned businesses where she could make a difference."

Maybe he doesn't mean it, but the douche sounds condescending. Perrie will make a splash wherever she's employed, not just in "little" corners of the workplace. Besides, none of that sounds like they'll fulfill the dreams Perrie expressed before she left for school. "Sweet pea?"

She shrugs. "I'll figure it out. It's a big city with a healthy economy…"

And a lot of rain. She's always loved the desert's heat, sun, and stark beauty. To her, storms ruin a gorgeous blue sky. And Derek wants to take her to one of the rainiest cities in the country.

Does he know her at all?

Sure, she might be willing to make that sacrifice if she really loves him. But the way she seems reluctant to look at the guy, much less touch him, leads me to wonder if she does.

"Well, that all sounds wonderful," Dan says when Derek finally shuts up. "Are you excited, Perrie?"

"Thrilled."

She doesn't sound like it. I'm calling bullshit.

"So was your engagement your big announcement, sweet pea?" I ask her directly because I don't want Asshole thinking I'm talking to him.

"Part of it." She swallows nervously, then finally cuts me a sidelong stare. The flare of awareness when our eyes meet shows all over her face. Then she turns to Dan and squeezes his hand. "We'd actually like to get married here, with your permission."

"I'd love that." Dan looks like a pleased, proud father.

I want to throw up. "When?"

She hesitates. "Saturday."

In six fucking days? That's how long I have to see if tying herself to Derek would be the biggest mistake of her life and stop her?

"Oh, wow. Well…" Dan rubs his hands together. "We have a

lot of planning to do, then. How about we sit down to dinner, and you can tell me what you're envisioning."

While Perrie's father wastes his time with that, I'll figure out how to get her alone so I can hear her side of this clusterfuck—without her fiancé butting in.

Perrie

HAYDEN CAN SEE right through me; I'm sure of it.

I escaped the tension of the dinner table to do the dishes, but I'm still a nervous wreck. Hayden glared at Derek throughout the entire meal. I know the million and one reasons my fiancé doesn't like my childhood crush. And my father seems oblivious to the undercurrents.

Could this get any more awkward?

Unfortunately, yes. If Hayden discovers my secret, it will be a hundred times worse.

As I tuck the last of the silverware into the dishwasher and slam the door shut, I wonder if I've made the right choice. Maybe I should explain everything. But I run the risk of shocking and disappointing my father. Ugh, I can't deal with that now. After eight hours of travel and one of the most stressful evenings in memory, I'm beat.

Thank goodness my father and Derek were gung ho to scout out the backyard for the perfect ceremony site—and that Hayden seems completely focused on dissecting my fiancé. I don't expect that to last. He'll soon turn his attention on me, and then…I'm almost afraid to ask.

I'd been hoping I wouldn't feel any of this crazy lovesickness when I set eyes on him. But now it's painfully clear that I'll have to deal with these nagging feelings until Saturday—just like I've done for the past four years.

"Perrie."

Speak of the devil.

"Hayden." I don't look at him as he saunters into the kitchen, his stare glued to me. Unfortunately, I can't shake the certainty that I'm transparent. *Please don't let him see my heart shivering and naked in front of him.* "What's up?"

He takes hold of my left hand—jolting me with his touch—and stares at my engagement ring. It's huge and not at all what I would have picked. Even under the kitchen lights, it both sparkles and screams that I'm someone's woman—which is exactly what Derek wanted.

Without a word, Hayden releases my hand and pins me with the sort of stare that makes me squirm. "Tell me what you're doing."

"What does it look like? I'm doing the dishes."

"Don't play dumb. Three months, sweet pea? What's your rush? And don't give me that one-thing-led-to-another bullshit. You're not usually impulsive."

"I appreciate your concern, but Derek is great. Don't worry."

He scowls. "Did you think that script would work with me? It makes Dan and his daddy-guilt feel better to believe you, but I'm going to be a tougher sell. Do you love him?"

God, he's more direct than I remember.

I reach for the dirty pans. "Pass me the dish soap, please."

Heaving a frustrated sigh, Hayden grabs my shoulders. "The fucking dishes will wait until we've talked."

He's too close. I can't take it.

I wrench away and shake my head. "You don't get to do this. I gave you an opportunity—"

"You were too young."

"That didn't make what I felt any less real. But if you think you can swoop in four years later and take me up on my stupid offer now that I'm 'old enough,' you're sorely mistaken."

"Does he make you happy?"

"Derek has been so good to me. And for me." It's the truth.

"Are you kidding? He fucking patronized you. He made your career seem like something cute and barely worth his notice. That can't be okay with you. I know you way too well to believe that."

"You don't understand."

"Maybe *you* don't," he argues as he advances on me again. Backed into the kitchen, the stove behind me, I have nowhere to go. "You deserve someone who's so proud of you he's willing to shout your praises. Hell, you deserve a man who worships you. I don't think that's him."

"It's not you, either, so it's none of your business."

"What if I make it my business?"

My heart stops. "What does that mean?"

"Can you look me in the eye and tell me you love this man?"

"I love Derek."

Hayden grinds his teeth as he scrutinizes my expression, taking me apart second by second.

What if he really can see through me?

"Does he make you breathless as a lover? Are you eager to marry him? Do you want to have his children? Are you in *that* kind of love with him? Because so far, I'm not buying it."

"Why can't you stop playing twenty questions, congratulate me, and let it go?"

The smile that plays at his lips makes me nervous as hell. "One reason: I think you still have feelings for me. And you know what? I'll come clean. I wanted you back then, too. That hot-as-fuck kiss has haunted me since you left, and if you'd had any idea how close I was to tossing you on your bed and being the first—and last—man inside you, it would have scared the hell out of you."

My heart chugs in my chest, and I cross my arms to hide my trembling. "Why tell me now?"

"Because I don't think you and I are through."

I shake my head. "I'm getting married."

"I know you think so. But I want to see just how attached you are to him."

He charges into my personal space and seizes my face in his hands, his lips hovering a breath above my own. We pant. Our breaths mingle. He's so, so close…

Oh, god, Hayden is going to kiss me. I'm ashamed to admit how desperately I want it.

The slamming of the back door and the rumble of Derek's voice blending with my father's sends me wrenching from his arms. "Leave me alone."

He curses softly, then holds up his hands as if he's giving up. "For now."

But I know better. Once Hayden decides he wants something, he'll stop at nothing to take it. He will come at me relentlessly until I get married…or get weak.

God help me.

CHAPTER TWO

Hayden

Over the next couple of days, Perrie is gone more than she's around. I can't decide if she's hurriedly dashing here and there to whip this wedding together or to avoid me.

Either way, it hasn't escaped my notice that Derek hasn't lifted a finger to help her to plan their nuptials.

Lazy asshole. If I were marrying her…

But I can't go there. That thought only drives me insane.

The bottom line is, I don't like it—and I don't like him. Am I jealous that he's had the woman I'm aching for? Sure. But he's also a jerk, holing himself up in the study and pounding on his laptop, phone seemingly glued to his ear. Does he think he's too important to help her? I don't get what she sees in this guy.

It's time I found out.

Making my way down the hall, I spy Derek in the study, working frantically, hair disheveled, tie thrown across the room.

I don't bother with hello. "I need to talk to you."

"It will have to wait. Would you mind telling Perrie that I can't go with her to the cake tasting? A damn conference call just cropped up, and it's really important."

But your wedding isn't?

It's all I can do not to roll my eyes. "If you give me five minutes, sure."

It shouldn't take me that long to figure out why Perrie said yes to this asswipe, but I'm giving myself extra time in case he proves to be as slimy as I suspect.

From what I've seen, he's done nothing but put her last. He's a younger, shinier version of Dan. But if Derek bailing on her— yet again—convinces Perrie not to marry him, I'm happy to pass the message along.

"All right. What do you need?" Derek looks ready to dive back into work now that he's found an errand boy to blow off his fiancée for him.

I've gone from wanting to punch him to wondering what's the worst that can happen if I do.

"Oh, for fuck's sake, would you stop looking at me like that?" Derek snarls.

"Like what?"

"You're judging me. It's not as if I wanted work to explode the week Perrie needs me most."

"I'm sure she understands." But I don't. It's a matter of priorities.

"Look, if this deal goes through, it will solidify our future. I don't owe you an explanation, and Perrie knows what's going on. But I'm filling you in so you'll lighten up."

Derek's tone says he isn't fond of me—and he knows the feeling is mutual. Did Perrie tell him that she once had a thing for me? Or has he sensed the undercurrent of attraction still between us?

"Tell me what you love most about her."

"Everything. She's beautiful, man." He shrugs. "Sweet, kind, funny, wicked smart. Everything I could have dreamed of… almost." He sends me a speculative glance. "But sometimes she's distant."

I sense Derek trying to turn the tables. I'm curious; I'll bite. "Yeah?"

Her fiancé nods. "I worry she's not as emotionally invested in our relationship as I am."

Is he kidding me right now? In the last forty-eight hours, she's waited on him hand and foot while singlehandedly planning their small wedding. And don't get me started on what I imagine she's letting him do to her in her childhood bedroom where *I* kissed her first.

"Why would you say that?" I finally ask.

"A couple of weeks after we met, she opened up to me about once having been in love with this guy back home. She said they used to be close. But apparently, he didn't want her. I've been wondering all this time who it could be. I didn't really think I'd meet him on this trip since he rebuffed her and all. But here you are, right under her nose, putting off the *hey, baby* vibes while looking at me like you'd love to rip me in two." Derek leans closer and sends me a sharp, narrow-eyed stare that proves he's a good salesman because he can read people. "Let me tell you something. You had your chance to make her happy. Now it's mine."

He wants to measure dicks? Totally not interested. What's fascinating, though, is Derek's admission that Perrie can be distant. If she felt the need to tell her boy toy about me four years after I let her down, then it's entirely possible she still has feelings for me.

If that's true, why is she engaged to this corporate drone?

Because you rejected her, dipshit. She's marrying this dude because of you.

Fuck. I have to stop her.

"I don't think you can make her happy," I say finally.

Derek scowls. "I don't care what you think."

"That's the first thing we've agreed on," I remark. "I don't care what you think, either."

"You turned Perrie down, old man. She's no longer your concern. So why don't you get out of my face?"

"I turned her down then because she was too young. But you know what that means? I was her first choice."

"Fuck you."

And fuck you, too, pal. "Did you know Perrie hates the rain? Or that she's ambitious as hell? Did you consider *any* of that before you decided on this grand move to Seattle, apparently without consulting her?"

"Back off. You don't get to play the I-don't-want-her-but-you-can't-have-her game. She's not a trophy you win if you run me off. She's a woman who wants a man to love her. You've already proven that's not you. So in four days, she'll be Mrs. Kingston, and you'll be a memory."

He's dead fucking wrong, and continuing this conversation is a waste of both my breath and time. "If thinking that helps you sleep better, have fun." I turn to leave.

He leaps out of his chair. "Where are you going?"

"To find Perrie."

"Don't you dare fuck with her."

Derek looks worried. He should be.

I flash him a satisfied smirk and a mocking wave. "Enjoy your conference call."

With a whistle, I leave. I've got a girl to win back and only a few days to do it. The good news is, I know exactly where to start…

Perrie

ON THE BACK PATIO, I try to absorb the blinding blue June day. I sandwich my phone between my ear and my shoulder, half listening to the caterer's quote. "Uh-huh. I like that."

I really have no idea what I'm agreeing with. I'm way too focused on what Hayden will do next.

During dessert the other night, he "accidentally" brushed against me a hundred times, until my body was aching, every nerve ending on fire.

When Derek and I retired to my childhood bedroom afterward, he wanted to talk about the move to Seattle and the future. I pleaded a headache, hopped into the shower, and masturbated through a trio of orgasms that left me wrung out and teary but distinctly unsatisfied.

Yesterday, I tried to focus on the details for this admittedly small but important event. The flowers were easy since I really only need a bouquet to carry and a few arrangements to line the trellised arch that will serve as the makeshift altar. I rented tables and chairs for roughly twenty-five people. I texted a few friends from both high school and college to invite them. But I still don't have a dress, an officiant, a photographer, or a cake. I've got at least a hundred other details that need addressing.

Derek is god knows where in the house, so it's up to me to finish them, but I'm way too distracted to check anything off my list.

Why did I think this was a good idea?

"What?" I say to the caterer because I totally lost my train of thought to Hayden.

It happens a lot.

Thankfully, she offers to email her food suggestions and her quote, then we hang up. I'll read everything when I'm more focused.

"Hi, sweet pea." Hayden strolls up in ripped denim shorts and a tight tank that shows off the fact he works with his body for a living. The sun loves this man. The skin over his bulging muscles is a rich golden brown that reminds me exactly why I always looked forward to our days at the water park. Hayden in a bathing suit is a work of art.

I try not to drool. "Hey. You're not working today?"

"I'd rather spend time with you. How's the wedding planning?"

He knows exactly how to make me melt. "Slow."

"Need help?"

I shoot him a suspicious glance. "Why? Two days ago, you told me I was marrying the wrong man. Changed your mind?"

"No. I just had a chat with Dipshit—I mean, Derek. I'm more convinced than ever that I'm right. By the way, he told me to tell you he can't come with you to test cakes."

I sigh. "We both worried this week would get crazy. He and his business partner are trying to wrap up a big negotiation before the move."

"Business comes first. Got it." Hayden shoots me a stare full of mock confusion. "I thought you didn't want to marry someone like your father."

He's not wrong, but I don't dare validate him now. "Did you come to pass judgment or to help?"

"To help. I'm all yours…"

The way he smiles tells me he doesn't just mean to assist me in wedding planning, but *anything* else I want. I'd love to ask him about his relationships and sex life…but I can't say in one breath that I'm not interested and get personal in the next.

"Thanks. Know a good photographer or officiant?"

That perks him up. "Actually, yeah. My sister moved here last year. I don't know if Dan told you…"

"No, but I doubt she wants to shoot my wedding pictures. That's way below her pay grade."

Hannah is a fashion photographer—one of the best in the business. Her pictures are stunning. She's great at capturing both striking angles and emotion with every shot.

"She'll do it. Promise." He winks. "So cross that off your list."

"That's amazing. I really appreciate it. But why would she move here?" She's lived in New York forever and constantly traveled the world. "Phoenix is hardly a fashion mecca."

"She gave me a lot of mumbo-jumbo about her reasons for relocating, but ultimately it has one appeal she couldn't resist."

"You?" I'm sure my stare reflects how skeptical I am about that.

"Not even close." He grins. "I'm not supposed to know this, but she and your father are…together."

I gape. "Are you sure? My dad works. He never dates."

"Ever since Hannah came to visit me last spring, he does. They hit it off, and I'm pretty sure they hooked up. After that, they started talking and…I think it's getting serious."

"So you're saying she'd shoot my wedding as a favor to my dad, not you?"

"Pretty much."

"But neither of them has actually told you about their relationship?"

"Not in so many words. They think I'm blind or something. It's funny. But the good news is, Dan finally started working a lot less." Hayden takes my hand, and I smother a gasp at the fire his simple touch ignites. "He didn't learn to put the people in his life first soon enough to save his marriage to your mom. Or to give you the childhood you deserved. But he *has* learned since Hannah."

"Now that I think about it, he's been around a lot more in the last couple of days."

"It took your dad twenty years to figure out what was most important." He shoots me a speculative stare. "How long will that lesson take Derek? Do you really want to marry someone who will put you last for years? Decades?"

"Stop." It's all I can say. Every moment I'm with Hayden, I feel so weak.

"I'm right, and you know it."

I snatch my phone off the table and grab my nearby car keys. "I have to go or I'll be late to the cake testing."

"How about some company?"

Oh, he's tempting me—on purpose, I'm sure. I shouldn't let him get too close...but it would be nice to have another opinion. At least that's what I tell myself. "All right."

The way he smiles says he's up to something. "By the way, our office manager, Linda, has a son who's an associate pastor. He could probably perform the ceremony. Want me to call?"

"Have you met him?"

Hayden nods. "Nice guy. Young, funny. He'd be good."

"Sure. I'd appreciate it. Let me grab my lipstick and my wallet so we can go."

"My truck is blocking your rental. I'll drive."

"Fine." I disappear to gather my belongings—and my wits.

I'm still suspicious of the reasons he's being so helpful, but Hayden has always been the first to lend a hand to people who need it. He's a great problem solver, a good networker, a fabulous friend, and he has an uncanny ability of convincing everyone to see things his way…

That last trait worries me. He knows exactly how to push my buttons.

By the time I reach the foyer again, he's smiling and tucking his phone back into his pocket. "Linda's son, Josh, is open to meeting you this evening and seeing if you'd be a good fit."

"Great," I say as we head out the door. "If I can check one more thing off my list…"

"I'll set it up for five thirty?"

"Perfect."

He sends off a text just before he unlocks the truck and opens the passenger door to help me inside. It's a perfect Arizona day, cloudless and blue. The slight breeze ruffles my hair and my skirt. I'm drinking in the blessed sunlight. My earlier peek at Seattle's forecast showed days of gloom and rain ahead.

The ten-minute drive to the bakery is full of classic grunge tunes and awareness-heavy silence. Hayden steers a vehicle like he leads his life—competently, confidently, and without much apology. It's one of the things that most attracts me to him. He doesn't spend a lot of time second-guessing himself. If he gets something wrong, he just fixes it.

Is that what he's trying to do with me?

When he opens my door and holds out his palm, I realize we've arrived.

I attempt to brace myself before I put my hand in his, but it's useless. Hayden's impact on my restraint is nuclear. Trying not to be affected by him is like trying not to notice a mountain directly in my path.

Impossible.

When our fingers touch, I shudder. It's pathetic. And his little grin tells me he knows I'm not immune.

I slam the car door and head for the bakery. "Don't gloat."

"Not wasting time with that. Are you even going to try convincing me that he satisfies you in bed or are you just going to cede that point to me?"

"What we do in bed is none of your business."

From behind, he grabs my shoulders and presses my back against his chest, hard from years of physical labor. There's absolutely no missing the singe of his firm fingers on my skin or the press of his steely erection against my ass.

It's all I can do not to melt against him.

"Stop it." I mean the protest to come out forcefully. It's totally breathy instead.

God, it's been four awful years since he turned me down. Why can't I get over this man?

"Give me a chance to make you feel so much better," he whispers into my ear.

I don't dare. "We're here to focus on cakes. If you have sex on the brain, you're going to be sorely disappointed."

"When you're around, I always have sex on the brain." He opens the door to the shop for me, revealing a long glass case full of sugary temptations under a fascinating floral ceiling painted in a wash of white, grays, and pale pink. "But I'll be a good boy while we're here."

His words do crazy things to my equilibrium. For years, I've fantasized about being naked with Hayden, about his large, capable hands gripping my hips as he pushes his way inside me and makes me his for the first time.

With his hot palm settling on the small of my back as he ushers me into the cool, white interior and sets my good sense ablaze isn't a good time to think about that.

I should resist baiting him. I should...and yet I send a quelling glare his way. "Zip it. I already know you're all talk."

Hayden laughs, something low and throaty and totally self-satisfied. "Oh, sweet pea, I'll be happy to show you how wrong you are. All you have to do is ditch the deadbeat, and I'll be all over you all the time. And I won't just fuck you until you have an orgasm. That's too easy. I'll fuck you until I've imprinted myself on your soul."

He's already managed that without ever touching me.

But I'm saved from replying when a competent thirtysomething blonde wearing a French twist and a smile appears from the back of the bakery to stand under a modern chandelier. "Can I help you?"

"I'm Perrie Atkins."

She smiles and shakes my hand. "My last-minute bride. Welcome. I'm Misty, the owner." Then she turns her attention to Hayden and sticks out her arm in a professional greeting. "And you must be the impatient fiancé. What was your name?"

"Hayden." He doesn't correct her presumption that he's my groom.

"Actually—"

"We're really eager to taste cakes today and check one more thing off our list." He wraps his arm around me and pulls me against him. "Aren't we, sweet pea?"

I'm not sure what the devil he's up to, pretending I'll be marrying him this weekend. But instead of making a scene about something that doesn't matter, I shrug him off. "I really don't have a flavor in mind, like I said on the phone. So I'm eager to try some samples and make decisions today."

"I'm glad I can squeeze you in. Since your cake only needs to feed thirty or fewer…"

"The event will be really intimate," Hayden cuts in.

"And I want the cake to reflect that. It should be simple but elegant. I found some things I like on Pinterest."

"Perfect. That will help. If you'll show me your pictures, I'll get your tasting tray ready."

When she disappears, I reach for my phone and launch the picture-based social media app, all too aware of Hayden beside me. "You let her think you're my fiancé."

"You didn't correct her."

"Not worth the argument. She only cares about the cake."

"Would you be more excited about this weekend if you were marrying me?"

I turn to him, mouth agape. "Why would you even ask that question?"

"Fine. I won't make you answer that aloud when I already know the answer."

"You don't. That's so far out of the realm of possibility…"

"Is it?"

He's actually suggesting there's an alternate universe in which he and I would be joining hands in a few days and exchanging till-death-do-us-part vows?

"Here we go." Misty returns with a giant baking sheet lined with nearly a dozen beautifully frosted petite cupcakes and two bottles of chilled water. She sets it on a wide desk tucked in the corner and motions us to the chairs in front. "Would you like me to walk you through the flavors?"

"Please."

"On the left is our most popular type for weddings, white. I can serve that with an almond cream filling that's deliciously light or we can go with something fruitier like strawberry or raspberry, which will also add some visual panache to your cake. Down the row, I've got red velvet, chocolate, lemon, carrot, pink champagne, coconut, marble…"

After she goes on about each and tells me all the available fillings, I'm reeling. I thought this would be a simple matter of telling her what I wanted the cake to look like and picking a flavor that most people should enjoy. But like with everything I've run into while planning this event, the selections are more complicated than I thought.

"Do you have specific recommendations?"

"They're all good. It's just a matter of personal preference. I brought you one of everything to taste."

"Hayden is allergic to coconut," I blurt, then get annoyed with myself. Will he even eat the cake?

"I'm glad you told me. Let's remove that sample." Misty plucks one of the mini cupcakes out of the middle of the line. "Once you pick the cake flavor, we'll test some fillings. I'll pull any with coconut, so you don't need to worry."

"Thanks." Hayden smiles like he's totally enjoying himself.

"Of course." Misty nods like she's ready to get down to business. "If you're still not sure where to start, maybe you can tell me some of your favorite desserts."

"My girl loves a sinful bread pudding," Hayden offers.

He remembers that?

Misty nods enthusiastically. "Me, too. The Capital Grille—"

"Has the best, right?"

"Definitely. Oh, my gosh…"

"But Perrie is really all about the ice cream, the lighter and creamier the better."

"That's helpful. Do you like the fruity flavors, the more traditional ones, or—"

"The unusual ones," he puts in for me. "We found a place

once that made a lemon biscotti flavor that had her groaning the whole time she was eating it. We didn't have any alone time that evening, so it made for a long damn night."

I stare at him, wide-eyed. That night, shortly before my high school graduation, is etched into my brain—and only in part because of the amazing ice cream. I remember being days away from turning eighteen and so, so aware of Hayden as a man, of wanting him until I ached and hating the fact he didn't see me as anything but a child. "That's not true."

"You loved that ice cream."

"I meant the way you felt about me."

"I had you fooled." He smiles. "I won't embarrass Misty with the thousand and one filthy things I thought that night. I'll tell you later."

My cheeks turn unmistakably hot. They match the rest of my body, which flashes with need.

I squirm in my chair, not daring to say a word.

Misty clears her throat, looking amused. "We can start with the lemon. I've got a biscotti-flavored filling I can add if you're partial to that flavor combination..."

Over the next twenty minutes, Misty and I chat about cake flavors in between testing each delectable bite. Beside me, I'm aware of Hayden licking frosting from his lips and watching me with an unnerving stare.

"I don't think the carrot cake is for me," I say.

"That was marble." Hayden's smirk says he knows he's rattling me.

"Oh, sorry." I smile at Misty to cover the awkward moment.

"Not at all. It's a lot of flavors at once. I may have saved the best for last..."

Before I can reach for the final confection, Hayden plucks it from the tray, unwraps the paper from the spongy cake, and breaks it in half. One piece he plops in his mouth with a groan. The other he holds inches from my lips. I rear back, silently insisting I can feed myself.

He cups my nape and pulls me closer. "Open up, sweet pea."

Swearing I'm going to get him back for this subterfuge and forced intimacy, I accept the bite. The second the cake hits my tongue, it melts into the most delicate sweetness balanced with a teeny hint of tart from the cream cheese frosting.

I groan. "I'm in heaven. What is *that?*"

"Pink champagne."

"Wow." I'm in love.

"This is spectacular. But I know how it could taste better." Hayden swipes his thumb across the corner of my mouth and comes away with a few crumbs and a dollop of frosting. I watch, unblinking and breathless, as he sets the digit in the middle of his tongue, closes his lips around it, and groans. "Now it's perfect."

Heat coalesces and sharpens into an insistent ache between my legs I can't pretend I don't feel.

When I realize Misty is staring, I swallow and try to find two coherent words to string together. "What kind of filling do you recommend with that?"

The baker looks amused. "Probably vanilla or almond. Both are good. Almond is a bit more unexpected and less sweet." She reaches around to find a sample, then sets two little paper cups with a tiny plastic tasting spoon in front of me, then does the same for Hayden.

As we dip the small utensils into the samples, then onto our tongues, a look tells me we're on the same page.

"Almond, for sure," I tell Misty.

"I agree."

It's startling to realize that Hayden and I just agreed on a wedding cake flavor together—after he practically ate some off my lips. It's so intimate...so couplish. And when he drops his hand to my thigh with a smile for Misty, I'm reeling—with confusion, with desire.

Abruptly, I stand. "I think we're good here. You know the cake size."

"I didn't get a good look at your Pinterest board."

"I'll send you a link." I'm eager to escape...until I realize I'll be all alone with Hayden in the small cab of his truck with nothing but a mere eighteen inches separating us.

If he touches me again, how am I going to resist him? Worse, what does my weakness bode for my future?

Suddenly, Hayden takes my hand in his and seems all too happy to hustle me outside. "Thanks for your help, Misty. We'll look for you on Saturday at nine a.m."

"I see a lot of brides and grooms, so I have a sense of who will make it. You two belong together. It seems like you know each other really well, but still tease and have plenty of fire. It's a good recipe for success." She smiles and waves. "See you this weekend."

Is that something she says to all the couples who come through the door? I don't think so. Misty seems professional, yes. But pretty dang honest, too.

Could Hayden and I be happily married?

I shouldn't even consider the idea...but it's hard not to.

The minute the door closes behind us, I'm overwhelmed by the nagging worry that I'm wearing my heart on my sleeve for him to see. And if Derek could read my thoughts now, what would he say?

"There's no need to put on an act for Misty anymore." I glance back to verify we're around the corner, then tug my hand from his.

He grabs it again and pulls me closer. "Who says I'm acting?"

Before I can object, he swipes at my bottom lip with his thumb again, a slow, sensual sweep that leaves me tingling, weak-kneed, and desperate.

"Hayden..."

He doesn't answer, just drops his stare to my lips, which automatically part to welcome him. His eyes darken. Intent stamps his face.

He's going to kiss me.

I should push him away, say no. I know that.

But this may be the only time in my life I'll ever know what it feels like when Hayden Hughes voluntarily kisses me like a woman. How can I pass it up?

"God, that look. You're killing me." His rough voice sounds strained.

"What do you mean?"

"Your eyes. They're eating me up." He rakes an agitated hand through his hair. "You need to be kissed by someone who knows what the fuck they're doing—and clearly that isn't Derek."

"I'm engaged." But when I'm this close to Hayden, it's hard to care.

His dark eyes drill into my soul. "To the wrong man. Give me one good reason not to kiss you."

I should have a million...but I can't think of one.

From the purse dangling on my shoulder, my phone rings, disturbing the moment. I can't decide whether I'm furious or grateful for the distraction. A glance at the screen tells me it's Derek.

"Hi," I say as I pull the device free.

Can he hear my voice shaking?

"I'm really sorry about the cake tasting. Did you already pick a flavor?"

"We did. We're just leaving."

"We?"

I hesitate. "Hayden came with me so I'd have a second opinion."

"I'll bet that's not the only reason," Derek mutters.

It's not, and what am I supposed to say? "We're on our way back for dinner. Did you finish work for the day?"

"About that..." The grimace in his voice is impossible to miss. "I'm sorry."

"You have to go to Seattle?" I don't really have to guess. This isn't my first rodeo with his last-minute business trips.

"There's a flight that leaves at seven tonight. I have to be on it. I'll be back Saturday morning."

Is he kidding? "That's the day of the wedding!"

"I know. I feel horrible. But this is my entire future..."

I close my eyes and do some mental math. If we have to push the ceremony out a few hours it's possible, just ridiculous. "What time will you be back?"

"There's a flight that leaves Seattle at six a.m. I'll be back at your dad's house with time to spare before the ceremony at noon."

What if the plane is late?

There's no sense in asking him. He doesn't have an answer.

I try to tamp down my disappointment and be supportive. He's doing his best. "Be safe. Hope everything goes well. I'll see you just before the ceremony."

"You will. I'll come through." He pauses. "Call me with any updates."

"Will do."

Then I hear three beeps and the connection goes silent.

I don't even have to look up to see Hayden's condemnation. Of course he overheard everything.

"He's leaving you the week of your wedding, and he doesn't even have the balls to tell you that he loves you before he goes." Hayden shakes his head. "You need to think really hard before you say *I do*. Because I'm pretty sure it won't be long before you're calling an attorney and starting your life over."

"Don't do this." I march toward his truck, more than ready to go home and crawl into bed with a bottle of wine.

Hayden wraps his fingers around my elbow and pulls me against his body. "Don't what, be honest?"

"Don't get in my head."

"Someone's got to stop you from making this mistake."

"The wedding is already planned. What would you have me do?"

His face softens as he filters his fingers through my hair. "Marry me instead."

CHAPTER THREE

Hayden

Well, that was smooth, fidiot.

Beside me, Perrie retreats into herself on the drive back to Dan's place. I grapple for something to say.

"I'm serious," I finally tell her. "In case you thought I wasn't."

She turns to me with red-rimmed eyes. I know her expressions well. She's trying not to cry. "No, you aren't."

"Why would you say that?"

She rolls her eyes. "You didn't marry Jackie What's-her-name after two years of banging her like a drum. You're not going to marry the girl you've only kissed once."

This I have the perfect answer for. "We can fix that right now. There's a Hilton down the street."

"I'm still engaged."

"And I still think you're marrying the wrong man. Let me prove it."

She scoffs. "Even if we checked in and fucked our brains out all night, there's still the issue of my dad. You told me once that I wasn't worth losing a friend over."

Those words I tossed at her four years ago in my desperation to push her away make me wince now. "I'm sorry I said that. I was wrong. No, I was lying so you'd back down. But neither Dan nor our business is the issue between us. The twelve-year gap in our ages doesn't mean a damn thing anymore, either. The only thing stopping us now is you."

"I can't take you seriously. The notion of marrying me never occurred to you until today."

"That's not true."

"Okay. Not before this week."

I can't refute her.

"That's what I thought. You've always tried to 'save' me in some way or another—from being lonely as a kid, from starving if I forgot my lunch money, from sucking at video games. If you sacrificed yourself simply to rescue me from marrying Derek, we'd both be miserable. Just drop it."

She has it all wrong. But when she crosses her arms over her chest and looks out the passenger window at the passing scenery—tuning me out—I realize nothing I say now will convince her she's wrong.

The rest of the trip is silent.

When we arrive back at Dan's place, Derek is gone. Perrie disappears into her room.

My best friend frowns as he watches her go. "She's upset. What happened?"

"We should talk."

Dan frowns, then shrugs. "Sure. It's beer o'clock. We can sit out on the back patio."

I'm not eager to see all the wedding prep progress, but we can talk out of Perrie's earshot there. "Sounds good."

A few minutes later, Dan and I are settled around the patio table, taking in the sunset. I'm too distracted to appreciate the vivid oranges, pinks, and yellows coloring the sky. I take a deep breath and prepare to blow up my entire personal and professional life with one sentence.

"I'm in love with Perrie."

Dan pauses mid-sip, then lowers his beer can again. "I know."

Not only am I shocked, his response gives me zero idea how he feels about that.

Feeling the need for liquid courage, I pop open my brew and chug half in a few swallows. "And…I'm going to do everything I can to put a stop to this farce on Saturday. I don't want to lose you as a friend or a business partner, but to be honest, Dan, if you don't approve, that's not going to stop me."

Absently, he fingers the rim of his can. "What does Perrie want?"

"Not to disappoint you. So I'm telling you what's up, man to man. I'd like your blessing, but if you can't give it to me, please don't give her your disapproval. It will crush her."

"You think she's in love with you, too?"

"She's done her damnedest to hide it, but yeah."

"Still?"

It's my turn to frown. "You knew…"

"She had a crush on you before she left for college? Hell yes." He lets out a long breath. "She told me. And I'll tell you what I said to her back then. If my two favorite people in the world make each other happy—when the time is right—that would make me happy, too."

Warm relief slides through my veins. "I want you to know I've never touched her. She kissed me once but—"

"I'm impressed. I wondered for years whether you slept with her that summer before she left."

If I had, would everything be different now?

"You would have killed me."

"At the time, yes. In retrospect, maybe it would have been for the best. To be frank, I don't like Derek. No, that's not true. He's okay; he's just not right for her."

"Of course he's not. He left on a business trip days before their wedding. He doesn't love her."

Dan shakes his head. "And Perrie doesn't love him. I figured that out in the first five minutes."

"She says she does…"

"She probably wants to because marrying him would be easier since he's not you. I admit she's attached to him in some way I don't understand. But I'm not blind; I know her heart has been yours for a long time."

"Do I have your blessing, then?"

Suddenly, Dan smiles and thrusts his hand toward me. "A thousand percent. You've always felt like family. It would be nice to make it official."

A two-ton weight just lifted from my chest. "Thanks. It would be great."

"Got a plan? She's a stubborn thing. She's going to keep marching ahead with this wedding to Mr. Metrosexual unless you *make* her change her mind."

"I've got some ideas, and I might need your help. But I'll get back to that. Since we're clearing the air… Speaking of not being blind, I know about you and Hannah."

"Seriously? Oh, thank fuck." Dan's visible relief is almost comical. "I have been wracking my brain for months to find a way to tell you."

"You two and your incessant eye-fucking made it obvious over New Year's Eve. I suspected way before then but…"

"It's funny. You and I have both been worried that the other would think we're too old for the women we love. After all, I'm thirteen years older than Hannah."

I shrug. "My younger sister is very much an adult. If you two make each other happy—"

"We do." He winces. "She's pregnant. Seven weeks. We just found out last Friday. I was going to propose anyway, but we should speed things up now. With your blessing."

It's impossible to stay in my chair for that news. Dan gets to his feet, too, and we share a long bro-hug. It's the most emotion I've seen out of him in a decade, and I can't help but think my sister has been good for him.

"You got it. But dude, this is weird. If it all works out, you'll be both my father-in-law and my brother-in law."

"It sounds creepy." He laughs. "But I can't think of anything better than Hannah and me finding a place together to raise a rugrat or two. I'll be a better father this time because I'm ready and I know all the ways I fucked up the first time. Plus, if you convince Perrie to be your wife, she'll be back for good."

"Not if, when. I'll do whatever it takes to convince her to marry me. But I have to be honest, words aren't working."

"Ah. So…you're plotting something underhanded? That's something I've always admired about you, that talent to know when and how to be thoroughly unscrupulous."

That makes me laugh. It sounds funny coming from upstanding Dan. But he's not wrong. "I'm thinking truly down and dirty…"

"Tell me. I'll see how I can help."

Three days later

Perrie

MY WEDDING IS tomorrow and nothing is anything like I imagined. Except my bestie, Kayla, all of my college friends let me know they won't be able to fly in last minute. They're too busy or broke. Turns out my high school friends and I don't have that much in common anymore. Most are either still in college or think I'm crazy for settling down so young. So no epic bachelorette party for me, which is actually fine. I'm not into exotic dancers or drunken party games. But my fiancé is still out of town. My dad has been conspicuously absent for hours. And Hayden is who knows where. I thought at least one of them would spend my last night as a single lady with me, but no.

I feel wretchedly alone.

That's not precisely true. I have plenty of regrets to keep me company. They're piling up and telling me that every choice I've made has been wrong.

My phone dings, interrupting that cheerful thought. I glance down to see a text from Derek.

`Meetings all over. Everything went great. It's not official yet, but I think Brian and I nailed this account.`

`That's great!` I type back.

`Sorry again I had to ditch out this week. Everything ready for the big show tomorrow?`

My fingers hesitate over the screen. I'm so close to calling everything off. Of course, right after I got everything into place. I finally found a dress off the rack—with Hayden's help. He's been weirdly supportive the last couple of days. And as if he realized the error of opening his mouth, he's been absolutely silent about marrying me after his impulsive proposal.

I shouldn't have gotten my hopes up. I'll press on and pray for the best, but I'm well beyond second thoughts. I'm on the billionth now.

Yes. Are you still okay with this wedding thing?

Of course! Don't give up on me. I'll be back. We got this.

Thanks.

Anything for you, darling. He sends a wink emoji with it.

With a faint smile, I darken my phone. Derek won't let me down. He never has. I wish I could have fallen in love with him, at least a little.

Adding that to my pile of regrets, I pad barefooted to the liquor cabinet and pop open a bottle of red. The sound of vino sloshing into my empty glass is a sad one, but I drown it out by tossing back half the wine, then heading to the kitchen to find my last supper. After tomorrow, I'll either be happy...or totally brokenhearted.

While I choke down some leftovers from last night's roast chicken before I lose enthusiasm for food, I reach for my phone. It's stupid and impulsive and likely to end in misery, but I tap out a message to Hayden.

What's up?

No answer. When I mentioned something yesterday about maybe having a gathering tonight, he was oddly vague about his plans and changed the subject. Does he have a hot date? A hookup with a fuck buddy? Or is he just over me?

It's a depressing thought.

With a sigh, I clean up my solitary dinner, plop onto the sofa, and stare into my nearly empty glass. While I contemplate pouring another, the doorbell rings. By the time I peer out the peephole, I see a driver climbing back in his van and driving away.

I open the door and find a bouquet of flowers on the porch, a colorful profusion of gardenias, pink lilies, cabbage roses, and orchids. It's huge and breathtaking.

Who sent this?

I don't know but I find myself smiling as I carry the flowers into the living room and root around for the card. I pull it free from its envelope and find three simple words.

SMELL ME NOW

AUTOMATICALLY, I comply. The beautifully dizzying scents swirl in my head and make me desperate to know who had them delivered to me. The card isn't signed. Derek wouldn't send me flowers; I know that. In fact, I can only think of one person who might have.

Hayden.

That possibility ricochets through my head as the doorbell rings again. I reach the peephole in time to see a local courier drop off a bag from a liquor store. When I retrieve it and peek inside, I spy a bottle of very swanky champagne. There's an attached card with another three-word instruction.

Chill me now

Beside that, I find a plain white oblong box with another unsigned note.

Don't open me yet

Did Hayden send these mysterious gifts? Since I can't be sure, can he actually get mad if curiosity gets the best of me? As my brain twists the question around like a pretzel, I dutifully slide the bottle of bubbly into the fridge and set the box, wrapped with a silken red bow, on the kitchen counter.

I've barely finished before the doorbell rings yet again. What the hell is going on? Are all these gifts Hayden's way of letting me down easy?

If so, I admit it; I'll be crushed.

When I pull open the door again, the courier is standing there once more. He's a teenage kid with an acne problem and bulging eyes. When he spies me in shorts and a tank top, he can't seem to operate his tongue. Poor guy. I remember that awkward age...

"Are you supposed to give me the box in your hands?"

"Huh?" He swallows, then nods. "Um, are you Perrie?"

"That's me."

"I thought you'd be an old dude."

I smile. "I get that sometimes. The box?"

"Right. I almost forgot." He shoves it in my direction. "Have a good one."

With a last long look, he jogs back to his idling hatchback still blaring an R & B tune. I shut the door, shaking my head.

Maybe I should look on the bright side. Though my life is still upside down, it could be worse. I could be sixteen again… and have six years of unrequited love for Hayden yet to endure.

The truth is, I have a good life. I've got some great people in my corner, like Kayla. Even though my bestie is now coupled up with Oliver, the guy she crushed on for years, she'll always be there for me. I'm fielding multiple job offers in major cities all over the country, so I have choices if things don't work out as planned. I'm young, healthy, and resilient.

I'd just rather not add brokenhearted to that list.

Sinking onto the living room sofa, I pluck at the frilly, pristinely wrapped package in my grip. The sticker affixed tells me it's from a local store with a very sexy reputation. The little card tucked under the pale pink ribbon contains three more words.

WEAR ME NOW

MY HEART STUTTERS. Did Hayden send me lingerie? Is that possible?

I yank the box open and tear through the dainty tissue paper. The white gossamer fabric and lace make me gasp. It's stunningly soft.

When I hold up the piece by its spaghetti straps, the box falls at my feet, forgotten. The baby doll is completely sheer. The two cups designed to "cover" my breasts are trimmed in a playful yet delicate dotted lace. Under that, a tiny white bow, placed where the fabric gently gathers, pretends to hold the fluttering sides together. But that bow is purely for show because the sucker is split open with a scalloped hem that runs down the length of the torso and trims the bottom edge, which will barely skim the tops of my thighs.

I bend and scramble through the box for another card or anything that tells me who my mystery gift giver is. All I find is a tiny scrap of matching panties. The strips of lace over the hips echo the design meant to hug my breasts. The rest, including the material over my pussy, is so see-through I'm wondering why it's there at all.

The tease factor on this getup is times a million. It's lingerie meant for seduction. I've never owned anything like it.

There's no question whether I'm going to put it on. I can't wait to.

As I slip into the bedroom and tug off my shorts and tank, I hope and pray I'm donning this for Hayden.

If I'm being honest, I came back to Phoenix for him. Everything is always for him.

The garments feel like a silky cloud of nothing as I slide them on. When I stand in front of the full-length mirror, I'm stunned to see the lace hugs me perfectly, clinging and revealing even more than it conceals.

I feel like a goddess, a temptress. Like the woman who could put a big, satisfied smile on Hayden Hughes's face.

From the living room, I hear music begin to play—something I can't identify from this distance. But it's slow and sexy and lures me downstairs because, other than my dad, only one person has a key to the front door.

Trembling, I make my way across the house. When I round the corner, the man I never fell out of love with stands in the archway, waiting. When Hayden sees me, he sucks in a breath. His jaw drops. He doesn't speak, just blinks and swallows hard. I risk a glance down. He's unmistakably excited by what he sees.

"Hi," I whisper.

"Oh, sweet pea..." His gaze wends its way back up to mine. "Wow..."

Electricity sizzles across my skin. The air seems alive with it. The charged current bounces between us. He hasn't put a finger on me yet, but I'm already so drugged with arousal I struggle to breathe.

"You sent this to me?"

He nods, seemingly looking for his brain. It would be funny if I wasn't so nervous.

"Yeah, along with the flowers and champagne. Maybe all that's cliché, but I'm late to the romance game with you, so I'm starting here. Damn, you're even more gorgeous than I thought."

"Why?"

The question comes out wrong, but he seems to understand that I'm not asking why he thinks I look good or why it's taken him so long to sweep me off my feet.

"Because everything I said the day of the cake tasting was honest and serious."

So...he wants to fuck me until he imprints himself on my soul? Persuade me to marry him instead? Or both?

Regardless, I have a decision to make.

But do I really? I've known what—and who—I want all along.

Still, I can't throw away all my plans before I get some

answers. And I shouldn't make this easy on him after all the torment he heaped on us. "Why?"

Again, he doesn't pretend to misunderstand or waste time. He jumps to the heart of the matter. "Because I love you."

Shock whooshes the air from my lungs. He's never said those words to me.

"Hayden…"

"I have for a long time. And you love me. Still." He puts one foot in front of the other, slowly closing the distance between us. "Don't you?"

I always have.

His eyes are all over me, mentally undressing me, until I feel as if I'm no longer wearing a single filmy stitch. Even his stare makes me dizzy with anticipation. I have no doubt in that moment that he sees me as a grown-up. His equal. The object of his desire. The woman who owns his heart.

"You know it's not that simple," I murmur.

"Ah, Derek the dipshit." He scowls, expression harsh. "Take it off."

"The lingerie?"

He shakes his head. "We'll get there soon. Right now, I mean that rock of his."

I didn't even realize I was still wearing the engagement ring. It has become second nature.

Slowly, I slide it off my finger and set it on the coffee table. "This doesn't mean I'm not marrying him. Or that I'll sleep with you."

"That's exactly what it means."

I raise a brow at him. But it's hard to be angry when his stare rakes down my body with a visual caress that leaves me aching. My nipples turn hard. My pussy softens and floods. I ache for him.

Somehow I manage to shake my head. If he wants me, he'll have to prove it. A few words and gifts won't suffice. "We're just having a conversation."

He scoffs. "Before I take you to bed and prove you belong to me."

"You're assuming."

"You're wearing the lingerie I chose, knowing damn well I intend to seduce you."

"That's not true." But it is. "I was just curious."

Suddenly, he smiles. "All right. We'll play this your way. But the Perrie I know would never go back on a promise."

What's he talking about? "Exactly. I promised Derek till death do us part."

"You haven't yet. Besides, you made a solemn vow to me four years ago." He reaches into his pocket and extracts something that pings with a metallic clink when he tosses it on the coffee table beside me. "You promised I could return that to you when and wherever I wanted, and you would show me that you're all the woman I need. I'm cashing in—right here, right now. Come here so I can finally kiss you the way I've wanted to."

I glance down to find the final token from the water park's arcade, which I impulsively shoved in Hayden's hand the night of our last visit there. "You kept it?"

It's probably silly, but I'm stunned and touched.

He nods. "You told me to look at it, feel it, and remember you. I have—every fucking day."

I'm way more thrilled than I dare let on. "A girl said those stupid words."

"No. A young, incredibly wise woman told me to give this back when I wanted not just her pussy but *her*. So here I am, admitting I want all of you. I always have."

"Your timing is lousy. I'm getting married tomorrow."

"Not to him. I've got all night to make sure of that." He takes a half step closer and points to the ground in front of him. "Come here. Meet me halfway."

How can I resist?

On bare feet, I tiptoe toward Hayden and find myself staring up into his familiar beloved face. I've fantasized about him making love to me for longer than I should admit. Is it really going to happen now?

"Good girl." He cups my face in his hand. "Are you taking the token? Are you saying yes?"

I blink, staring up into his devilishly dark eyes. This is my decision point, my make-or-break moment, but what else can I say? "Yes."

"Thank fuck. I feel like I've waited a hundred years to touch you."

"I've waited longer." I wrap my arms around his neck and press myself against his body, lips a breath away from his.

Hayden is already impatient, fists wrapping around the gossamer fabric as he closes the final inch between us and covers my lips with his. He doesn't waste time seeking or searching. He plunges deep to prove that he can, that I'll let him. That he owns me. It's the kiss of a man staking his claim.

I sway and swoon into him, eyes closing as I dissolve into instant bliss. His throaty groan tells me he's every bit as impacted as I am. We melt into each other as if we were always meant to share this moment.

Dragging in a heaving breath, he pulls away and peers deep into my eyes. "Jesus, Perrie. You kiss exactly the way I remember."

Is that a good thing? "Yeah?"

"How is that fucking possible?"

I have no idea what he's asking. "Will you kiss me again?"

"Oh, yeah. And this time I won't stop until I know the feel of you gripping my cock as you shout how much you love me."

"What if I don't?" I can't resist teasing him. The truth is, I've always loved him, and all it takes for me to dissolve into a puddle of need is to look at him.

He sends me a smug smile. "You better understand right now, sweet pea, that I'm going to be relentless. I have a little more than twelve hours to prove to you that you're engaged to the wrong man. I'm going to use every second. I'm going to leave you so boneless and sated. And I'm not going to leave your bed or your side until you admit that you love only me."

I'm willing to admit that now, but I don't. There's no way I'll let myself miss out on Hayden turning all his determined focus on me.

"You're welcome to try."

That makes him laugh. "You never did know when to stop baiting the bear, did you?"

Probably not, but his resolve makes me downright giddy.

I push him against the wall. "Shut up."

Before he can respond, I tighten my arms around his neck and leap into his embrace. He catches me, both hands gripping my ass, and lets out a stunned *oomph*. I plaster my body against his and seize his lips.

His grip tightens. He moans, encouraging me. I should let him show me what he has in mind, let him prove how badly he wants me. But I can barely tamp down my brimming anticipation, especially when I wriggle and rub my clit against his steely cock.

"Fuck." He ends the kiss with the gasped curse. "I can't be patient right now. Have you fucked Derek in your bedroom?"

"No."

He looks puzzled by that. "Not even once?"

"No." That's all I dare say now.

Resolution crosses his face. "I've dreamed so many times of having you on your bed…"

Still holding me tight, he makes his way down the hall, his lips skimming up my neck, over to nip at my lobe, before dropping to nibble on my shoulder.

At the foot of my bed, he releases me to slide down his body. I feel every hard inch before my feet finally touch the hardwood floor.

Everything in this room looks exactly the way it did when I was a teenager. The walls and tufted headboard are similar shades of pristine white. My black-and-white polka-dotted sheets shout youth and happiness. The blush comforter with its coordinating lace-trimmed shams seem so innocent. The leopard pillow and bold chandelier break up all the sweetness with attitude.

This room was a perfect reflection of me. In many ways, it still is.

This is exactly where I want to make love to Hayden, too. None of my fantasies included him seducing me with the last of the day's sun slanting through my window, tossing golden rays all over his strong face and lighting up the fire in his eyes. But this is way better than any shadowy midnight I envisioned.

"I'm nervous," I admit.

"Don't be. This is for us. Tell me everything you want and feel. I will, too. We're not just fucking; we're joining. And after this, I'm never going to let you go, Perrie. You understand that?"

So far he's made me hot, but his words now touch me deep.

As I nod, he skims my cheek with his knuckles, brushing his way back to cup my nape and lift my lips to his. Then I'm falling, dissolving into him, losing myself in his kiss. One bleeds into the next, then another, until my lips feel swollen, bruised, and tingling.

His hands aren't still, either. It's as if he's intending to sensitize me to his every touch, starting with a drag of his fingertips over my shoulders, then down my arms, across my collarbones, before slowly drifting up my throat and under my jaw. Finally, he swipes his thumb across my bottom lip again.

"So that's what you look like when you've been well kissed." He smiles, terribly pleased with himself.

"Are you going to make me blush or kiss me again?"

"You should know the answer to that."

I do, and I brace for more of both. Instead, he surprises me by easing the strap off my baby doll. His lips follow in a seduction so slow and patient it makes me want to cry. He does the same with the matching strap on the other shoulder until the garment is barely clinging to my breasts. Not that it matters. He can see through it anyway, especially with the sun beaming across our bodies.

"You have the prettiest fucking nipples." Finally, he drags his knuckles across one.

The sensation is so instant, so hot, I gasp. "Hayden..."

He's barely touched me, and I'm panting. Every inch of my skin is on fire. God, how will I feel when he's surrounding me? On top of me? Inside me?

"Hmm, sweet pea." Through the fabric, he does the same to the other nipple. "These are so hard. I love how sensitive you are and the way you respond to me."

I barely manage a nod before he grips one rigid tip between his thumb and forefinger and squeezes. My instant yelp has nothing to do with pain and everything to do with pleasure.

"Yes," he croons as he pinches the other, then slides the baby doll's straps off my arms, one after the other, exposing my breasts to his hungry stare. "So fucking perfect."

With firm, hot fingers, he cradles a breast in his hand and lifts it as he leans in.

Oh, god…

The first touch of his tongue is like a jolt from a live wire, somehow unexpected and shocking. But then his lips close around my sensitive tip. He gives it a tug and draws it into his mouth with a strong pull.

I'm a goner.

Without any conscious thought at all, I sink my fingers into his short hair and yank him closer. He obliges me with another tug of suction, a follow-up caress of his tongue, then a little bite that has me digging my nails into his scalp.

"You like that," he murmurs against my skin. It's not a question. "Oh, Perrie, I'm going to be at these nipples all the time. Holy fuck…"

When he switches to the other bud and all but inhales it into his mouth, I cry out again and realize that I've not only lost my heart to this man for the rest of my life, but I'm about to lose my body, too. By morning, every part of me will belong to him. I'm both thrilled and terrified by that notion.

As he continues to nip and sip at my tips, pulling, tugging, pinching, laving, they grow tight and pleasantly sore. I didn't know such a state existed, but I *feel* my body. My skin is alive. My blood races. My heart is full. I'm all woman right now. He's like a drug, and I want more.

Heat swamps me. My head buzzes. I'm dizzy, disoriented. On fire.

Hayden's scorching palms skim the baby doll down the bare skin of my torso. The way he exposes my body to his singeing gaze leaves my chest tight. I'm breathless, achy. And so ready.

"You're beautiful." He thumbs my navel, palms the curve of my hip, eats at the hollow of my waist. "And you're mine."

"For tonight." I'm not giving in easily.

"Keep thinking that if it makes you feel better."

I'm still trying to rub two brain cells together to form a snappy comeback when he skims his knuckles across the gauzy fabric covering my pussy. I'm shocked to realize it's clinging wetly to my flesh.

"You're soaking, sweet pea." Hayden groans as he drops to his knees in front of me and plasters the sheer sodden fabric to my skin. "Look at you…"

I tremble as he leans in and fastens his mouth over the saturated triangle and laps at me with the flat of his tongue.

Sensations jolt through me. The immediate shock of pleasure burns my veins. Tingles cascade behind that, leaving me reeling and staggered. It's twenty times more agonizing when Hayden slips his thumbs under the elastic front of the tiny panties, spreads my lips apart, and prods my most sensitive spot with the tip of his tongue.

"Hayden!"

"Jesus, you're sweet. Has any man ever made you come in his mouth?"

"N-no." I can barely gasp the word out.

Against my flesh, I feel him smile. "Oh, I'm going to enjoy the fuck out of this."

When he wraps his arms around my hips and stands, lifting my feet off the ground, I squeal. I don't have long to be startled since Hayden quickly drops me flat on the mattress. With impatient jerks, he drags the itty-bitty thong from my body and kneels beside the bed.

My heart pounds as he drags my hips to the edge and positions my thighs over his shoulders. Then he plows his tongue through my folds, letting loose a deep, satisfied groan.

"Oh my god!" My back arches. I fist the comforter. My eyes roll back in my head.

How can I possibly keep from shattering into a million tiny pieces?

The way Hayden devours my pussy, centering all his attention on my clit with the most skillful nips and licks, makes me realize it's impossible. He's fracturing me, tearing down all the barriers he thinks I've erected between us, making me his.

I can't stop him...and I don't want to.

He's merciless and unceasing, swiping, licking, sucking. He manipulates my reaction, my body, my mind, until I'm twisting in agony and chanting his name. Until I no longer care about anything except Hayden, how he makes me feel, and finding a way to make this ecstasy last forever.

Suddenly, he backs away and presses an almost chaste kiss to the pad of my pussy. "No, sweet pea. The first time you come for me, I'm going to be inside you."

As much as I want the orgasm now, I nod. I'd rather we be joined, me feeling him deep when I come apart.

"Hurry." I attack his zipper.

"Wait, Perrie. Sweet pea. Just a— Holy shit!"

Yeah, he probably didn't expect me to shove his pants and underwear around his knees and swallow the crest of his cock between my lips. But I groan because I'm so glad I did. He's salty and musky. Manly. And he's built big. I'm stretching my lips as wide as I can, but within seconds, the hinge of my jaw begins to protest. Still, I don't care. I want to taste this man. I want his flavor on my tongue. I want to please him.

I lick him like an ice cream cone, reveling in his hiss as he fists my hair and guides me up and down his rigid length. "Oh, fuck. Yes. Hmm…"

Since my mouth is otherwise occupied, I smile on the inside as I suck him deeper, molding my lips to his shape and pressing him to the roof of my mouth as I work him. Then I rear back, graze the underside of his crown with the tip of my tongue, worrying a spot that instantly sends him reeling.

He pulls free with a snarl. "Did Derek teach you that?"

"No."

"Then where the fuck did you learn to give head?"

I gape, so glad in that moment that a few of my former college roommates proudly called themselves whores. They hooked up a lot, with anyone who interested them. And they weren't shy about sharing details. I listened…

"No one."

He frowns. "Are you saying you've never given a blow job?"

"Never," I whisper.

I wonder how long it will take for him to figure out the rest of my secret.

Hayden's suspicious stare tells me he's already puzzling his way to the truth.

"But it doesn't matter. I just want to please you." I lean back in.

He's too fast and gives my hair a tug, stopping me before he urges me flat onto the mattress again, then covers my body with his. He stares deeply, intently. I can practically hear his mind working, so I lurch up and press my lips to his.

Instantly, he uses his own to pry mine open wide and sweeps inside, chest rumbling with need, as he forces himself into the deepest recesses of my mouth—and my soul.

Finally, he wrenches away and takes my face in his hands. "Do you want me?"

"Yes," I gasp. "So much."

"Do you need more proof that you belong to me?"

"No." I don't want to play games anymore. I just want Hayden. "I'm yours."

"You're not marrying Derek, right?"

"I'm not."

He sighs with visible relief, then caresses my lip with his thumb. "You going to marry me instead? I've already talked to your dad. He's given us his blessing."

My heart catches in my throat. "Really? You're seriously asking me?"

"I'm not letting you go again. The first time was the biggest mistake of my life."

"Oh my god..." This is real.

"Is that a yes?" he demands.

"Yes." I nod as it sinks in. I'm going to be Hayden's wife. "Yes!"

"Oh, sweet pea. Thank fuck. I love you."

"I love you, too."

He skims his kiss across my jaw, seals our bond with a sweet press of lips, then reluctantly releases me to meet my gaze. "Do you want kids?"

"Of course." I didn't love being an only child, so I've always pictured three or four little ones I could nurture and spoil.

"Me, too. I want them with you."

I smile. "I'd love that."

His expression turns serious. "I want them now."

Suddenly, I grasp what he's saying. "Right now?"

"We've already waited years. You really want to wait more?"

A million thoughts flit through my head. We'd be newly-weds. I'm trying to start a new career. We need to adjust to living together. I'm still pretty young.

But we've known each other forever, so how much do we really need to get to know or adjust to one another? I can still work and be a mom; lots of women do it well. And worrying about age is for people who don't know what they want out of life. I totally do.

"You're right. Let's start now."

He laughs, then smacks a kiss across my mouth that's meant as a celebration. It soon lingers, then worships. I'm sucked back into a vortex of passion I can't escape. I have a feeling that's how it will always be between Hayden and me.

When I'm melting, panting, and red-cheeked, he settles his body between my splayed thighs and peers deep into my eyes. "The night you gave me that token, you said you'd be saving yourself for me. Perrie?"

I know what he's asking. I swallow. "I'm a virgin."

A smile softens his face. "I should have guessed sooner. You're a girl who always keeps her word. You're not actually engaged to Derek, are you?"

"No."

"And you never have been?"

I can't quite look Hayden in the eye. "He's a really good friend. I do love him...but he's like a brother to me."

"So why did you come here and..."

"And pretend? Derek offered me a job at his new start-up in Seattle. Before I accepted, I had to come here and see if there was any chance that you could finally want me. He offered to help."

"I always wanted you...even when I shouldn't have. So this farce was for me?"

I nod. "I figured if it didn't matter to you now that I belonged to someone else, it never would. Then I could move to Seattle and try to get on with my life."

"You need to turn down his job and tell him to go to hell."

I laugh. "He won't be terribly surprised. He's only flying back tomorrow because—"

"He's not even fake marrying you at noon."

I shake my head. "He's not. He just needs to get his stuff and say goodbye."

Hayden raises a brow. "If he wants to stay tomorrow and watch me marry you—just so he knows you're off-limits—I'm all for that."

"You mean…you and I get married? For real?"

"Why let a perfectly good wedding go to waste?"

I giggle, giddy with happiness. Hayden is giving me everything I could have wanted. Well, almost. I'm still waiting for him to join our bodies and make me his in the most primal way possible.

"I love it," I murmur. "I love you."

"I love you, too. In a few hours—if I can stand not being inside you—I'll get the engagement ring I bought you out of my pocket and slip it on your finger. Then we'll open that bottle of champagne and drink from the glasses I sent with it, the ones that say Mr. and Mrs." He flashes me a self-deprecating smile. "I was thinking positive because there's no one else I want to be Mrs. Hughes except you."

"That sounds great. But right now…"

"Right now, I've got to have you. I feel like I've waited my whole fucking life."

"Me, too."

Then silence falls between us. Hayden lowers his head and takes my lips again in a kiss both solemn and passionate. His hands roam, outlining the curve of my waist, then he grips my hips as he braces himself and nuzzles my neck.

After tracing an erotic path over my pulse point, his lips drift to my ear while he aligns his naked cock against the entrance to my small, aching pussy. "Tell me you're mine, Perrie."

"I'm yours." I close my eyes in anticipation.

I'm only seconds away from feeling that on a deep, visceral level.

"Open," he insists. "Your eyes, your cunt, your heart. Spread them all wide for me."

I lift my lashes with a flutter and part my legs wider under him. My heart is already open; it has been for years.

He pins me with a commanding stare that makes me shiver. "Tell me you'll be mine forever."

"I will. And you'll be mine forever, too," I insist.

"I will." He speaks the words like a vow.

My heart pounds and traps my breath in my chest. Time slows. I know only this man. And I'll remember the way he's looking at me in this moment for the rest of my life.

Finally, he bares his teeth and shoves his way past the thin barrier of my hymen with one rough push. Even as he tears into my body and I gasp at his invasion, our joining mends the fracture he left in my heart four awful years ago.

The discomfort between my legs is a small price to pay for the feel of Hayden working himself inside me, inching and pushing, only to withdraw and sink in again, this time deeper, more insistent.

"Oh, god… I've never felt anything better, sweet pea. Ever."

I raise my hips to meet him as he slowly strokes downward again. Even though I feel packed full of him, he's still not completely inside me. The stretch of my flesh to accommodate him burns and stings, but I welcome it.

"Deeper…" I moan.

He hisses as he balances above me, his dark eyes burning

with both passion and the strain of holding back. "You're so fucking tight. And it feels so different bareback."

I'm shocked. "You've never…"

"Not without a condom, no." He eases out, then forces his way back in—finally to the hilt.

We both groan. I feel him everywhere—inside me, around me, overwhelming me. I throw my head back, cling to him, dig my nails into him.

"I can't believe I'm finally inside you," he breathes. "I fantasized about being your first, sweet pea. I've wanted to make you mine for so long. The fact we're together now, that there's nothing between us, and you could get pregnant tonight…" Impossibly, he swells inside me. "Oh, fuck, yes."

I manage a little mental math. "The timing would be right."

"Really?"

"Is that okay?"

"Okay?" Suddenly, he thrusts into me like a wild man, claiming me with a hard, ever-increasing pace that fires all my nerve endings. "I'm going to stay inside you all night, make you come for me until you're wrung out, and fucking fill you every chance I get. I'd love for you to be pregnant when I marry you tomorrow."

"Yes…"

All talking stops then. He pumps me deep, one strong push after another, increasing his pace into something raw, primal, insistent. Teeth bared, he groans as he grinds his way inside me, claiming me masterfully and turning my body inside out. Every shove of his wide cock scrapes nerve endings inside me that has my eyes flaring, my body tensing, my heart thundering.

"You're tightening on me."

"You're unraveling me," I manage to cry out between labored breaths.

"Good. I want to watch you come." He rolls onto his back and grips my hips until I'm situated on top, straddling him.

He's so huge, I swear I can feel him everywhere inside me.

"Now be a good little girl and fuck me."

I sense Hayden is holding back a bit since it's my first time, and it's sweet. But he's giving me a glimpse of the fact he'll be dirty and raw in bed.

Yeehaw!

As I move carefully over him, my hair brushes sensually over my back. I splay my palms across the solid width of his workingman's chest and drink in the sight of tribal ink around his thick biceps. As he guides my hips, my breasts bounce and my pussy catches fire. Incredibly, I feel him in places I didn't before. And when he tightens and slams up inside me in rapid-fire strokes, my desire churns out of control. I start to come apart.

He hurries my loss of sanity with a thumb over my clit. "Come for me. Yes. Oh, fuck. Yes, just like—"

I can't hear the rest over the pounding of my heart. I tense and cry out as I feel the storm gathering between my legs and need tearing through my veins. It spills over and sends me skyrocketing to an ecstasy where I'm only aware of pleasure and Hayden deep inside of me providing it. It jolts me. I shudder, disintegrating before him, and scream my throat raw until a heavy roll of satisfaction hits me and I feel utterly boneless.

A split second later, he tosses me on my back again, jackhammers into me as if he can't fill me deep or fast enough, then an animal growl rips from his throat as he impales me with one last powerful thrust, shudders, and floods my womb with his hot seed.

The moment is perfect, powerful, profound—and far more

amazing than any teenage fantasy I ever had about making love with Hayden Hughes.

A moment later, he catches his breath and tucks a strand of hair behind my ear. "Feel good, sweet pea?"

"Yeah."

"Happy?"

I smile. "Yeah."

He shoots me a sly grin. "Is that token you gave me good for more than one ride?"

The curl of my mouth turns naughty. "It's good for the whole night."

"Hallelujah. How about we break out the bubbly, I slip that engagement ring on your finger, then you can spread your legs for me again so I can make you deliciously sore and ensure you look well fucked tomorrow when I marry you?"

There's my Hayden—audacious and challenging and perfect for me.

I wriggle under him, earning a hiss, then whisper in his ear, "I can't think of anything I want more."

CHAPTER FOUR

Hayden

I'm in heaven.

Six days ago, Perrie came home, "fiancé" in tow, and forced to me re-examine my feelings for my best friend's sweet, virginal daughter. Thank god I don't have to fantasize anymore what being deep inside Perrie is like. After last night, she's all woman—*my* woman. And as she walks down the aisle to me, looking stunning in a simple white satin floor-length sheath with lace insets along the back and the thigh-high slit, I could swear she's glowing even more than usual.

Fingers crossed she's pregnant.

Yeah, maybe it's wishful thinking, but the notion makes me pretty damn ecstatic.

"I've never seen either of you look so happy," Dan murmurs in my ear as he stands beside me.

"Thanks for being my best man."

He nods. "Happy to. I'm honored to be beside you both as you become man and wife."

"Will I be returning the favor soon?" I look at Hannah in the front row. "My sister looks teary-eyed…and she's wearing a rock on her left hand that didn't used to be there."

"I proposed last night. She said yes. We're going to Vegas next weekend."

"Perrie and I will be there."

Dan claps me on the back and falls silent as my bride glides toward me. I only have eyes for her. And my full heart is exclusively hers, too.

Finally, she reaches the front of the aisle. Beside her, Derek—who barely made it in time for the ceremony—lifts her veil and kisses her forehead. "Be happy, darling."

"I will." She glances at me with love in her eyes before regarding her friend one last time. "You find your person and be happy, too, huh?"

"Someday," he murmurs before he takes his seat in the front row.

On the other side of the altar stands her best friend from college, Kayla, who came to be Perrie's matron of honor. And the way she's eyeing her new husband, Oliver, tells me they're very much in love. Perrie tells me they're already expecting, and I see they're both thrilled.

I tuck a finger under Perrie's chin. "You ready to become Mrs. Hughes?"

"Yes. Come on, slowpoke. Let's get hitched."

"Slowpoke?" I raise a brow at her. "Who got us a last-minute marriage license on Saturday morning so I could marry you now instead of waiting until Monday?"

"You," she concedes, then glances down at the two-carat

cushion-cut diamond I picked out yesterday. "And you've made me the happiest woman."

"I'm going to keep doing that for the rest of your life."

"And I'll make you the happiest man, I promise." She smiles, then whispers my way as we face the officiant. "You know I never break my promises."

I know. And as I promise to love, honor, and cherish Perrie for the rest of my life, I figure she'll learn soon enough that I don't break my promises, either.

SEDUCING
THE
Stranger

New York Times

Shayla
BLACK

Bestselling Author

SHAYLA BLACK
Steamy. Emotional. Forever.

ABOUT SEDUCING THE STRANGER

Will a hot night with a stranger spark something that lasts forever?

I'm Calla.

I'm responsible. I plan. I'm cautious—always.

Until I see him, the gorgeous stranger with the rugged hands and the dark mood.

Instantly, I'm drawn. I can't stop staring. I can't stop wanting.

When he makes me an indecent proposal, I do something shocking.

I say yes.

I follow a man whose name I don't know to his hotel room so I can surrender my body.

But what have I gotten myself into?

And what will happen when I accidentally discover the identity of my sexy stranger?

Enjoy this Forbidden Confession. HEA guaranteed!

CHAPTER ONE

Las Vegas
4 p.m.

Calla

The tall man with the dark beard and even darker eyes striding into the swanky hotel bar might be the most gorgeous man I've ever laid eyes on.

Oh, dear god.

I sit up a little straighter in my barstool and cast a sidelong stare as the stranger stops six feet from me. He motions the bartender for a beer, then slams his hands on the bar and hangs his head. I can't help but notice his hands—big and bronzed with pronounced veins running from hair-roughened forearms to blunt knuckles. Long fingers taper to clean, brutally short nails.

I shiver. I'm in lust. I have a thing for hands, and his are the stuff out of my fantasies.

Though his head is down, nothing about him seems despondent. Or heartbroken. But he's feeling something… Frustrated? Exasperated?

Finally, he raises his head and stares straight ahead. I glimpse his expression in the massive mirror over the bar. He's angry. Incredibly, blazingly pissed off. The fury in his eyes should scare me. It could launch rockets and scorch earth.

Perversely, I'm even more aroused. Or maybe that's just his overall effect on me.

As if he suddenly realizes he's not alone, he shifts his regard. Our gazes meet in the mirror. My heart pounds. I should look away, let him have a moment of privacy to deal with whatever's troubling him. But I can't seem to pry my stare free.

He turns his head, eyes narrowed, and all his considerable attention falls on me. My breath catches.

Has any man ever affected me this way?

The simple answer? No. Never. Not once.

And I'm loving every moment I spend pinned under his stare.

"What?" His confrontational bark startles me. His voice is as rough and merciless as his expression.

"Are you okay?"

He says nothing for a long moment, and I'm convinced he's going to blow me off. I doubt he's feeling conversational. And I'm sure the zing of attraction is completely one-sided.

Finally, he growls, "What's your name?"

I swallow. "Calla."

His gaze dips to my nearly empty tumbler. "What are you drinking, Calla?"

"Amaretto."

Just then, the bartender sets a frosty mug of some dark,

imported beer in front of the gorgeous stranger. I realize then he never told me his name.

"Get her another," he tells the bartender.

I should refuse. I came off the plane from LA three hours ago, and I still haven't eaten lunch. I know without looking that dinnertime is fast approaching and I should find something to fill my stomach before I drink more. But if this shiver-worthy stranger is buying me a drink, I'm going to smile at him, partake, and continue to stare my fill.

"Thank you," I murmur.

When the bartender steps away to mix my cocktail, the gorgeous man cocks his head. "Has anyone ever made you furious beyond words?"

I consider his question. While I had a college roommate who came close once... "No."

But disappointed me? Oh, yeah. All the time.

"So you don't have any advice?" He gulps half his beer, giving no hint that he's actually enjoying it on the way down.

"Other than to say it's not smart to try drowning it in booze, no."

He grunts before he downs more of his brew. "I should have guessed you've never been that angry. You've got a halo."

"What does that mean?"

"The overhead lights reflect off all your shiny blond hair. When I walked in the door, it was the first thing I noticed. Makes you look like you have a halo." His eyes narrow again. "You've got an angelic face to match."

Is that a compliment or a sneer?

The bartender sets my fresh drink beside the empty one, then sweeps the first tumbler away. I see a smile lurking at his mouth before he disappears into a back room, leaving me alone with the surly stranger.

"I'm no angel," I argue.

He raises an inky black brow and studies me so intently I have to struggle not to squirm under his gaze. "You're under twenty-five. You have a steady job. Your apartment is somewhere between clean and spotless. You've probably never had more than a parking ticket. And"—he leans in, dark eyes drilling down through mine as if he can read my mind or see into my soul—"I'll bet you've had fewer than five lovers. You've definitely never had a one-night stand. Where I come from, that basically makes you an angel."

My mouth hangs open. Yes, I'm gaping, but...how did he guess so much about me? "What makes you think all that?"

"More than fifteen years in law enforcement. You get good at reading people. You going to try convincing me I'm wrong?"

"This isn't about me." I clear my throat. "I'm sorry if I butted in. I saw you were angry, and I asked if you were okay. If you don't want anyone to care, then I won't."

Finally, he slides onto the stool next to mine and polishes off his beer. The heat of his thigh close to mine makes it hard to focus on anything except him.

"I didn't say that, angel. I'm just looking for a way to deal with my anger since I can't beat the hell out of my dad for being a stubborn asshole."

"I kind of get that. I know I told you that drinking your anger away wouldn't work, but I'm basically trying to do the same. My mom is...an idiot."

He barks out a laugh. It comes with an expression that's not precisely a smile, but it's close. And it makes him even more stunning. His eyes warm. I'm even more drawn to him.

"So I'm furious, and you're...disappointed, I'm guessing. If drinking doesn't work, what's our next best option?"

"What would you normally do to purge anger?"

"Hit the gym. But I'm only in town for thirty-six hours, so I didn't bring my gym clothes. What about you?"

"I'm only in town until Sunday morning, too."

"No, I mean what do you do to get rid of your anger?"

"I try to meditate." But I'm not very good at it.

He snorts. "Yeah, that's not for me."

"I sometimes drink chamomile tea or watch a comedy."

Two more things I can't picture him doing.

He shakes his head. "Yeah...no. I have to figure out how not to be incredibly pissed—at least enough to act civil—by tomorrow afternoon."

"Can you really stay angry that long?"

"I have a slow, hot fuse. It takes a lot to set me off, but once I'm there... I just came from seeing my dad. I already know I'm going to be pissed for a while." He sighs. "I don't even know why I came to Vegas. He called, and I thought I could save him. I'm a dumb ass."

"I'm in a relatively similar situation. My mom is so irresponsible and impulsive. She makes the same mistake over and over. Like now."

"And you're here to stop her?"

I shake my head. "It's too late for that. I'm only here because she guilted me."

"And you're not angry about it?"

"I am, but I guess I just expect it at this point."

"My dad's idiocy is something new. I'm not a fan." He taps his thumb on the bar. "I have to figure out how to deal quickly. But we've ruled out booze, workouts, tea, and TV. Any other suggestions? I've only got one, and I doubt you want to hear it, angel."

The low note in his voice makes my breath catch. His suggestion is probably the same one screaming fire through my head.

"Tell me," I murmur.

He stares at me with black eyes. The moment seems frozen. The overhead speakers pipe down the vaguely familiar strains of a rock guitar riff that's both soft and provocative.

"Sex."

I swallow. My heart pounds. I feel myself blush. Would I have it with him? If he asked, that is. I'm still not one-hundred percent sure he's interested. I'm not convinced he's not, either. But I'm attracted to him. Very. Deeply. Utterly.

Whatever the gorgeous stranger's name is, he's right. I've had a handful of boyfriends, most thoroughly underwhelming. I put romance on the backburner to focus on my career as a food blogger these past few years. I haven't had sex in longer than I'd like to remember. And I've never had a one-night stand.

I'm suddenly eager to make an exception for him.

"Yes."

He peers at me. "Yes…that's a reasonable suggestion? Or yes, you'd let me have sex with you?"

I gulp down half my drink and go for broke. "Both."

He doesn't immediately jump to his feet and hustle me out of the bar. "Why?"

"It's"—I shrug—"a feeling. That I should. That I'll regret missing out on you if I don't. But you may not have meant me at all, so—"

"I did." He leans closer, and I can't stop staring at his glittering dark eyes or ridiculously long lashes. For a man, he's beautiful. "I wanted you the instant I walked into the room."

My breath catches in my chest. "Same."

"Are you staying in this hotel?"

I shake my head. "My mother is. I'm down the Strip."

"I'm upstairs if you're really game, Calla. But one thing."

Am I going to do this, be intimate with a man whose name I don't even know?

Yes, I really am. Me, the girl who's never done anything impulsive? I'm going to live on the edge for once. "What?"

"I'm not a gentle man, even on a good day. And, Calla, this isn't a good day." He cups my chin with a touch so restrained, I shudder. "I won't hurt you…but I won't go easy on you."

He's exactly the sort of man I've been secretly fantasizing about—larger-than-life, take-charge, brimming with testosterone. Base. Alpha. Savage.

Since college, my friends have been insisting their lives are much better without men and marriage, attending rallies and marches, and insisting their soy-boy co-workers are so masculine it's toxic. I've smiled and nodded, fully agreeing that women should receive equal pay for equal work and that women can be every bit as capable as a man. But my educated brain is in constant conflict with the primal urges of my body. I crave a man who oozes aggression to turn all his barely contained sex drive on me.

I've hated these desires. I'm ashamed. My friends would be aghast and demand that I evolve beyond them immediately. I've tried. A lot. I even took their suggestion to buy a better vibrator.

It's not working. Nothing is.

Maybe this stranger will cure me. He'll either scratch my itch or prove my fantasy ridiculous. Whichever happens, I'll be better off. Besides, if I don't try surrendering to a man who makes every inch of my skin spark, won't I always regret passing him by?

"I don't want you to," I murmur.

Something on his face changes. The hesitation in his black eyes suddenly melts in a blaze of heat. "Then there's nothing left to talk about. Let's go."

When he calls out for the bartender, I lay my fingers on his arm. It's every bit as warm and steely as I imagined. "There is. One thing."

"What?"

"Are you married or taken?" I couldn't live with that.

He's not wearing a wedding ring, nor do I see a tan line where one once lay, but that doesn't always mean anything.

"No."

He doesn't hesitate and he doesn't look away. I don't know this man at all, but every gut instinct tells me he's being honest. "Thank you. Don't you want to know if I'm single?"

He shakes his head. "I know your kind. You wouldn't have said yes if you weren't."

"I wouldn't," I agree, voice trembling with anticipation.

He quickly pays the bartender, and I mull everything I've ever heard about safely hooking up. I'm supposed to tell someone where I'm going and with whom. I'm supposed to create check-in times and backup plans.

I don't do any of that. My gut says I'll be one-hundred percent safe with this sexy stranger. Maybe that's stupid, and I'll regret it. But for once, I'm shutting off my logic and relying on instinct.

He wraps his hand around mine, grip firm, and leads me out of the empty bar and through the smoky noise of the casino before stopping at a bank of elevators. There's a collection of businesspeople checking in to attend a convention downstairs, as well as a family gearing up for their weekend away. Despite the fact it's late afternoon, a pair of girls are already completely trashed and hitting on a casino attendant passing by.

When the elevator doors open, a cross-section of humanity tumbles out, then the others waiting beside us jump in. I move to follow, but the stranger tugs me back against his body. His erection prods the upper curve of my ass as he eases my hair over one shoulder and whispers in the opposite ear. "We'll take the next one."

As soon as the door closes, a ding a few feet away tells me there's another car waiting. He hustles me to it, all but carrying me when my stilettoes prevent me from matching his long-legged, ground-eating pace. Once we're inside, he sets me down and stabs a button to close the elevator door. Then he turns with a dark, burning stare, sexual intent plastered all over his face. He's going to use me to the fullest and relish every moment of turning my body inside out.

My heart stops. My brain screams at me to exercise caution and back out.

I don't say a word.

He wraps one arm around my waist. With his free palm, he grabs my nape, manhandling me until I look up, snaring myself in his gaze. "Last chance."

To back out? "I said yes for a reason."

"Don't say I didn't warn you." He pushes the button for the twelfth floor and the car begins to whoosh up.

I should probably ask questions or tell him I've never had a lover overwhelm me. Or simply plead with him for mercy. But I don't want any. I don't know even one man like him among the coffee-drinking, beard-growing, enlightened granola males in my circle of acquaintances. I'd be lying if I said I wasn't curious and excited…and ready to indulge in all my fantasies.

"Duly noted."

His eyes turn impossibly darker as he crowds me with his big body. He's hard and overwhelming. He smells like wood, leather, and pheromones. The way he wraps his fists around my long hair and tugs until my scalp tingles excites me. Then he pins me against the wall of the elevator and shoves his knee between my legs, my pencil skirt scraping up toward my hips. My heart races as he twists me in his big grip and settles my wriggling weight on his thigh.

"You're in trouble, angel."

God, I can barely breathe past my excitement. "What are you going to do?"

"Make you come for me before we leave this elevator."

When I gasp, he swallows the sound with his mouth. He doesn't merely lay his firm lips over mine. He surges inside my mouth, overtaking it as thoroughly as he overtakes my will. He kisses like he owns me. He makes me his with one sweep of his tongue. I can't find a shred of will to resist.

Then he guides my hips to rock on his thigh. Heat flares between my legs, firing out to the rest of my body and incinerating my good sense. My skin threatens to liquefy under his touch.

It seems impossible that, after one endless kiss and a barely thirty seconds of his knee against my sensitive flesh, I would be not only aching but on the edge of climax. I can't deny it, though. I feel it—blood pooling, need gathering—right between my legs.

I grip his big shoulders through his dress shirt, nails digging in as he tunnels into my mouth relentlessly again and increases the pressure against my throbbing sex. Pleading mewls escape me. I've never heard myself make those sounds. I don't think anything has ever made me whimper so needily. But I can't stop myself, not any more than I can stop squirming on his hard leg to chase the climax just out of reach.

"Come," he growls.

As if his voice opened my floodgates, I suddenly can't hold the orgasm back. I let go against him, my entire body jolting and shuddering as he swallows my long, agonized groan of satisfaction with his greedy mouth, holding me suspended during the shocking, unfightable ecstasy.

It's a long moment before I fall limply in his arms, gasping for breath.

"How do you feel?" I can't miss the satisfied smile on his face as he steps back and smooths my skirt down my thighs, just in time to hear the elevator ding. The car jolts to a stop.

I blink up at him, wondering who the hell he is and what kind of man is capable of making me—buttoned-up Calla Blair —orgasm in a potentially public place, much less so quickly.

"Stunned," I whisper. "I should be afraid."

"Are you?"

"No."

The elevator doors rush open. The stranger takes my hand and leads me past a trio of waiting businessmen who instantly cease their animated conversation to stare. I have no doubt my blouse is wrinkled, my cheeks are flushed, and my lips are swollen. They know what we've been doing.

For once, I don't care.

The stranger wraps a protective arm around me and glares their way. Instantly, all three look elsewhere and settle into an uncomfortable silence as they shuffle into the car we just vacated.

How does he have that effect on people? His presence seems to simply overwhelm everyone around him. They seemingly give in to his silent will with a mere glance. What is that? And why?

The elevator doors shut behind us, then his hands tighten on me again. He plucks me off my feet and lifts me against his body. It's a self-preservation instinct to wrap my legs around his waist and hold on for dear life.

"What are you doing?" I demand.

He looks at me, those black eyes glinting. "Jesus, I can already tell you're going to be sweet and I'll have a hard time keeping my mouth off you."

"You can kiss me," I say because he looks like he wants to.

The smile that splits his face can only be called filthy. "I wasn't talking about your lips, angel."

It only takes a second for his intimation to hit my brain. My eyes widen. "Oh."

"If the wet spot on my thigh is any indication, your pussy is beyond juicy. So, hell yeah, I'm going to get my mouth on it."

As much as I'm horrified by the thought I've stained his pants, I'm even more excited by the notion of having his head between my legs. Of having his tongue against the most intimate flesh on my body.

But... "Fair warning. I've never, um...responded much to that in the past."

He snorts. "Then someone was doing it wrong, and I'll be happy to prove he was an idiot."

As the stranger stops in front of a door in the middle of the hall, he sets me on my feet to dig a key card from his pocket. He doesn't waste more breath telling me how good he can make it or that I should give him a chance. He simply inserts the key, sweeps the door open, and urges me inside with a hand at the small of my back.

The second the door shuts behind us with a thud, he attacks the buttons of his gray dress shirt. Vaguely, I'm aware that I should do something besides stare. But I can't. I just watch as he reveals inch after bronzed inch of steely, muscled flesh.

As he shrugs off the garment and hangs it over the back of the nearby desk chair, I gulp. His torso is like something out of a magazine. Broad shoulders bulge and give way to thickly corded arms. The hard pecs between swell with powerful strength. His ridged abs are a testament to a fit life and a very clean diet. My stare drifts down, down—and I find myself gaping at his obvious erection. It's as big and rigid as the rest of him.

Even looking at him, I feel faint.

"I've died and gone to heaven." The words slip out before I can stop myself.

He laughs. "Or I might torment the hell out of you, angel. And by morning, you'll know every inch of the devil."

Oh, pretty please...

"Got any objections?" He prowls toward me and lifts the strap of my purse from my shoulder, then sets it on the nearby dresser.

"No." I shake my head. "None."

"Good. I want you naked. And I want to hear your scream as you come for me."

His words make me hot all over. But I shiver and swallow back the assertion that he probably can't make me come twice in one night. No man has ever managed to. Even my trusty battery-operated boyfriend struggles at times.

Suddenly, I don't doubt this stranger. I'm convinced he can melt me, make me putty in his big hands, and manipulate my body to do whatever he wants.

"I'm going to take your blouse off," he mutters as he skates a hand up my torso and skims his knuckles against the side of my breast before zipping his thumb across the taut crest.

Sensation zings through my body. I suck in a sharp breath. My nipples have never been particularly sensitive. But for him? One touch, and I'm ready to beg.

What else is this stranger going to be able to do to me before the sun comes up? I don't know, but I have a feeling it will change my entire concept of sex.

CHAPTER TWO

Quint

I can't stop staring at Calla's exquisite face. Regardless of what she says, she's an angel, and it's taking every bit of my will not to ravage her where she stands. If she doesn't open her tempting, red-painted lips and say something soon, I'm going to grind my teeth into goddamn dust. Or toss her on the bed, root deep inside her, and keep at her until she cries her throat raw.

"Calla?"

"Yes," she breathes. "Please. Take it off."

Thank fuck.

Less than thirty minutes ago, I headed into the bar for a much-needed drink, but I stayed for her. To stare at her. To talk to her. To touch her. I didn't think she'd actually agree to let me fuck her. Sure, I said that sex would calm me, but being near her only revs my libido. I feel like a rabid dog jerking against its chain. My need to consume this delicious panting morsel of female is bordering on dangerous.

There's something about her I can't walk away from.

I drop my hands to the winking pearl buttons down the front of her blouse, taunting me. One by one, I unfasten them, never taking my eyes off her. It's gratifying as hell to hear her breathing pick up, see her cheeks flush, and watch her pulse pound at her neck. I don't know who she's been to bed with in the past, but I'm determined to make her forget every one of those bastards. I don't know why. The urge is completely irrational. But if I put all my focus into making her scream for me all night, maybe I'll forget—at least for a while—that my dad is stubbornly set on making the biggest mistake of his life tomorrow.

And maybe I'll be the best fuck she's ever had. Maybe she'll never forget me.

I unmoor the last button at the bottom of her white blouse and push the garment off her shoulders. She's wearing a sensible tan-colored bra. No lace. No embellishments. The size of her breasts is average, which is fine because, first, I'm an ass-man. And second, nothing about the rest of her seems average at all. Her skin is like velvet. The lines of her body are lithe, almost graceful. I'm craving the chance to explore her.

"Lose the shoes and skirt," I demand.

She bites her lip and kicks off her heels as I head to the floor-to-ceiling window and draw the sheers beneath the black-out drapes. I have a sick view of the Strip, which is great. But I won't allow some perv in one of the nearby towers to peek in and see what's mine right now. On the other hand, I want to bathe Calla in light. I want to see her halo encircling her as I fuck her dirty and raw.

By the time I turn back, she's stepped out of her skirt and

draped it over my shirt on the back of the chair. Her panties match her bra—modest and practical—but her breathless stare threatens to strip away what little composure I have left.

I pad back across the room, reveling in the way her nipples get harder the closer I come. "Don't look at me like that."

"Like what?" She frowns.

"Like you're waiting for me to touch you."

"But I am," she murmurs, making me sizzle hot. "I'm just sorry I'm not wearing something sexy."

"You're in your skin, aren't you?"

A little smile flits across her lips. "I'll bet you're a real smooth talker."

"No." I don't normally waste my time. "I want you naked, Calla."

"What about you?"

Maybe she doesn't realize that her shy, flirty question is only torquing me up. That everything about her makes my cock impatient and hard. Or that once I take my pants off, I'll be shoving my way inside her.

She'll figure it out.

"Trust me. You're going to get every inch." I take her by the shoulders—fuck, she's so soft—and peer into her face, deep into those blue eyes. "Any hard limits? Things you won't do in bed?"

"No."

Oh, fuck. She might as well have just lit me on fire. "You might regret that answer, angel."

"*You* might," she counters. "I'm not usually very…sexual."

Her words ping around my brain. Not very sexual? Says who?

"But for some reason," she continues as she reaches behind her back and unclasps her bra, "I feel different with you."

Yeah, I feel different with her, too. More dialed in. More…

connected. More determined to give her a better experience than she's ever had.

As she slides the underwire garment down her arms, I hold my breath. It falls to the floor. Then she's standing half-naked before me, golden tresses tumbling well past her trembling shoulders. I lose my goddamn mind.

Her tits are perky. The round undercurves look lush above her rib cage. Her button nipples are topped with hard candy crests. I want them—in my hands, in my mouth, surrounding my cock.

I crook my finger at her. "Come here."

On graceful footfalls, she complies, her stare fused to mine. When she stops in front of me, she raises a soft hand and skims her fingertips over my shoulder. Her free hand lifts to the other, and her touch turns to a caress. I have to try not to shudder. I have to work even harder not to throw her flat on her back and bury myself inside her. Since I plan to do a lot of thoroughly filthy things to her tonight, I let her take me in and get comfortable with my body, with the feel of my skin on hers.

"I want to touch you everywhere," she whispers.

"I won't stop you."

A smile skips across her face as her fingertips skate down my pecs, float over my ribs, trail down my abs...and flirt with my waistband.

I suck in a breath. "Angel..."

"What?" She plucks at the button of my pants.

"You're playing with fire."

Her smile widens. "Am I?"

Oh, so she's trying to tease me? "You know you are."

And two can play that game.

"Are you going to let me?" She pops my button free and reaches for my zipper.

I grip her wrist. "Be very sure."

She ignores me and eases my fly open with a quiet hiss, then slips her hand inside to wrap around my cock. "I think your bark is worse than your bite."

Her touch burns in the best way. I suck air in through my teeth to counter the sizzle. "If you keep that up, you're going to find out how wrong you are."

"That sounds ominous." But her sultry stare from under the fringe of her dark lashes says otherwise. So does the way she leans in to press butterfly kisses along my pecs and shoulders.

"Calla..."

"Yes?" She strokes me softly, rhythmically, as her little pink tongue peeks out to lave my shoulder before she nips it. "You keep warning me. I don't think you mean it."

"You're dead fucking wrong."

I wrap my hands around her small waist and lift her off the floor. She yelps and releases me, blinking and sputtering as I shove the duvet aside and plant her, back flat, on my sheets. Before she's even stopped bouncing, I hook my fingers into the waistband of her panties and yank them down, tearing them past her feet and sailing them across the room with an absent flick of my wrist.

All my attention is on her slender thighs and the soft, sweet pussy in between. The dusting of blond hair tells me the pale tresses on her head that hang in gentle waves damn near to her waist are natural. She's slick, her folds puffy.

"Fuck, you're like a buffet. It all looks so good I can't decide where to start."

A little blush steals up her cheeks, and I'm fucking glad no other pervert has corrupted her. Suddenly, I'm wishing I had more time to do the job properly, but I'll damn sure make good use of tonight.

"What do you want?" Her silky feminine voice taunts me.

To let you know who's boss in the bedroom. "I want to spank your ass."

I don't give her even an instant to respond, merely sit beside her and lift her squirming form facedown over my lap.

She lifts her gaze to me, eyes wide with shock. "You're serious?"

"Never been spanked?"

"Of course not. Men really do this?"

She's so innocent, I have to laugh. But all hint of humor dies the instant I see her world-class ass across my lap. Taut, round, firm, pale. Kissable. Edible. Fuckable.

I start to sweat.

I don't know who the fuck she's been dating or why he hasn't managed to locate his dick, but... "Oh, yeah. Men definitely do this, angel. Get ready."

With a nudge, I steady her by planting one hand on the small of her back. With the other, I smooth and squeeze the luscious globes—testing, prepping, fondling.

"Will it hurt?"

Since I'm a dirty, degenerate son of a bitch, the tremble in her voice only turns me on more. "Sting. For a minute. After that... Well, you'll see."

"O-okay."

I wonder at the trust she's placing in me. She still doesn't even know my name. But for some reason, she's willing to surrender everything to me.

Does she feel that inexplicable tug between us, too?

She must. It's the only explanation.

I would never hurt Calla, but make her feel? Push her to the limit? Abso-fucking-lutely.

Breath held, I lift my hand, then bring it down with a soft

smack to her left cheek. I do the same to her right, then settle into a rhythm. Every time I land my hand, the blow turns a little harder, a little louder, until her cheeks begin to turn satisfyingly pink.

At first she tenses, then—a few spanks in—she starts to gasp and soften. Wiggling follows. When I pause to press my palms against her hot, stinging flesh, she moans. I smile. Then, fuck yes, I hasten the pace and the intensity of each smack until she starts breathing heavily, her ass slowly turns red, and she lifts herself to me for more.

I rub and squeeze her tormented cheeks until she hisses. "If you want me to keep going, Calla, ask for it."

The long, heavenly hair bobbing around my feet tells me she's nodding. "More," she gasps. "I don't know why, but I need it."

She probably doesn't know. I do. She's proving to be the softly sexual yin to my dirty-as-fuck yang. Even if I'd special ordered her, I'm not sure I could have found a woman who dovetails as nicely with my proclivities as this one. I'm eager as hell to show her everything she's been missing.

"Good girl," I praise as I pinch and knead her sensitive backside.

When she whimpers, I swat her with more force and sting than before. She jerks again. Her keening gets louder. I get even fucking harder.

Minutes slide by. My palm stings. Her backside looks sunburned red. And I wait. I suspect I'm approaching the edge of her tolerance, but I may not be quite there yet. I hope, anyway. I'm enjoying the hell out of seeing my bronzed hand connect with her pale, supple ass, hearing her groans and gasps, feeling her wriggle and jolt. I suspect she loves this every bit as much as I do.

"More?"

"Yes." The word rushes out with her audible exhalation. "Yes."

"You're going to be sore." And because I'm perverse and I can't resist, I give my fingernails a gentle drag down her flushed skin.

She sucks in a sharp breath. "I don't care."

I smile. She will care a lot more tomorrow when she tries to sit down, but if she remembers me a bit longer, I'm all for it.

"I warned you..." Then I don't give her a chance to change her mind, just unleash a fresh dozen blows on her throbbing ass, loving the way she rocks and digs her nails into my calf as her voice lifts to broken, strangled cries every time I lay my palm across her sensitive flesh.

When I stop, she's shuddering and struggling to catch her breath. A light sheen of perspiration covers her skin. Her ass is all but glowing. I could happily keep going for half the night. But whether Calla knows it or not, she's had enough. And her well-being comes first.

Even so, I can't resist the opportunity to kiss her backside, which throbs hot under my tongue. I run the tip up one blistering cheek, then nip at it until she yelps and begs.

"Oh. My god. Do something..." She struggles to sit up.

I plant my palm on her back more firmly to hold her in place. "Why?"

I know the reason, but I want to hear her say it.

"I'm on fire. I'm dying..."

That makes me grin. She really is perfect.

I help her upright, onto shaky legs. She stumbles to find her balance, planting her hands on my thighs and blinking at me with dilated eyes like I'm something between a monster and a god. I tuck a long strand of her hair behind her ear, marveling at how fucking beautiful she is. I wonder what her last name is, where she's from, what she does for a living, and how it's possible no red-blooded man has seen who and what she is, then snapped her up for his own. "You need to come?"

She nods, then stops, frowns, and finally shakes her head. "I need to touch you more."

Before I know what she's got in mind, she drops to her knees between my thighs, reaches into my fly, and wraps her hand around my cock. Her mouth follows, enveloping me into her slick, hot depths, sucking like she's desperate to inhale me.

I let out a long, low growl of appreciation and fill my fists with her silky hair. "Yeah. Fuck, angel. Suck me. Oh, that feels so damn good."

She whimpers, head easing back in a slow, thorough stroke. She circles the head, then sucks me back in deep, her lips pursing around the base before dragging the shaft back up her tongue and repeating the process all over again.

My heart revs. All the blood in my body rushes to my cock. The sight of Calla, hair mussed and pale as her head bobs between my legs, damn near unwinds all my self-control. I hoped she would want more of the chemistry between us. I prayed she'd go crazy in my arms. I felt sure she'd make me insane. But I didn't expect her to engulf me in her mouth as if her life depended on it.

It's not merely the pleasure itself that's melting me but the way she gives it to me like she's aching to. The way she's worshipping me, caressing me everywhere, every chance she gets. It's heady and addicting. And so fucking easy to lose myself... But I don't just want a blow job from this woman. I want to be inside her, as deep as a man can get. I want to stay there as long as she'll let me. I want to mesh our bodies together until she no longer cares where she ends and I begin.

"Angel." When she ignores me, I tug on her hair just enough to stop her stroke and get her attention.

She sits back on her heels and looks up at me with blinking blue eyes, a glossy red mouth, and a pleading face. "I don't want to stop."

"I know." I thumb her pouty lower lip. "But we've got all night. Let me touch you. Let me make you feel good."

Let me give you what you need.

Slowly, Calla nods and casts her eyes down. She can't possibly know what that does for me, but I'll reward her anyway.

Hooking a finger under her chin, I lift her gaze again and make her meet my stare. "Stand up, angel."

When I hold out my hand to her, she takes it. Her little gasp tells me she feels something sizzling between us, too. It's crazy and not like anything I've experienced before.

When she rises to her feet, I pull her in. Her breasts are inches from my face. *Holy shit.*

I cup one and bring it to my lips, caressing it with my tongue. And as she sighs, her body swaying toward me, I drag the crest into my mouth. She's both soft and firm. Her nipple tightens between my lips. And when I nip at the sensitive tip with my teeth, she yelps and presses her thighs together like she can barely contain the ache.

"Oh, my god," she murmurs as her eyes slide shut and her head lolls back. "Please."

I turn my attention to her other breast, still cradling the first in my hand. "Please more?"

She answers with a whimper as she clutches my head and draws me closer. "What are you doing to me?"

"Everything you'll let me." I run my tongue up the side of her breast before I take her nipple back into my mouth.

She grips me harder. The little sounds she makes at the back of her throat get louder. She shifts her weight and presses her thighs together again.

Good luck relieving that ache until I'm good and ready to end it…

In fact, I'm eager to add to her torment.

Sliding my palms down her body until I'm cupping her thighs, I lift one and set her foot on the edge of the mattress beside me. She stiffens and clutches my shoulders as she teeters to find her new center of balance.

I grip her hips to steady her. "I won't let you fall. I promise. Relax."

As if she only needed my words to reassure her, she does, losing herself again the moment I take her nipple back into my mouth and suck deep. I hear her soft sigh, watch her eyes close as pleasure furrows her brows and parts her lips.

Then I drag my thumb across her clit and make two thrilling-as-hell discoveries. First, she's deliciously slick and ripe for fucking. Second, her bud is beyond hard. And when I touch it, she jolts like I've touched her with a live wire.

"Oh!"

I do it again.

"Oh, my…" she groans. "Yes!"

With a smile, I find her opening and shove two thick fingers inside her pussy as I begin rubbing relentless circles against her clit with my anchoring thumb. She digs her nails into my shoulders and bites her lip, but the pleading sounds still escape.

"Are you going to come?" I know the answer, but I want to hear her say it.

To my shock, she shakes her head. "I-I had my…oh, orgasm for the night. I probably won't…ah!" She gasps. "Not again. But it feels…"

"Like you're going to come?" I root my fingers deeper inside her and concentrate my effort on her clit. "You are, angel. You may think you won't, but I know better."

"Usually—"

"Does anything about this feel like the usual to you?"

"No," she admits with a little cry.

"Me, either." I suck her breast into my mouth again and toy with her nipple. "In the elevator, you came when I told you to. Want to bet you'll do it for me again?"

Her lashes flutter open, and she looks at me with big, dilated eyes above the pink blooms of her cheeks. "Maybe you're right."

I know I am. For some reason, she thinks she's only capable of one orgasm a night. That's somewhere between laughable and ridiculous. And it will be my distinct pleasure to prove otherwise.

Regretfully, I release her breast, then hook my palm around her nape to haul her down to me. Her mouth is right there, and I can't not taste it.

The moment I slant my lips over hers, I push in, shove deep, and take control. Bless her, she lets me. She gives way entirely, allowing me to pillage at will as I continue to stroke her clit. And all the while, she rewards me with more breathy, needy little noises that drive me fucking wild.

Finally, her tense body and erratic breathing tell me she's on the edge. I ease back just enough to delve into her eyes and I press where her moans and gasps have told me her pussy is most sensitive. "Calla?"

"Yes," she pants, staring at me as if I control her world.

Right now, I do.

"Come for me, angel. Come hard."

Another drag of my thumb, another scrape of my fingertips over her G-spot, and another deep suckle of her nipple—and she releases her pleasure. The clamp of her cunt on my fingers and the steely hardening of her clit tell me so just before she wails out in low-throated bliss.

Her body jerks. She struggles to stay upright, digging her nails into my shoulders in the most delicious little sting. But the best part is the way she looks at me helplessly as if she doesn't understand my mastery over her body and silently surrenders herself to me.

It's beyond delicious.

When her womb stops clenching and the tension leaves her, I smile and pull her onto my lap. She melts against me, cheeks hot, and closes her eyes.

"I've never felt anything like that."

"I enjoy making you feel good." I nuzzle her neck and press a kiss to her nose. "I want to do it again."

"If you were anyone else, I would say you're crazy. But our chemistry…"

It's fucking strong. I've never felt anything like it. "I know."

She cups my jaw and presses her lips to mine for a lingering kiss. "Why aren't you inside me yet?"

"I will be soon," I promise because I intend to fuck her like she's never been fucked before. That doesn't sound romantic, but when I'm done, I'm determined she'll feel thoroughly adored and possessed. "I haven't finished exploring you yet."

Calla frowns. "But you've had your hands all over me."

"And my mouth is jealous." I slide her off my lap and ease her onto the mattress beside me. "I'm going to fix that now. Lie back."

CHAPTER THREE

Calla

Is he crazy? I can't stop wondering.

With my last boyfriend, orgasm was something between a duty and a trial. I often faked it because the time it took to reach the real thing was exhausting. But with this man? I still don't even know his name, but that doesn't matter. Everything inside me tells me he's important. Maybe that's only true tonight; I don't know. But he's already undone me twice, and just looking at him now makes me feel as if a third climax isn't impossible.

Coming upstairs with him may have been the best decision ever. Not just for the pleasure, though that's amazing. But he's setting the gold standard for future boyfriends. If someone I'm seeing can't make me feel this way, maybe that's my clue I don't belong with them.

At the thought of not seeing him again tomorrow, everything

inside me rebels. I don't want to let him go. I called this pull between us chemistry, but somehow it feels like more.

Fate?

"Calla?" He raises a brow at me.

There's a hint of displeasure on his face I immediately want to soothe. "I'm sorry. What?"

"I asked you to lie back. Is that a problem?"

So he can make me feel amazing again? I shake my head and quickly comply, looking up at him with what I'm sure is a loopy, lovesick stare.

He smiles, then stands above me and kisses the insides of my knees. My heart flutters at his gentleness. He's big and sexual and commanding, but the gesture is so tender I can't help falling under his spell a little more.

It takes me a hot minute to realize he's used the action to part my legs so he can step between them. Then he kneels at the edge of the bed and cups my thighs, spreading them even wider, before flashing me the dirtiest smile I've ever seen.

"That is one pretty pussy, angel."

Even his words incite my ache again. It's as if I didn't just have the biggest orgasm of my life. As if I haven't already experienced ecstasy twice tonight. And when he bends to plant a chaste kiss at the top of my mound before looking up my body to meet my gaze? I swear my womb melts and my ovaries explode. I want this man. I want him deep. I want him gentle and rough. I want him however he wants me.

"This is insane," I murmur.

"This is heaven. That's why I call you my angel." He drags his fingers through my wet, sensitive folds, and I see satisfaction in his eyes. "I need to taste you."

I tense. I was being honest when I said I wasn't a fan of receiving oral sex. Not only does it take a long time to find satisfaction this way but it's disconcertingly intimate. Yes, I fantasized about having his head between my legs earlier. But now that he's leaning toward me and licking his lips, I worry. Am I too wet? Will I respond the way he wants? Will he like this with me?

He bends closer. I freeze up.

"Relax," he murmurs.

I try…but it's not that simple.

"Whatever you're thinking, stop. Everything will be fine." He breathes against my inner thigh just before he kisses it softly, his lips lingering. "If you don't like it, tell me. I'll back off."

"Okay."

But the swagger in his posture and the grin on his face say he's absolutely confident I'll end up putty in his hands.

I'm beginning to believe he's right. So far, everything he's done to and with me has been exactly what I need. It's as if he's decoded the mysteries of my body no one else has managed to —even me. Maybe I simply need to trust that, when it comes to pleasure, he's right.

I slide my feet farther apart and lift slowly to him in offering.

"What a good girl." His approving stare belies his rough growl of arousal. "I'm going to reward you for your trust."

Before I can decipher his meaning, he rakes his tongue between my folds, lingering at my opening. He moans as he laps at me, then licks his way up to my aching nub. He flicks it, toys with it, then sucks it slowly into his mouth, tormenting me with heat and friction.

The blinding pleasure is immediate. I let out a startled gasp as I arch and my hips jerk up involuntarily to him. He takes full advantage, clamping his fingers even tighter on my ass to keep me in place, then licking my pussy with greedy strokes as if he's never tasted anything sweeter.

"Oh!" The sound slips out, startled and breathy.

"Oh…" His low reply sounds like something between a come-on and *I told you so*, which he accompanies with a slick-lipped smile.

Then he seems to latch his whole mouth over my aching sex, as if he can kiss it every bit as thoroughly as he kissed my mouth. I gasp.

My god, what is he doing to me? This definitely isn't anything like the polite, half-hearted oral sex I've experienced in the past. This stranger isn't remotely reluctant. As I glance down my body, it's as if he's put all his strength into my pleasure, spine arching, shoulders twisting, hands clutching possessively. Being with him feels amazing, eye-opening…and slightly forbidden.

My veins heat. My heart chugs. My toes curl. I flash hot all over. And suddenly the climax I was so sure would be impossible to feel barrels down on me. I can't help myself. I dig my fingernails into his scalp with a cry as my spine twists. My blood begins to jet and boil and pool right between my legs, where I swear I've never felt an ache quite as shattering or exquisite as this.

"Please…" I manage to squeal out between ragged breaths.

"You even beg pretty."

Though he's speaking, he doesn't relent. Not even a bit. He merely drags his thumb over the sensitive tip in a lazy sway that has my entire body tensing.

"Please!"

"You said earlier you didn't much like oral. Change your mind?"

He knows the answer and is simply tormenting me. But it makes these moments he holds me suspended in his grasp even sharper.

"Yes. Oh, my…yes."

He chuckles, and the vibration of his low rumble skitters across my nerves and ups the stimulation where I already ache. "Glad to hear you've stopped doubting me."

I nod enthusiastically. I can't even find the breath to plead anymore.

"Ready to come for me again?"

Beyond. I give him another jerky nod.

"Beg me one more time," he demands.

Are you serious? I want to screech the question, but I don't. First, my brain is too scrambled to speak a complete sentence. Second, instinct tells me he'll delay giving me the ecstasy I'm dying for if I don't comply.

And the way he's bending me to his will is a shockingly huge turn-on.

"Please," I pant. "Please…"

He rewards my compliance with another lash of my clit with his tongue, then slowly sucks me into his mouth.

Maybe I'm crazy or just beyond rational thought, but I'd swear every move he makes is calculated to dismantle my self-control. I've never felt anything like the ecstasy he's giving me. I don't have any way of fighting it. I don't want to. All I want is the pleasure he alone seems capable of showering on me.

"*Pleeeease…*"

"There it is," he praises as he licks his way up my center again. "That's what I wanted. Come, angel. Let me watch."

The sensations he heaped on me were enough to send me over the edge, but his command is like kindling to my restraint. Knowing he's watching me? That's the gasoline on top.

The pleasure coursing through my system converges between my legs and explodes. I wail; there's no other way to describe my sobbing cries that echo off the walls. I writhe. I buck. I don't even control my body anymore. This man does. A stranger. He holds my next breath and my sanity in his hands. He balances them on his tongue. I feel his eyes all over me and I know that he's completely aware of his power over me.

It's both heady and terrifying.

My body hurtles over the pinnacle, then slowly eases back down as I fight for breath and coherence. Slowly, I open my eyes. He's still between my legs, easing my float to the ground with his tongue, his black stare still on me.

Finally, he backs away with one last kiss to my mound. "That might be the prettiest thing I've ever seen."

He makes me blush. I both love it and hate it. I'm hardly a girl, and I'm not a virgin. But somehow he strips away my disillusionment and wipes the jaded side of me clean, leaving me shiny and new and frighteningly naked.

I have to do something to balance the power between us. At least that's what I tell myself. But I'm aware that I'm trembling with the need to make him feel good, too.

Sitting up, I splay my hands on his thighs, wishing he wasn't half-hidden by his zipper. "That was amazing. Do I get to finish what I started and return the favor now?"

He shakes his head and stands, towering over me, as if he wants me to understand who's in control. "Later. I want inside you now."

I've just had the orgasm of my life. How is it possible his words renew my spark of desire?

"Now?"

He doesn't answer verbally, simply pulls a foil square from his pocket, drops his pants, and kicks them aside with his shoes.

My eyes bulge. His sculpted torso alone was stunning—all muscles, bronzed skin, and the tribal tattoo I now see bisecting his ribs along one side. But seeing him head-to-toe naked? I swallow. He's big, hard, and ready. And tonight, he's mine.

I don't say another word. I simply lie back and spread my legs. Without being told, I know that's what he wants. His silent approval moments later fills me with a pleasure that's distinctly different from the arousal he lavished on me minutes ago.

"Such a good girl," he praises as he slips the condom over his cock and leans above me, palms flat on either side of my head. Then he covers me with his body and uses his knees to spread my legs farther apart. "Keep them wide. I want to enjoy every second I'm inside you."

I want him to enjoy it, too, but I can't find the words, so I just nod.

"God, the way you're looking at me..." His eyes darken as he grips my hips and fits his fat crest against my opening. Then he swallows like he's every bit as turned inside out as I am. "We just met and this makes no sense, but this is more than a fuck." He nudges my opening. "Right?"

"Yes." I feel myself tighten on him, trying to suck him in deeper.

Nothing about this makes any sense, but I don't argue. I can't. Something's happening between us. It isn't just that he makes my body sing—but oh, hell, he does. It's as if he stares into my eyes and, as he's penetrating my body, he penetrates my soul.

I gasp as he stretches me, filling me, seeming to complete me. Which makes no sense, but I can't escape the feeling that all other men have left me cold because I was meant for this one.

He tunnels deeper, deeper, finally pressing in to the hilt and bottoming out. "There. Now you're mine."

He feels it, too, this inexplicable connection. I see it on his face.

"Yours." Names aren't important. We'll get to them, but right now we're leading with our hearts. With the love we're making. "Oh, that's good…"

His smile lights up the shadowy corner of his room.

"I'm going to make you feel even better, Calla," he vows as he eases out in a molasses stroke that nearly has me whimpering.

I believe him.

Then we don't need to talk. He plants his elbows on the mattress beside me and grabs for my hands. I give them over, melting when he links our fingers as he thrusts even deeper into my body.

Again and again, he fills me slowly. The pleasure builds until need starts to burn once more. I should be past the shock that he can ignite me so quickly and so often. But I blink up at him as the desire ignites. Suddenly, I'm breathing hard and rocking with him. My heart lurches when he slants his mouth over mine and kisses me. His tongue is as thorough as his cock, exploring deep and conquering me totally. With every touch, I feel all my usual defenses crumble to dust. Instead, my very chest seems to open up. When all the feelings I normally hold back pour in, for once I welcome it.

"Look at me," he demands.

I open my fluttering eyes wide and lose myself in the black depths of his glinting stare. "This is insane. I've never felt…"

He doesn't need me to finish the thought to understand. "Me, either. I don't know what's happening but I'm not stopping."

Even the suggestion that he might makes me clutch him tighter.

His strokes pick up pace. His body crashes into mine over

and over. His strength of will ensures that, even if I wanted to hide my feelings from him, I couldn't.

"Calla?"

"Yes."

"You with me?"

"Yes…" I pant out.

He drags his lips up my neck before stealing my mouth—and my thoughts—again. Everything inside my body is tightening and heating. Nerve endings I didn't know I had awaken and tingle for this man. I can't think. I can't breathe.

All I can do is feel—and surrender to—him.

"We're going to do this together."

"What?" I've gone from stimulated to electrified. My fingers grip him. My lips dust his jaw. My hips lift to each thrust. My sex clenches.

"Come," he insists, teeth bared. "Now."

I have no idea what it is about this man or the way he talks to me, but his demands are the key to unlock my body. Suddenly, all the tension inside me shatters in a primal release unlike anything I've ever known.

Arching, I toss my head back and cry out so loud I'm sure everyone on the floor can hear how good he makes me feel. My beloved stranger presses his lips over mine. I feel his body tense and shudder. He shoves inside me even deeper and groans into my mouth as he swells and jerks, giving himself over to me.

We take a collective breath, and our hearts slow together. Then he opens his eyes and soothes stray curls from my damp forehead and hot cheeks. "Hi."

I smile, stupidly, deliriously happy that I met him. "Hi."

"I'm Quint. Thought maybe you should know the name of the man who's fucking you. You know, for next time."

I have to laugh. "Hi, Quint. It's nice to finally know your name. And that sounds great. Next time."

My sigh probably sounds half lovesick, and I don't care. If something good comes out of this craptastic weekend, then I'll call him my silver lining and be grateful. Because I have no illusions; tomorrow afternoon will suck.

"Hey, where did your smile go?"

"Sorry. Thinking that I have to do something unpleasant tomorrow. I'd rather not think about it at all."

"Same." He presses his forehead to mine and holds me tighter before kissing my brow. Then he eases free and trashes his condom. Before I even have time to miss him, he returns and cuddles me against his hard body. "But I'd like to spend the rest of the weekend with you."

I don't have to think at all. "I'd love that."

His smile blinds me. "Where do you live, Calla?"

"LA."

He grimaces. "What do you do?"

"I'm a freelance food blogger. What was that scowl about?"

"That's a long way from home for me, and I hate LA."

"Actually, I'm not that fond of it anymore, either. The traffic is horrible. The cost of living is ridiculous. It's just… It seemed normal when I was growing up there. Now…" I shrug. "Meh. Where do you live?"

"Outside Santa Fe. I lived in Denver for a while, but I like Santa Fe's smaller town feel. I'm a homicide detective."

So my instinct that he wouldn't hurt me, no matter how much I put myself at his mercy, had been right. "I can picture that. You like it, don't you?"

"It can be grisly and sad, but yeah. It's like a calling. How did you know?"

"Tell me I'm not the only one who feels this strange connection—"

"Like we've known each other forever? You're not."

I let out a sigh of relief. "Exactly. It's so odd. I've never felt this way."

"Me, either. I'm usually a perfectly happy loner."

"Well, not a total loner," I point out. "You obviously know your way around a woman's body."

Quint is manly as hell, but the self-deprecating grin that crosses his face could almost be called boyish. "I said I was a loner, not a monk."

He was already gorgeous and solid, but he's got a sense of humor, too? Be still my heart. "Clearly."

Something on his face changes. "You haven't dated a lot, have you?"

"I did. Well, I tried. I just never found anyone I clicked with."

"Until me?"

"Yeah. Does that sound crazy?"

"It does. But I know it's not since I'm feeling it, too."

I bite my lip. "What do we do about it?"

CHAPTER FOUR

Quint

"Good question." We live in different cities, in different states. I'm not sure how we deal with that. But the longer she bites that plump pink lip, the less able I am to problem solve rationally. I drag my thumb over her pouty mouth. "Stop that."

"Why?"

I can't help but notice she asks the question with a hint of sass, which I'll be happy to spank out of her later, but she complies immediately. Does she have any idea how perfect she is for me?

"Because you look sexy doing that and it distracts the fuck out of me."

She laughs. "You're not sated?"

"For the moment, maybe." But not for long. "You think you are?"

Calla rolls her eyes. "I've never had four orgasms in one

night. You're like the Superman of the bedroom. After all that, there's no way I'll be able to manage round two."

Oh, she of little faith. "Wanna bet?"

Suddenly, the smile leaves her face. "No. If anyone can prove me wrong, it's you."

"Not if, angel. When. I will definitely be proving you wrong, but not until we have food. I'm starving."

"Me, too. I didn't get to grab lunch before I caught my plane."

"Same." I shift a sidelong stare her way. "Go out...or stay in?"

"There are a ton of amazing restaurants here in Vegas, and the food blogger in me thinks I should hit at least one before I leave Sunday morning, but...stay in."

"God, you really are perfect for me." I hold her close and kiss her nose. "I want to know everything about you."

"And I want to know about you. How do we cram all of that into a few hours?"

"We'll do our best." I bound out of bed and prowl around the room, stark naked, searching for the room service menu.

I feel her eyes on me. Given the way she's staring, I'm not sure she cares what we order for dinner. I don't much anymore, either.

"You're gawking," I point out.

"You're hot." She grins.

That makes me laugh. "If you keep flirting, you're going to get fucked again."

"I wouldn't hate that, but you promised me food first."

"I did." I sigh and hand her the menu, then sit on the bed beside her. "What sounds good?"

Calla glances down at the pages with a frown. "Whoever did their photography is second-rate. It's distracting. Why don't you tell me about your scars instead? It looks like you've led an exciting, if harrowing, life."

"You could say that." Probably more than she can imagine.

"By contrast, all I've ever done is beat a path between my kitchen and my computer, photographing and writing about what I've cooked. You must think I'm so sheltered." With a sigh, she sets the menu aside and fingers a round scar near my ribs. "Tell me about this."

I thumb through the menu and realize she's right about the photos. "Once you've picked some dinner. Because if you keep touching me like that, dinner will never happen."

She giggles. "Fine. Do they have a burger?"

"Yeah. What do you want on it?"

"Just ketchup and lettuce."

"Sounds good." I make the call, aware of Calla's gaze on me. As I finish and hang up, the curiosity in her eyes is just another turn-on to add to the list of things I'm digging about her. "Forty-five minutes to an hour."

"Good. That gives you plenty of time to tell me about your scar."

Her tenacity makes me laugh. "I got shot here about three years ago. Want to see the rest of the collection?"

"Since that means I get to peruse your whole body, yes."

I walk her through another shooting, this one even further in the past, a trio of stabbings—all by the same killer trying to escape capture—and a stupidly reckless motorcycle accident in my twenties that landed me in a coma for two days. "What about you?"

"Scars?" She grimaces. "I fell as a toddler and hit my head." She points to the faintest pucker at her hairline.

I lean in. "It's basically invisible. That's it?"

"More or less. I probably have a few on my hands where I've burned myself cooking. Want to see my blog?"

"Hell yeah."

She seems sweetly nervous when she launches the site from her phone. Pictures of all the dishes she's created appear, many themed around holidays, traditions, virtual vacations, or zany culinary experiments. I take my time studying what she's done. After all, this is important to Calla. I read some of her articles and even play a few of the videos she's shot.

Finally, I darken her phone with a smile. "You're really good."

"Thanks. I keep trying out for TV shows to increase my exposure. I made it onto a cable competition where I was judged by three really talented chefs. But I lost to another home-trained cook who used to be a stripper…and dressed accordingly."

"So all the chefs judging you were male?"

"Two of them. The other was a female who had a passion for Indian food, which my competitor made perfectly." She shrugs. "Maybe I'm not meant to be on TV. That's okay."

"I think you'd be great." I pull her closer and tuck long strands of her hair behind her ear. "And I think you're beyond gorgeous."

"How are you still single?" She sighs.

"I didn't really look. I was always married to my job." *And I never found anyone who seemed right for me…until you.*

She nods. "I've been guilty of ambition, too. I figured I have tons of time."

Of course she did, which makes me wonder… "How old are you?"

"Twenty-four. You?"

I grunt. God, is she going to think I'm an old lech? "Thirty-six. Does that bother you?"

"Actually, I'm relieved."

That surprises me. "Because?"

"Most guys in their twenties are still playing stupid games I don't have patience for. They don't know what they want and they aren't ready for anything real."

"That's not me."

She nods again. "I like that about you. Plus, my mother always dates guys who are younger than her. She was a cougar before the term was a thing. She was always fixated on looks and sex way more than emotional connection. I couldn't relate. Then again, we're not super close. She didn't have me until she was forty. I was a surprise. She's not even one-hundred percent sure who my father is."

And that bothers her; I can tell. "So you're the opposite, only wanting to date responsibly and seriously?"

She nods. "You're the first truly impulsive thing I've ever done in my life. I didn't start dating until I was eighteen. My ex-boyfriend and I were together almost two years before we had sex."

"And I'm guessing it wasn't good?"

"Horrible. And the last few guys just didn't wow me. I tried, but… What about you?"

"Never been interested in settling for something less than my parents had. They were married for thirty-three years before we lost my mom to cancer a few years back."

As if she senses the pain I still carry, she tosses her arms around me and gives my back a comforting stroke. "I'm sorry. You miss her."

This woman gets me. "All the time. She was amazing." I peer at Calla again, marveling at how right it feels to have her in my room, in my bed. "She would have liked you."

She gives me a warm smile. "I'm sure I would have liked her, too. Do you think you get your personality more from her or your dad?"

"My dad. I look like him. I talk like him. I think like him." I laugh at myself. "When I was a teenager, I was determined to be anyone and everyone other than him."

"Rebellious, huh?"

"Oh, my god. I was a horrible kid. Full of angst and defiance." I roll my eyes at how stupid I was. "But as I got older and started seeing the world as an adult, I realized he was right and I'd been an idiot. At least until lately. Now I'm convinced he's gone off the deep end."

"Well, if you need advice on handling *that* parent, let me know. I've always had to manage my zany mom, who never thinks anything through."

We laugh a little, kiss a little, pet a little. I go from wondering if she'll let me make love to her again to being sure she will. The knock on the hotel room door puts a stop to the fun.

"Shit. I'm naked," she shrieks as she darts for the bathroom.

"I won't let anyone see you." I grab a pair of shorts from my nearby suitcase, then motion her to shut the door. "I'll get everything set up and let you know when it's safe to come out."

"Thank you," she sighs.

Calla

I LEAN against the bathroom door with a huge grin. The way Quint protects me from even the little things makes me melty. I can see a future with someone like him. It really sucks we live so far apart…

You could move, a voice in my head suggests.

For a guy I've known all of three hours? That makes all of the stunts my mother has pulled over the years seem completely rational. At least she knew husband number three a whole four days before they decided to elope. Over my sixteenth birthday. And not tell me where she'd gone for the entire weekend.

Good times…

A few minutes later, he knocks softly, then opens the door, waiting for me with open arms. "Coast is clear, angel."

He's so handsome I can barely stop myself from smiling at him. "Thanks."

The scent of the burgers and crispy fries fills the room. He ordered a bottle of wine, too—a delicious red that will totally elevate our bar food. He leads me to a chair that flanks a little table in the corner and holds it out for me.

I send him a sassy gaze. "A caveman in the bedroom and a gentleman in the dining room?"

He grins. "Something like that. Complaining?"

"Nope." Actually, I love it. I feel protected, like he'd always look after me if I let him. For the girl who had almost no parental boundaries or sense of security growing up, I'm here for it.

"Good. Because that's probably not going to change," he drawls as he lifts the stainless domes off our dishes.

I dig out the condiments as he pours the wine, then he sits down to eat. We start talking. About friends. About our jobs. About some of the most embarrassing moments of our lives. I can't picture him streaking through a pal's house party, but in fairness, he was fifteen, super drunk, and lucky he didn't get arrested. He gives me a sympathetic grimace when I talk about my run for seventh-grade class president and having to give a speech in front of my whole school—which ended with me losing my lunch all over the podium. We talk about our worst dates and our happiest memories.

As if by silent agreement, we don't talk about anything heavy. And I absolutely don't bring up my mother or mistake number five she's hell-bent on making tomorrow.

We polish off our burgers and chat through the last of the wine. When the bottle is empty, he orders another. Together we open it and imbibe before kissing our way to the shower, where we both get squeaky clean. After we towel off, we tumble back into bed and get deliciously sweaty again.

I'm panting after yet two more orgasms that completely rock my world when I look over at him. "How have I lived this long without you?"

Something tender softens his black gaze. "I was wondering the same thing about you, angel."

He kisses me long and slow before he turns out the light, wraps his arms around me, and settles my naked body against his. I burrow closer, not wanting an inch of space between us.

Sure, the wine softens my mood and makes me less resistant to Quint's charm. But he'd already pried his way past my defenses and started climbing into my heart. This isn't simply alcohol induced. That means one of two things is happening: I'm either falling in love or I'm turning into my impulsive mother.

Both possibilities are terrifying.

He drops a kiss onto my shoulder. "You're tensing."

"You're changing my life," I blurt.

He doesn't reply, but I feel him smile in the dark before he lays a tender kiss on my lips. "Good night, angel. Sweet dreams."

CHAPTER FIVE

Quint

I wake to the sweet scent of female. She's curled against me, soft around me. Instantly, I'm hard.

When I pry one eye open, I see a long blond braid and a slender neck above the graceful curve of her shoulder. Her hip fills my hand. Her ass cradles my erection. Her nearness fills me.

Calla.

I'd half hoped when I went to bed last night that I'd wake this morning feeling completely different about her. Half of me wanted to have fucked her out of my system so I could return to Santa Fe single and resume my normal life, since I don't take to change well or easily.

But that half of me didn't get its wish.

Gently, I roll Calla to her back so I can study her face. I'm mesmerized by the long sweep of her brown lashes on her cheeks and the smooth skin of her face, beautiful even devoid of makeup.

I could happily wake up to her for the rest of my days.

Jesus, I sound ridiculous. I need to slow the fuck down. I've known this woman for barely more than twelve hours. There's no such thing as love at first sight, and no sane man wants to tie himself to a woman forever after less than a day.

At least that's what I used to think. Now? I don't know anymore.

Calla shifts in her sleep, and the sheet dips, the top barely covering those pretty breasts I remember sucking last night. My mouth waters. The rest of her is under that starchy white linen—her flat stomach, sleek thighs, tight pussy, and that glorious ass. No doubt, she's gorgeous and she physically turns me on. But I'm actually even more attracted to her as a person. I love the way she's both calm and prim—until I unravel her. I love the spark and the hint of sass—until she yields to my will. And I love her honesty. She doesn't play stupid head games. She would never lead me on or fuck me simply for the sake of fucking with me. When she gives her body so openly, I can tell it means something to her.

She doesn't know it means everything to me.

"Stop staring," she mumbles, eyes still closed. "I look horrible in the morning."

I laugh. "You look beautiful."

Calla scoffs and opens one eye with a frown. "Sure. Sheet marks pressed into splotchy cheeks are sexy. And who can resist bedhead? I'm sure I need a toothbrush, too."

"If you keep suggesting that I shouldn't want to be inside you right now, I'm going to prove you wrong. And you know I'm perfectly capable of making my"—I press my erection into her hip—"point."

Her lashes flutter open, and her blue eyes are like a visceral punch to my gut. Her lips are so softly pink, like the first flowers of a new spring. Yeah, that's really fucking poetic for me, but I like this color so much better than the va-voom red she was sporting yesterday in the bar.

"You're crazy," she says. "I'm ridiculously pale without makeup. I'm sure I'm bloated from the wine. And I'll bet I looked way better last night than I will in full sunlight this morning."

I roll her onto her hip, facing me. Then I give her luscious behind a hearty slap. "You're saucy this morning. Do you need a spanking *and* a fucking?"

A little smile plays at her lips. "I just might." Then as if she remembers something horrible, she sits up, clutching the sheet. "Shit. What time is it?"

I look at the clock on the nightstand. "Nine thirty."

"What?" Her eyes bulge. "I never sleep that long."

"Me, either." I'm lucky if I sleep more than four hours a night. Last night? Nearly nine hours. "What time do you have to be at…wherever you're going today?"

"With my mom?" She wrinkles her nose. "I told her I'd meet her for lunch at one. What about you?"

"My dad wants to have a drink with me about three. But I should be free again by seven at the latest."

She shakes her head. "I won't be staying that long. As soon as this farce is over, I'm leaving."

I don't know what shit show she's facing today, but I like her idea. "Good point. I'll book out of there right after dinner. Give me your number, angel. I'll call you as soon as my command performance is over."

I grab my phone, and she rattles off her number. I send her a quick text so she has mine, too. When it dings, she slides out of bed, all pink and totally unselfconscious, then smiles when she sees my message.

"Perfect."

"Not yet." I set my phone aside. "It will be perfect when you come over here and let me prove how gorgeous you are to me this morning. I'll put a smile on your face, too."

"You sweet talker..." She grins as she saunters toward me, all swaying hips and intriguing allure. "But afterward, you have to feed me. It will be a very bad day if I have to face my mother's stupidity on an empty stomach."

"I pre-ordered last night. It will arrive at ten thirty."

Her smile widens. "You might be the most wonderful man on the planet. Until the eggs come, I'm all yours."

There are a million things I want to do to Calla. Sweet things like kiss her until she swoons. Filthy things like bend her over the nearby desk and fill that tempting ass with my cock until she cries out in agonized bliss. And if I keep feeling about her the way I'm feeling right now, I'll move heaven and earth to spend more than the weekend with her. I'll make her mine so I'll have eternity to do every romantic and dirty thing to her I can think of.

Right now, I just want to be close to her.

"Come here." I sit up and I loop my fingers around her wrist, drawing her in between my spread legs.

"What?" She bites her lip.

Her come-hither expression lights me on fire.

I press kisses to the swells of her breasts, then coax her to lean in so I can trail my lips up her neck. With my free hand, I reach onto the nightstand for a condom.

Calla moans and offers me the graceful line of her throat.

I love melting her. "How about you be a good girl and straddle me so I can fuck you?"

Her breath catches. "Wouldn't that make me a bad girl?"

"No, it's going to be damn good for me. I'll make it good for you, too."

"You always do."

I smile as my mouth wends back down to her nipples and I take them in my mouth, one after the other, in long, lingering licks that soon have her tightening her fingers around my shoulders even as she melts onto my lap. I rip the foil packet open and sheathe myself just in time to lift her up by her small waist and down onto my stiff cock.

She takes in my length with a sharp, agonized gasp. "Quint!"

"You sore?"

"A little, but...oh, who cares?" Her lashes flit open to show me her eyes are already wide and her cheeks are flushed.

Fuck, she really is the most beautiful, feminine thing I've ever held. She's like something out of my fantasies. But I'm trying like hell to be noble. "I don't want to hurt you."

"You could only do that if you left me."

The earnest way she speaks the words tells me she doesn't mean right now or this fucking. She wants us. Together. Beyond today.

I think that's what I want, too, angel.

Logically, I realize a few hours away from her spun-sugar lips and sensual-as-fuck body would be good for my common sense, but I can't imagine feeling differently about her than I do right now. I can't imagine not wanting her in my future. Sure, I could write this off as lust. I've felt plenty of that before.

This isn't it.

"That's not going to happen," I whisper.

The smile that transforms her face takes my breath away. Then the clouds part, the sun slants in through a crack in the drapes, and her halo is all lit up again. It's the perfect way to make love to my angel. After all, it's got to last me until tonight. Then…I'll figure out how to keep her beyond the weekend. Because I don't see any way I'm letting her go.

CHAPTER SIX

Calla

I knock on the door to my mother's suite at one o'clock, wishing I was back in Quint's room, wrapped in his arms. Following breakfast, he put me in a taxi to my hotel. After a quick shower, I slapped on my makeup and did my best to cover the love bite he left on my shoulder. Then I shimmied into a black dress I last wore to a funeral and headed back down the strip and into battle.

I'll be so glad when this afternoon is over and I can escape to Quint's strong arms again.

My mother opens the door with a bright smile, wearing a gorgeous cocktail dress in a rosy-beige color with sky-high heels. One thing about Iris Blair? She doesn't look sixty-four—not even close. She attributes that to her *joie de vivre*. I attribute it to a strict keto diet, a hair-color magician, and Botox.

"Baby girl, come in. I missed you last night."

"Sorry I didn't call again. I had a drink in the bar after we talked and…" No way am I telling her I met the man who might be the love of my life. It will really undermine my argument for putting an end to her impetuous charade.

"And?"

"I started drinking."

She sighs in disappointment. "That face tells me you spent the night in your room."

"Something like that," I demur because it's not important. I only have a few hours to save her from making another potentially colossal mistake.

"But it's Vegas!" my mother argues. "You're my daughter. Why don't you know how to have a good time?"

I don't bother pointing out that it's because of her I often can't. When I was growing up, *someone* in our house had to be the adult. That was usually me.

Instead of arguing, I switch the subject to one guaranteed to end the squabbling. "You look amazing."

"Don't you love this dress?" She twirls to show me every bit of it, including the peekaboo plunging back.

"It's really something." I nod, but I can say one thing honestly. "I love the color on you."

"I wore that soft green number for my last wedding. You remember? But I wanted something totally different now. This says spring bride to me."

Sure. Why not? "Where is your fiancé? I was looking forward to meeting him."

Not that it matters. Given my mother's track record with husbands, he'll be "wonderful" through the spring, "fine" this summer, a "pain in the ass" as fall sets in, and her ex by Christmas. She's got a routine. I can pretty much set a watch by it.

"He's with his family. You'll get to meet them after the ceremony. So how about I open this bottle of champagne, and we toast?"

There's something really tempting about the notion of attending my mother's fifth wedding sloshed, but I want to be sober and awake for my time with Quint later. Besides, I should try to talk sense into her now.

I shake my head. "Tell me about this man you're marrying first."

"Curtis Dean is *everything*. He's it. He's the one!"

I've heard this speech before, so I'm unmoved. "Why do you think that?"

Her face softens. "Because I've been around long enough to know what's important in life and when it's real. When I'm with him, I feel as if I've finally found the man I've been searching for my whole life."

Okay, so that part of her speech is new. Is it possible she's truly learned that relationships aren't just about wine, song, and good times, but the *person* you're with?

"That's great, Mom. I hope that's true, but I have to ask... If he's the one—for real this time—what's your hurry? You've known him for how long?"

Her expression tells me she's annoyed but clamps it down. "Actually, we met a couple of months ago."

Wow. Typically, she falls head over heels in a matter of days. A couple of weeks is a steady relationship for her. A couple of months might as well be an eternity. "That's great."

"We met online." She nods as if she's proud of herself for her use of technology to expand her dating pool. "A singles' site for seniors. I saw his picture and reached out. He's a retired fire-fighter. Widower. Even-tempered. Funny. So charming. We finally met face to face three weeks ago. We both knew right away. He's not like the others."

Frankly, he doesn't sound like the cheating, sponging douchebags Mom usually marries, but I'm still not getting my hopes up until I meet this guy. "Where does he live?"

"He's offered to move to LA...but I may move to Colorado with him. Start fresh. It's just nice that, for once, I have a man who wants to make me happy. Be faithful to me. Love me." Tears sting her eyes as she reaches for my hand. "I know you think I've been irresponsible in the past, and I wasn't always the mother I should have been. But I didn't know what love was until Curtis because I realize now I'd never been loved by anyone. Well, except you. You always stood by my side, no matter what. I was too wrapped up in myself and my love life to realize... I'm so sorry."

Wow, this is a totally different version of my mother. I don't recognize this empathetic woman with watery blue eyes, looking at me as if she'd do anything for my forgiveness.

I wish I could snap my fingers and just make all the bad memories and heartbreak go away. There's a part of me that's still angry with her, and I'm not really sure I trust that this two-dot-zero model of Mom is here to stay. But I would never wish her anything less than sublime happiness.

"I hope Curtis really is everything and that he makes you happy for the rest of your life." I hug her.

She sniffles and hugs me back with a tentative smile. Maybe she will make more effort going forward. And maybe she's just being sentimental on her wedding day. Right now, all that matters is that maybe she's turning over a new leaf, and hopefully, marrying this man won't be a mistake.

"I don't want to mess up my makeup." She dabs at her eyes. "Shall we have some lunch? I made us a reservation." Then she frowns as she takes in my funeral dress. "Is that what you're wearing to the wedding?"

Now I feel a little guilty about my silent protest. "Since I work at home, I don't have many dresses."

"Feel like fixing that?"

I frown. "I thought we were going to have lunch."

"We can. I made reservations at that place... It's on the tip of my tongue. Oh!" She rattles off the name of the restaurant owned by one of my favorite chefs.

"You planned to take me there?" My mother doesn't share my same interest in creative, upscale food, but this might be the first time she's listened to my wishes and put them above her own desires. I'm touched. "Really?"

"Of course. I know how much it means to you." Then she waves her hand at me. "You know what? I don't care if you're wearing black. You look lovely, and I'm happy you came. I can't wait for you to meet Curtis and his kids. They're coming, too. I haven't met them, but I'm hoping that after today we can all be one big family."

"Are you sure? I can tell this wedding is important to you. We can shop if you'd rather."

My mom shakes her head. "I don't know how many times we'll be in Vegas together, where the two of us can do something this special. I don't want to give that up. My maid of honor wearing black just makes the ceremony more elegant."

"Maid of honor?" Now I feel somewhere between guilty and sick.

"Well, of course. Nothing is more important than family, and no one is more dear to me than you. Curtis reminded me of that. In fact, his older son is going to be his best man."

I swallow. "That's fantastic. But...maybe we should rethink the dress after all.

"And give up what's-his-name's spectacular food? Or a good social media opportunity?" She shakes her head and squeezes my hand. "No. But…since we wear the same size shoes, maybe you could swap out your black heels for these?" She holds up a pair of patent cream-colored peep-toes.

"Sure." I slide them on, then look in the full-length mirror on the back of her door. Surprisingly, the shoes, along with the freshwater pearls around my neck and wrist, make my outfit seem almost spring-like, too.

"Perfect!" My mother exclaims as she takes my hand. "Now, let's go to lunch."

I smile, genuinely happy and hopeful that Mom and I are meeting in the middle and forging a new path together. Maybe Curtis has been good for her, after all.

"I'm excited. Let's go."

Quint

As I wait for my dad in the bar in the hotel, I can't stop thinking about Calla. I whip my phone from my pocket and send her a quick text.

How's it going there? I miss you.

I get a reply right away. Great! Having a surprisingly good time with my mom.

Then she sends me a picture of some very frou-frou food that's a work of art. Everything on the table has been fashioned to look like flowers, and in the middle of it all is a half-empty bottle of champagne.

Then her next message pops in. But I miss you, too. Soon?

Yes. All night.

She sends me a kiss emoji and a couple of hearts that make

me laugh. I would have sworn she was far too practical to be this giddy.

Suddenly, I feel a familiar hand slap my back. "Hi, son. Sorry to keep you waiting."

I turn. I was pissed as hell at my father yesterday. Today, I rein in my temper. It's not my life, and I need to back off. "Hey, Dad." We share a manly hug, then I look around. "Where are Ivy and Lacey?"

My brother, Jett, is finishing up a negotiation in London. This wedding was so last-minute, he couldn't get here in time. And after the backstab he endured in college, he's about ambition, not romance.

Dad rolls his eyes. "Your sisters are still getting dolled up since they had to get up so early to catch their flights this morning. Lacey looks hung over."

"Ah, to be twenty-two again." I have to smile. Lacey, the "oops" baby of the family, is in her last semester of college and partying hard—while maintaining her four-point-zero GPA, so I can't complain.

"No, thanks," Dad drawls. "And Ivy says she has big news to share after the ceremony, but she looks so peaked and refused to eat breakfast when I picked the girls up and took them out. I can only imagine she's going to tell us that she and Darrin are finally pregnant."

"That would be great." The older of my two sisters is thirty-three. She and her husband have been trying to have a baby for years. "But I'll do my best to act surprised."

"Good idea. Sorry I left you to your own devices last night."

I shake my head. "After the things I said yesterday afternoon, you had every right. I'm sorry. If you're happy, I'm happy for you."

"It takes a big man to admit when he's been wrong and apologize." He pats me on the back. "Thank you. But you'll see. This isn't a mistake."

I can only hope he's right.

Then we don't have time to exchange any more words because Ivy and Lacey appear, both in pretty springtime dresses. Ivy's is a dusty blue with sensible beige heels. Lacey, God help me, is wearing something hot pink, low cut, and getting attention from every corner of the bar.

After greetings and hugs all around, I catch up with my sisters. Ivy and Lacey both still live in Denver, not far from Dad. I can drive to see them in about six hours any time I want, but it's just far enough away that it's too far without a reason. So I don't see them often. I wish Calla was here to meet them. If she hadn't been busy with her mom, I would have asked her to come with me today and meet my family.

We'll definitely do it another time—soon. I make that promise to myself because I'm not giving her up. My impromptu shopping trip a few hours ago proved that. Now I just have to persuade her to say yes.

Will she think I'm as crazy as I feel?

"Where is this place?" Ivy asks, indeed looking slightly green-tinged.

"Follow me." Dad begins to lead us through the hotel, Lacey beside him, smiling.

I turn to the older of my sisters. "You doing okay?"

She slants me a frustrated glance. "I look fine, damn it."

I have to repress a smile. "You look as if you're trying to look fine. Mostly you look sick." I lean in closer. "Does that mean you're finally pregnant?"

Suddenly, a dazzling smile breaks across her face. "Darrin and I found out yesterday."

Slinging an arm around her shoulders, I give her a squeeze. "Congrats. I'm really happy for you two."

In my pocket, my phone vibrates again. I pull it free to see another text from Calla.

I might be a little later than I thought. It's nice to be with my mom, and this day is important to her. But I'll be there as soon as I can. Be waiting?

I'm disappointed because our time together has been so limited, but... I understand. Of course.

She thanks me with more emojis.

"Who's that?" Ivy asks. "Did you finally meet someone special?"

I want to go with my gut...but I temper my response until Calla and I have talked about this. She's everything I've wanted. Instinct tells me that. But I don't know how she feels.

I shrug. "Maybe. We'll see."

"Tell me about her."

"When there's something to tell."

Ivy nods. "Fair enough. What do you know about this woman Dad is mixed up with?"

Her question makes me grimace. "Not much. He's been tight-lipped." Mostly because I think he doesn't want his kids butting into his life. "She's divorced and has a grown daughter, who's going to be her maid of honor today. I think he said she's from Orange County. He says she's so kind and outgoing—exactly what he needs."

My father has always been a brooder, so I come by the propensity naturally. And he needs someone with the kind of zest for life that will bring him out of his cave.

Ivy looks as confused as I feel. "How long has he known her?"

"He was vague. A couple of months is my best guess."

My sister shakes her head. "I hope this isn't a giant cluster."

"Same. But all we can do is be supportive."

"I guess." Ivy doesn't sound any more convinced than I am.

The trek to the far reaches of the hotel seems to take forever. When we arrive, I peek inside. It's already set up for the upcoming wedding I still object to. Several standing arrangements of roses line the back and flank the rows of padded benches. White petals have been strewn along the softly geometric runner bisecting the chapel. At the front, a more elaborate flower arrangement livens up the otherwise plain cream-colored, low-ceilinged space.

We're escorted to a small room in the back for the groom and his attendants. I check my watch. The ceremony starts in thirty minutes.

"You sure about this woman?" I say to my dad as my sisters mill around before Lacey drags Ivy into her selfie.

"Yeah."

And now that I look at him, I don't remember the last time I saw him this happy. It was definitely before Mom's prolonged illness and death. Maybe I need to be less suspicious. Dad isn't easily duped. He's always been even-tempered and even-handed. It might really be possible to fall in love quickly.

I know because I'm doing it now.

"All right, then. Let's get you married."

Dad smiles, then pats his pocket until he produces the ring box and hands it to me. "Thanks for standing up with me."

"My pleasure." I pocket the ring. "I'm sorry Jett can't be here."

His face clouds over. "I am, too. But Lacey is going to loop him in on FaceTime, so he'll be here virtually."

Despite the fact it will be very late for him? "Great."

Dad rubs his hands together. "I've been really self-absorbed this weekend. You doing okay?"

I nod and debate the wisdom of opening my mouth...but I don't much like that my father hid his romance from us until it was serious. I can't do the same and then bitch, especially when this thing with Calla is moving so fast.

"Really good, actually. I might have met someone."

He looks taken aback. Then he smiles. "Someone serious?"

"It's looking that way."

"When do I get to meet her?"

"Soon."

"Why didn't you bring her with you this weekend?"

I give him a self-deprecating smile. "Actually, we just met last night."

Dad raises a brow at me. "You mean after you browbeat me about falling in love too fast?"

"Yeah. Ironic, isn't it?"

"Karma is a bitch." He laughs. "You think you're in love with her?"

"It's definitely feeling that way. You don't think I'm crazy?"

"A few months ago, I would have. Not now." That makes him laugh again. "Tell me about her."

"Her name is—"

"Excuse me." An impeccably dressed man in his forties approaches with hands clasped and a cautious smile. "My name is Michael, and I'm the wedding coordinator here. We only have a few minutes before the ceremony starts. I've just settled the bride and her family into their dressing room. Do you need anything?"

"I'll let you handle this." I clap my father on the back, leaving him to finish the last-minute details with Michael, and head over to my sisters.

"Hey." Lacey grabs me and ropes me into a sibling selfie.

We chat for a few minutes. Then it's time for the ladies to head into the chapel, so they meander out to take their seats in the padded pews.

"Ready?"

My dad nods. "Very. But this conversation isn't over. I want to hear all about your girl soon."

I smile. "You got it."

Then Michael motions us to take our places at the altar, so I file out, Dad right behind me. While we're waiting, I observe my father. He isn't nervous at all. He's dead sure about this woman. He *knows*.

Is that why I'm not more nervous about Calla, too? Why I'm almost entirely convinced, despite knowing her a mere twenty-four hours, she's the one for me?

Suddenly, the music starts. The chapel doors at the back open. In walks a gorgeous blonde in a black dress with pale shoes and matching pearls—and familiar blue eyes.

Calla.

She's the maid of honor? Yeah. And that makes her the bride's daughter.

Oh, fuck.

I blink. This can't be happening.

But it is. The woman I'm falling for is about to become my stepsister. What are the fucking odds of that? And what am I going to do?

One step after the other leads her up the aisle. I see the exact moment she stops sizing up my dad as a prospective husband for her mother and her stare lands on me. Her eyes go wide. Her step stutters. She blinks as she smothers a little gasp behind her hand.

"Quint?"

My dad was right; Karma is a bitch. "Hi, Calla."

My father frowns. "You two know each other?"

"Yeah, Dad. She's the girl I was just telling you about."

At that, my dad tosses his head back and belts out a laugh. I'm glad he sees the humor in this. Calla looks horrified, I don't have any idea what to do, and there's no time to sort things out because the music changes, and Calla's mother starts walking up the aisle to make us officially family.

Calla

Is the world playing a cruel joke on me?

The question circles through my head while my mother and Curtis begin to speak the words that officially make my boyfriend—well, of sorts—my stepbrother, too.

This isn't okay.

Two hours ago, my biggest worry was finding a comfortable position for my sore backside on the restaurant's hard chairs and wondering when I'd get back to Quint. Now...I'm just stunned.

Somehow, I manage to smile and nod. Through the ceremony, I keep stealing glances at Quint. He's trying to work this out mentally, too. Clearly, he's no less shell-shocked than I am.

The next fifteen minutes feel like forever, but finally Curtis slips a ring on Mom's finger, they kiss, and the officiant pronounces them man and wife. They beat a path down the aisle, hand in hand, leaving Quint and me at the altar to stare at each other.

Finally, he sidesteps toward me and holds out his elbow. "Come on, angel. We can't figure anything out here."

"You're right." I wrap my trembling fingers around his forearm.

Is it bad that, even though we're related by marriage now, I can't help but notice how devastatingly masculine he looks in a navy suit with a crisp white shirt and a tone-on-tone blue tie?

I can feel his distress and confusion. It's a lot like mine. But he's still solid beneath me, not looking at me any differently than he did before he realized our parents were about to marry each other.

We only make it halfway down the aisle when two women I don't recognize assault me with hugs. "You're Iris's daughter?"

I nod. "Calla."

"That makes us sisters now!" says the younger with a squee. "I'm Lacey. This is Ivy. Our brother, Jett, is in London." She turns the phone around to show me an attractive man of about thirty in his hotel room. He looks a lot like Quint, but he's holding a glass of wine and waving. Though he's smiling, his eyes look both cynical and haunted.

"It's nice to meet you." What else can I say?

Lacey smiles. "And you haven't really met my brother, Quint."

"Actually, we met last night," he corrects. "Why don't you two let Jett go to bed since it's ungodly late in the UK, then catch up with the parents. Calla and I need to talk."

His sisters exchange a glance, like they finally grasp that something is up between us.

"Yeah. Sure. We'll...um, meet you in the restaurant."

They scurry out of the chapel. The door closes behind them with a soft swish.

Finally, we're alone.

"Fancy seeing you here," I try to joke.

Quint lets out a deep breath. "Obviously, neither of us expected this."

"No." But now that the shock is wearing off, I'm wondering what we should do. Technically, he's my stepbrother now...but we're not actually related. We don't share any blood. "It's shocking but—"

"I don't care," he insists. "I refuse to give two shits that my dad just married your mom. Why should that change anything between us?"

His thoughts are heading exactly where mine were. And he's right. It's unexpected. It's odd. It might even seem weird to others but... "I was just beginning to think that maybe this 'problem' isn't really a problem."

"Exactly." He grabs my shoulders and presses our foreheads together. "This weird twist of fate might be a practical joke from the universe...but it doesn't change the way I feel about you."

My heart catches in my throat. "It doesn't change the way I feel about you, either. When I first realized what was happening, all I could think about was how I was going to live without you. And everything inside me rebelled."

"I did those mental gymnastics during the ceremony. But I'm not giving you up."

"Then we agree."

A little smile creeps across his mouth. "Does that mean you're game to have sex with your stepbrother?"

I wince. "When you say it like that, it's so cringy."

He laughs and wags his brows at me. "But you still want me, right?"

"Are you telling me you're the kind of guy who would nail his stepsister?"

"Not usually, but I'll make an exception for you. And how

about we never mention that we're related by marriage in the context of sex again?"

"Deal." I grin. "How about you come here and kiss me?"

"Sure." He lays his lips over mine experimentally. Gently. We freeze, share a couple of rapid heartbeats.

Then passion takes over. It's as if my body is wired to respond to him—and him alone.

He nudges my lips apart. I suck in a breath and wrap my arms around him. Then his hands are in my hair and his tongue is teasing mine. My nipples are so hard they hurt, and the ache between my legs is ridiculous, considering how sore I am from all the sex. None of that matters. I'm still wishing we didn't have to go downstairs for this wedding dinner my mother planned. I'm still wanting to spend the night alone with Quint.

I love him, and I have no idea how—or if—we can work everything out.

With a last drag of his tongue and a low groan, he forces himself to pull away. "Calla. Angel..."

The gravity in his tone is heavy. Something's up. "What?"

"Maybe you think I'm crazy. Hell, maybe I *am* crazy. But I know myself. I know mere lust. And I know my feelings. This is completely different." He swallows and cups my face, fusing his stare to mine. "I love you."

I can't help but smile and throw myself against him. "Really? I was literally thinking just seconds ago that I love you, too. I've never felt this way. You know that."

"Yeah." He nods. "Neither have I."

I bite my lip. "What do we do?"

He shrugs. "We tell the family. Then we stop caring what they think and do what makes us happy."

I turn his words over mentally, but again, he's right. Ultimately, this isn't about everyone else, just us. They'll either accept us together or they won't. But I have a feeling they'll embrace us with open arms. I know my mom will be thrilled for me. "Yeah."

"You in?"

I nod. "One hundred percent."

He slides an arm around me and dips his head to kiss me again when a man behind us clears his throat.

"Sorry to disturb," Michael assures. "But we have another wedding in less than an hour. We need to prepare."

"Of course," I say. "Let me grab my purse from the bride's room and—"

"Are you all booked up tonight?" Quint asks.

My heart stops. "Are you serious?"

Quint pulls out a burgundy velvet box. "I bought this earlier today." He lifts the lid and gets on one knee. "Marry me?"

It's crazy and impulsive—everything I've scolded my mother for in the past. But this is Quint. It doesn't matter how long I've known him. He's the keeper of my heart. I've never been impetuous a day in my life—well, except this weekend— and I know what I want.

"Yes. Oh, my god… Yes!"

With a hearty laugh, he slips the ring on my finger. I glance down at the sparkling oval diamond haloed by a smaller cluster of the pale, glinting stones, all sitting on a simple white-gold band. It's beautiful. I love it. Then again, it could have come as a toy surprise in a Happy Meal and I would have been thrilled because it's from Quint, and he loves me.

He kisses me again, and we get lost in each other—at least until we see the rest of the family at the back of the chapel cheering for us and running to embrace us all with their happy hugs and hearty congratulations.

Just outside our circle, Michael smiles at Quint and me.

"How does ten p.m. sound? That gives you enough time to celebrate with your parents, get yourselves a marriage license, and make it back here."

I look at Quint. He looks at me. We both grin.

"I'm ready if you are."

It's crazy and it's wonderful, and I'm not second-guessing myself one bit. "Let's do it!"

SEDUCING
THE
Enemy

New York Times

Bestselling Author

SHAYLA BLACK

Steamy. Emotional. Forever.

ABOUT SEDUCING THE ENEMY

Once he takes his pound of flesh from her, will she steal his heart?

I'm Jett, self-made billionaire.

I have everything I could ever want—except revenge.

Eight years ago, my best friend and I planned to start a business together…

Until I fell for his little sister.

After he found out, he stole my idea and made a fortune.

She took his side and stabbed me in the back.

Now he's in financial straits, while I'm richer than I ever dreamed.

So I made Whitney a bargain: forty million dollars in exchange for a week of her body.

But now that she's in my bed, what if it's not animosity I feel?

What if I fall for her again?

Enjoy this Forbidden Confession. HEA guaranteed!

CHAPTER ONE

Dallas

4 p.m.

Jett

She's late.

Maybe she's not coming, asshole.

That's a distinct possibility.

What did you expect? You're the enemy.

I am, and she's too smart not to realize I'm springing a trap. She also knows I'm powerful enough to destroy her and all she holds dear.

But I'd rather not. Does she know that, too?

I shove the thought away. What's in Whitney Chancellor's mind—and heart—now shouldn't matter. She made a choice, and I'm going to make her regret it.

You made a choice, too. And she probably hates your fucking guts for it.

But that doesn't change anything. If she doesn't show today, I'll keep coming at her. I have ways to bend her to my will.

She *will* give me what I want.

I tap an impatient thumb on the charred wood of the hand-scraped bar. The faux-rustic room is designed to be a "laid-back" watering hole, but since it sits in the middle of a horribly pretentious hotel in an exclusive, five-star part of town, I'm calling bullshit.

I've been here ten minutes, and I already despise this place.

You're just nervous.

No shit. But this site is less than two miles from her house, so I'm here.

It's been eight years, and I traveled halfway around the world for this. For her.

That doesn't mean she'll come, especially since you ordered her to.

In hindsight, that may not have been my best strategy, but cushioning my approach would have been counterproductive. It's best if she understands I'm a world-class bastard, and nothing—not even her—will soften me.

Whitney has probably discerned that. After all, I've put her in a terrible position. One of two things will happen next: she'll sweetly capitulate like she seemingly did all those years ago...or she'll tell me to go fuck myself. With her, I've got a fifty-fifty shot.

I'm almost hoping she chooses the latter.

At the sound of heels clicking across the tile floors in the otherwise empty bar, I snap around.

And I nearly drop my jaw.

Holy motherfucking son of a bitch.

Why is Whitney still so beautiful that, when I see her, I struggle to string two thoughts together?

She approaches me, dark hair curling past her elbows, mouth

rosy, jewelry understated, ankle-strap heels classic—and black dress instantly sweat-inducing.

A band of fabric hugs her neck like a collar. Intermittent, gradually widening strips—strung together only by a loose lacing of satin playing a daring peekaboo with her exposed skin in between—tapers down, ending with a black leather belt that cinches her small waist. Her shoulders are covered. So are her tits—barely. But I can't not see their tempting swells or the soft valley in between. The skirt ends halfway down her sleek thighs where another subtle row of crisscrossed ribbons mirrors the bodice detail just above her flirty hem.

Two things are immediately obvious: I still can't look at Whitney without desperately craving her, and she isn't wearing a goddamn bra.

This dress would make any other woman look like a whore. Somehow, she elevates it to elegant.

Clearly, she came to make me suffer.

She stops at the bar less than three feet from me, and I'd be a lying SOB if I said my heart wasn't pounding.

"Whitney."

She turns to glance at me over her shoulder, hazel eyes full of anger. "Jett. What do you want?"

A dangerous question.

"To talk." *For starters.*

"I don't have anything to say to you."

She's lying.

"So you don't want to save your brother?"

Her expression spits hostility. "You know I do. Or I wouldn't be here."

Yes, just like I know she's incredibly loyal to him. She'd do anything for him. I'm banking on that.

Whitney sets her small, chic purse on the bar, laying her left hand on top of it. She's wearing an engagement ring.

Fuck. It's not even subtle. It's a statement rock, designed to flash a warning to every other man to back the hell off.

Too bad for her fiancé nothing will make me comply.

"Congratulations." I cast a pointed glare at her ring. "Who's the lucky dick?"

"None of your business. I presume you summoned me here to negotiate?"

I nod and try to keep my cool. I'd much rather seduce her—and she probably knows that. It kills me to remember I was the first man to lay his lips on hers. The first man to possess her mouth. She was a very sweet sixteen to my horny twenty-one. I was old enough to know better but too desperate to touch her to care.

Almost.

By sheer willpower, I stopped myself short of doing something her very affluent family would have insisted I go to prison for.

In the end, my restraint didn't matter. Nearly slipping that one moment cost me everything.

That seems like a lifetime ago.

Her hypnotic eyes aren't filled with innocence anymore. Nope, when she looks at me now, I see venom.

"What's your offer?" she demands.

"In a hurry? Why don't we have a drink? I haven't seen you in a long time."

She scoffs. "Let's not pretend I matter to you."

I raise a brow at Whitney. She does matter…but admitting that would only weaken my position. "Humor me. After all, it's my forty million dollars."

"Fine." She lifts one delicate shoulder like she doesn't care, but I can read her. On some level, I get to her and she hates that. "Vodka cranberry. Make it a double."

I acknowledge her with a curt nod, then I motion to the bartender, who takes our order.

"You're not drinking with me?" She scowls.

"I never drink." I haven't since that summer.

Whitney's gaze probes me for a long moment. "Because you're a control freak?"

You have no idea.

I smile. "You can call me names and divert the subject all day. That doesn't change why we're here."

"So you're going to lend Vance forty million dollars to save his company—"

"Which should have been *our* company."

"You lost that lawsuit."

"Because your brother is a lying, thieving snake." *And you helped him, didn't you?*

She arches her dark brow at me. "Is all this charm how you've become so successful?"

Life has apparently roughed up my sweet princess and given her a stronger spine. I like it.

Breaking her will definitely be more fun.

"No. I'm successful because I'm ruthless."

She says nothing, but her silence concedes the point. She knows. That's enough for now.

When the bartender sets her drink down, she grabs the elegant tumbler like it's a lifeline. That's the only outward clue that I make her nervous.

It's the perfect time to make myself clear. "The forty million is a buyout, not a loan."

"He won't agree."

"Then I can wait for him to go bankrupt and buy it up for pennies on the dollar."

She glares at me. "How do you know we don't have other financing?"

"If you did, you wouldn't be here."

The way she purses her lips is a confession. She's out of options. "Why do you imagine Vance will listen to me?"

"He needs the money too badly not to."

"He'll never sell to you."

Does she think I'm going to give either of them a choice? "I'll make sure he has the right incentive."

That sets her on edge—as it should. "Like what?"

"Leave that to me."

Whitney tries to shrug like it's irrelevant, but I see through her. She knows she's cornered.

That does my black heart good.

"Whatever," she says flippantly. "What's your proposal? What do I have to agree to so my brother gets the money?"

"We're having a drink first, remember?"

"*I'm* having a drink. You're watching me for reasons I can only guess at."

She shouldn't have to guess too hard, especially when she's dressed like that. Then again, she's likely baiting me for a reaction. Oh, she'll get it. But not now.

When I'm ready.

"Tell me what you've been up to since I last saw you." I keep the words soft, but there's an underlying command.

Whitney feels it. She stiffens. "Not much to tell that I'm sure you didn't find out for yourself. I finished high school. Then I attended Stanford and earned my economics degree. I stayed to finish my MBA. I've been home a handful of weeks, trying to help Vance unravel this situation. And here I am."

I knew all that. She's intentionally not telling me what I really want to know. Who has she dated? Who else has she kissed? Who fucked her first? Who fucked her last? Who does her goddamn heart belong to?

Patience, I tell myself, swallowing back all my questions. I *will* find out.

"What about you?"

There's the subject change again. Why? She can't possibly believe I'm going to give her anything she can use against me.

"After the last summer I saw you? I dropped out of college so I could bartend by night and spend my days developing an even more profitable intellectual property."

It was the perfect setup for me...almost. Entire days to push myself to create an even better app than the one Vance had stolen from me. Full nights of making money and hooking up with her acquaintances. That disappointed the hell out of my dad. Even my older brother, Quint, lectured me about throwing my future down the toilet. But Whitney was always in the back of my mind, haunting me.

I had everything to prove.

"I launched the following year." To success beyond my dreams, which spawned a massive tech company that now circles the globe.

"Tell me about your mother."

I sigh. It's the one weakness I'll show Whitney because, under all the animosity, she's too human to use my pain against me. "She died four years ago. Breast cancer."

That horrible night, I sobbed and held her hand, watching as she took her very last breath. It still fucking hurts every time I think about it.

Whitney's face softens. "I'm sorry. I know you two were close."

"Yes."

And I haven't been close to anyone since. I've tried. My brother and I have a better relationship now. My sisters, Ivy and Lacey, have reached out again and again. But it's me. Something inside me is dead.

I'm almost ashamed to admit that getting beyond my grief didn't cure my toxicity. Probably because my mother wasn't the cause. The poison is all about Whitney, about the way she stabbed me in the back and left me to bleed out.

"I understand. I miss my dad," she murmurs softly.

"I heard about his car accident. I'm sorry." I genuinely mean that.

She's had a terrible few years, too. Some part of me that still gives a shit about her—no matter how hard I've tried not to—empathizes. That part wants to reach out and hold her, soothe her, and tell her I'm here for her.

The rest of me has learned better.

"Thank you," she murmurs.

Silence falls again, and Whitney clutches her purse like she's nervous as she downs the last of her drink. Next time she looks at me, she's glaring. Her shields are up once more. "So now that we've caught up and you've watched me drink, what do you want?"

"In exchange for forty million dollars to save your brother's financial ass?" I smile tightly. "You."

She swallows like my words unnerve her, but she doesn't look surprised in the least. "I'm engaged."

"That's not my problem."

Slowly, she closes her eyes. To brace herself? To hide her fury from me?

Finally, she nods. "What are your terms?"

"One week."

"For me to be your whore?"

She's trying to bait me. "You putting an ugly spin on our arrangement isn't going to make me change my mind."

She clenches her delicate jaw. "What do you expect?"

"I'll send a car to pick you up at precisely nine o'clock. Bring *nothing* with you. Anything you need, I'll provide. When you arrive, the front door will be unlocked. Once inside, you will strip. And you will kneel. Then you will wait for me. You *will* be completely mine. While you're with me, you will forget two things: any other man who's ever fucked you and the word *no*. You will do *anything* I desire with, to, or for me during our week together. Am I clear?"

"You're a bastard."

"That can't be a surprise."

"No."

"Are you refusing?"

Whitney hesitates. "No."

Triumph spikes. I lay a twenty on the bar for her drink. "You accept? You'll get in my car tonight?"

She looks down at the bar like she's ashamed. She makes me wait and sweat and worry that she'll refuse. But we both know she won't. For her brother's sake, she can't.

"Yes," she finally whispers.

I settle a finger under her chin. "Look at me when you answer."

"Yes, I'll come be your forty-million-dollar piece of ass for the week." With a jerk of her head, she pulls away. "Don't touch me until then."

I smile at her show of spirit. It's intriguing—but it won't last. I'll make sure of that.

"You have four hours to get yourself in order. After that…" I trail off into a smile.

Let her imagine the worst.

I'm sure she thinks I intend to use her horribly and cause her pain. Quite the opposite.

I'm going to give her so much pleasure she'll lose her mind.

And surrender her heart?

Since I can't afford to listen to the mocking voice in my head, I shove it aside and slide a burner phone across the bar to her.

She picks it up, then frowns. "What's this for?"

"To contact me in case you choose to back out. If not, at quarter till ten, you will text me to verify your arrival. Make no mistake, Whitney, this device only allows you to call or text *me*. So don't bother trying to use it to contact anyone else so you can tell them where to find you for the next week." I send her a cold smile. "It will be our secret."

I toss those words she uttered to me long ago back in her face.

Predictably, she blanches. "I hate you."

"I don't care. I'll see you this evening."

I force myself to walk away. The rest is up to her. But I've dangled the carrot and I've cornered her. She'll come. She'll submit.

Then I'll make her pay.

Eight years earlier…

Jett

I SHOULDN'T PUT my hands on Whitney Chancellor. Really, I shouldn't…but the princess is right there, mere feet away by the shimmering pool, wearing a pink bikini and soaking in the sun.

Her long, dark waves brush the swells of her pert ass as she sways to *the* sexy ballad of the summer.

For fuck's sake, I need to keep my distance. But how, especially today?

Tiptoeing across the back patio, I sneak up behind her, cover her eyes, and whisper in her ear, "Happy sixteenth birthday, Whitney."

She whirls around and flashes me rosy cheeks and a flirtatious grin. She might still be too young, but nothing about the way I want her is innocent.

I'm twenty-one. I know better. I shouldn't make a move on my best friend's little sister, especially before she's grown. But during the past two months, she's been just beyond my reach, wearing next to nothing to combat this heatwave and tossing me come-hither glances. My impatience to have her under me chafes. I'm almost beyond caring what I "should" do.

It's bad, like masturbation-in-the-shower-twice-a-day bad. Still, I can't not wish her a happy birthday, right?

"Thanks! Is that for me?" Her gaze falls on the fluffy cupcake on the nearby patio table.

"Of course." I retrieve the pink-frosting confection and hold it out to her.

Unlike Whitney, I didn't grow up with money. Despite having five dollars left to my name, I used half of it to buy her something I hoped would make her happy.

I watch as she plucks it up. She licks her way through the frosting before taking a delicate bite. "Mmm… So good."

I swallow back a groan. It doesn't matter that I jacked off not an hour ago. I'm harder than ever for her.

"Thanks for remembering, Jett," she murmurs.

I try not to focus on the way her pretty pink tongue peeks

out as she licks residual frosting from her plump lips. "Yeah. Sure."

"It means a lot to me. I'm pretty sure my brother forgot. Tell me again why you're friends?"

Despite knowing she's teasing me, I'm still tongue-tied. "We're, um…going into business together."

She knows that, dumb shit.

Whitney smiles. "I remember the spiel. You've got the brains, Vance has the connections, and you're both ambitious as hell. You'll succeed. How's it going? Almost done?"

"Yeah, almost. We've logged in a ton of hours, but I've nearly finished the coding, and he's been writing up the business plan and making lists of people to contact. We should be ready to launch before we go back for our senior year. So just a few weeks now…"

Her smile dims. "I'll miss you when you're gone."

"You will?" She's always been flirty, but this is the first time she's stated her feelings outright.

"Sure." She backs up and gives me a suddenly nervous, nonchalant shrug. "It will be so much quieter when you and my brother are gone. Who will I nag about hogging the TV late at night while you play Xbox and refuse to share your tequila? Who will play Monopoly with me until four a.m. when I can't sleep?"

Maybe that's true…and maybe she's saying that in case she thinks I don't like her *that* way. But I have—from the moment I met her eight weeks ago, when I first stepped foot onto the Chancellor estate. Everything around here is ornate, too traditional. Stuffy. Perfect.

Except Whitney. She's all the beauty, but she's also a new spring breath of fresh air.

Vance would have my ass if he knew what I wanted to do to

his little sister. He's protective. But the way she's looking at me proves her thoughts aren't a little girl's. They're a woman's.

"I hope that's not all you'll miss about me." I tuck a strand of hair behind her ear. "I'm sure going to miss more than that about you."

"Yeah?" She bites her lip and sends me a flirty glance through her dark lashes. "If I wanted something for my birthday, would you give it to me?"

"I'd give you the world if I could afford it." But I can't.

I hate that I wasn't raised rich, like her. I barely have two nickels to rub together. She deserves better.

Whitney sets the rest of the cupcake aside and eases closer. She looks nervous as she shakes her head. "I don't want you to buy me anything. My parents have already given me tons."

That's true, but I admire that she's not a typical spoiled little rich girl who doesn't see her good fortune.

"Then what can I give you, princess?"

"A kiss." She looks so earnest. "Please. You'll be the first."

My heart stops as I stare at her tempting mouth. "I don't know if that's a good idea, Whitney."

I manage to get the words out, but my protest is weak. How can it be anything else when I want her so badly?

"Maybe not, but I think you want to. I see the way you look at me."

It would be easier to lie and tell her she's mistaken, but I can't crush her. "I want to, but Vance…"

"He has nothing to do with us. In case you hadn't guessed, I…like you. I just want a kiss."

It's wrong, and I know it, but I thread our fingers together for one simple reason. "I like you, too. I think about you a lot. But you're underage."

"I'm not a child."

She's really not. She's actually pretty mature. God knows her body has filled out in all the right places, like a full-grown woman's.

"You have no idea how badly I want to say yes."

A new smile brightens her face. "Really?"

"Yeah," I admit roughly as I stare at the three stories of windows that make up the back of the vast house. Vance could be watching us even now. "But we can't. Not here."

I drop Whitney's hand.

"Definitely not here," she agrees. "I'll be in my room, Jett. Waiting."

Then she takes her cupcake and her music and disappears inside. I heave a deep breath as I watch her go, the tiny triangle of fabric revealing more of her ass than it covers.

God, I want her. I crave her so badly I'm shaking.

I shouldn't give in. I should stop myself from even laying a finger on her.

But she's giving me the chance to kiss her, be the first man to take her lips. That does something to me. Lights my possessive fire. Makes me want to growl that she's mine.

It's wrong and it's dangerous and I should have my fucking head examined. Knowing the feel of her will only make my lust burn a million times hotter.

But I don't care. I'm going to do it.

I'm going to kiss Whitney Chancellor.

Dragging in a breath, I push my way into the house and look around. It's empty. Her dad is at work. Her mom is out getting stuff for Whitney's party tonight. Vance is in the study, on a conference call.

It's now or never.

Resolution firing up my veins, I march upstairs. Whitney's door is cracked. I see her pacing.

I ease in, heart pounding, and shut the door behind me.

She stops and blinks up, meeting my stare. "Jett?"

Am I going to kiss her? That's the subtext of her question.

I nod and stalk across the room, every move clipped. As if I need to leave all my doubts behind. As if I can't reach her fast enough.

Finally, I cup her cheek and slide against her body. My free hand palms her nape. Willingly, she tilts her head and meets my stare. It's not merely that she's looking at me, but the way she's doing it, like she's completely open to me.

Like she's completely mine.

"Whitney…"

There's nothing else to say when the candy lips I want are so sweetly parted just inches under my own.

I bend to her, dragging my thumb across her so-soft cheek, and watch her wide hazel eyes slide shut.

Fuck, this is surreal. But it's the best dream imaginable. Princess Whitney wants *me*, and all I have to do to please her is take her mouth with my own.

Yes…

Finally, I touch my lips to hers. I hear her little indrawn breath. She tenses against me, fingers digging into my shoulders. But the way she's wriggling to get closer tells me she's every bit as nervous and eager as I am.

This means something to her. Every bit as much as it means to me?

I sink into the kiss. She puckers, and it's sweetly unpracticed. I regroup and redouble my effort until she's less hesitant. Then I nudge her lips apart. She offers no resistance, shyly softening and conforming herself to me.

Need and impatience claw at my restraint. I'm slipping.

A groan tears free when I slide inside Whitney's mouth. She

welcomes me. And she's like sugar on my tongue. I clutch her tighter as I deepen the kiss.

She's with me, pucker for pucker, tongues stroking, lips clinging, breaths harsh.

Suddenly, she's sinking onto her bed. I follow her down, wholly unwilling to stop kissing her, especially when her body is under mine, we're alone, and she's so obviously consenting.

As if my hands have a mind of their own, my palms wander her curves, skating the valley of her waist, cupping her hips, clutching her thighs. Then her legs are around me. I'm pressing my unflagging erection against her damp bikini bottoms, and our bodies are moving together as one.

Fuck, I don't think I've ever been this hot.

Whitney gropes until she circles my wrist, then lifts my hand.

Suddenly, I'm cradling the tender weight of her breast in my palm. I groan. The subversive part of me needs to know just how aroused she is, so I thumb her nipple.

She breaks our kiss to toss her head back and cries my name. "Jett..."

"Oh, princess. You feel amazing." I squeeze her mound and close my eyes, letting go for this one moment. I haven't done anything irrevocable to her. I can stop any time.

Right?

Under me, she shimmies and rocks. Pleasure jolts me with every move. The minute I realize we're going through all the motions of sex with our clothes on is also the moment my hand seems to get its own ideas and shoves aside the little scrap of pink covering her breast. My mouth gets on the bandwagon and sucks the pretty dark nipple I just exposed, tonguing it until her back arches and her whimpers fill my head.

Jesus, I'm going to come.

"Princess..." I pant. "We've gotta stop."

She shakes her head, trembling when my exhalations fall on her straining nipple. "We don't. Please. I want you. I want all of you."

Whitney doesn't give me time to think, just wraps herself around me—arms, legs, lips—and wordlessly begs me for more.

I shake. The thought of being inside her nearly sends me over the edge.

Sure, I've had sex. Hurried-high-school sex. Drunken-frat-party sex. We-just-met-in-a-bar sex. Friends-with-benefits sex. Even screwing-an-ex-girlfriend's-mother sex. But I've never wanted any woman the way I want Whitney.

I'm in love with her. I think I have been half the summer.

"Princess..."

But what am I saying? I know what I *should* do, should say.

With Whitney, none of that seems to make much difference.

"Please don't say no."

I filter through all my arguments. Vance, her age, what's right and wrong... I've already hit those. They don't matter to her. I'm not even sure how much they really matter to me.

"You're a virgin," I finally say.

"So?" She blinks up at me, looking somewhere between earnest and tearful. "I love you."

"Oh, fuck." I hold her tighter. In all my wildest dreams, I never imagined she was feeling what I was. "I love you, too."

Whitney's smile lights up my world. Then she tosses off her bikini top. "That's all that matters. Make love to me."

"I can't give you anything."

"All I want is you." She clings to me and presses a kiss to my lips. "Please."

"I have to go back to college in a few weeks."

She nods. "I know. But I'll still be waiting here for you next summer. And I get that you're worried about Vance, but—"

"He's my best friend. He'd kill me for touching you."

She presses a finger over my lips. "It will be our secret."

There's a no perched on the tip of my tongue, but she muzzles it by lifting her hips to me and closing her eyes with a moan.

Shit. I've got to stop this.

Soon.

Just one more minute…

Then I lose myself in her kiss again, in the feel of her slender body undulating beneath me, in the way her gaze clings to me with love when I take her nipple in my mouth. She's all cotton-candy sweetness and sweet-sixteen perfection. I want her so badly, every fucking part of my body hurts.

Is going behind everyone's backs and rushing into this good for her?

No. I've got to stop this now.

I sigh. "Whitney—"

Behind me, the door to her bedroom slams open. "You son of a bitch. Get the fuck off my sister!"

Vance.

I jump to my feet and block his view of Whitney with my body. "It's—"

"Not what I think?" he sneers.

No, it's exactly what he thinks.

"Get out!" Whitney screams at her brother.

Neither of us budges. I won't leave her alone to endure her brother's wrath, and he won't leave me alone with temptation.

"I would never hurt her," I promise.

He snorts, silently admonishing me that it's too late. "When did you start fucking her?"

I hold up both hands. "Dude, I didn't—"

Vance silences me with a cross to the jaw.

"What are you doing?" Whitney screeches. "Stop!"

"Don't touch my sister again." He points a finger in my face. "Ever. I fucking trusted you…"

He did. He invited me into his house and let me stay with him so I would have all summer to write code instead of heading back to my hometown in Nowhere, Colorado, to make minimum wage shoveling horse shit or whatever my dad says "builds character." Don't get me wrong; I need the money. But if this app takes off like I think it will, money won't be a problem anymore.

"I can't believe this is how you repay me!" Vance gestures to Whitney, who's got her arms crossed over her bare breasts.

"I'm sorry."

Vance grunts. "You will be, asshole, once I take it out of your hide."

At the time, I thought he was just lashing out. I thought he'd get over his anger and we'd go back to normal. I thought Whitney would believe me when I told her at the end of the summer that none of my feelings for her had changed, to give her brother time, and we'd work things out between the two of us somehow. I believed her when she kissed me one last time and said she'd be waiting.

But I was wrong. So fucking wrong. I learned that weeks later when Vance, with an LLC he created alone, launched our app without me. My idea, everything I'd spent months innovating and coding, my one chance at being someone and crawling out of the blue-collar middle class I've always despised —all stolen from me. My best friend left me with nothing.

And when push came to shove, Whitney backed him up by taking his side in my lawsuit.

She ripped out my heart, too. I've never been the same.

After that humiliation, I launched my own creation the following spring. Over the next half a decade, I amassed a tech empire that far surpasses anything Vance has accomplished. But I've spent eight long, terrible years waiting for the day I could finally have my revenge. I waited for *this* day.

I smile coldly. Now, it's here.

And this time, when she's broken, when I've fucked her out of my system, it will end on *my* terms.

CHAPTER TWO

Present day

Whitney

As I watch the hands of the clock tick away the last of my freedom, I wonder if I've gone insane. That's the only answer that makes sense.

I should have refused Jett's insulting proposition. I should have spit in his face.

I don't have that luxury. While I can criticize my brother for this financial mess, I was away at school when he needed me. Some of the blame rests on my shoulders.

For the next seven days, I have to let Jett Dean use me in whatever way he wants and hope he doesn't destroy me.

Bitterly, I laugh. Every time he touches my life, it explodes into a fiery, horrific inferno, then leaves me standing in a heap of ash.

It took me years to pick myself up after he left the first time.

How much harder will it be this time after I share his bed? After I take him into my body?

And what about the secret I'm keeping from him?

A glance at the clock on my mantel tells me it's eight fifty-eight. A pair of headlights slow, turn into my driveway, and stop. The driver doesn't honk. I don't walk out right away. I have two minutes to decide what to do. On the table in front of me is my phone. Beside it sits the burner device.

Which am I going to pick up?

But I already know the answer.

With a trembling hand, I grab my phone and hit the button to reach the person I call most.

"Whit," my brother answers. "What's going on?"

I look at the clock. Eight fifty-nine. I have less than sixty seconds to give Vance an excuse. It's too late to explain the truth.

"I'll be gone for the next week. I'll call you when I get home next Saturday night."

"Where are you going?" He sounds confused.

"I can't say."

"Who are you going with?"

"I can't tell you."

"What the fuck is happening?" Now he sounds alarmed. "I'm coming over there."

"Don't. I won't be here. Just…trust me."

"I do, but this isn't like you."

"I'm doing what's best for both of us. Please try to stay out of trouble while I'm gone. Please. Don't do anything. Don't sign anything. Don't—"

"Yeah, yeah. You don't have to hound me."

Yes, I do, and we both know it.

"I'm sorry," I say finally. "I'll talk to you in a week."

"Can't you call me while you're away?" Now he sounds downright worried.

"No."

Even if I was allowed to bring my phone, I'm sure Jett will keep me too busy under his thumb—and in his bed—to even try.

Outside, the headlights in my driveway flash off and on again. That's my cue.

"I have to go."

"Are you going to be all right? You're not doing anything dangerous, are you?"

I don't lie to him, at least not any more than I already am. "I'll talk to you next week. I love you." That's something I never say because sentiment annoys him, but I need to get the words out...just in case. "Bye."

Then I hang up. I don't reach out to my fiancé. He won't miss me; he doesn't care. He's probably spending his weekend with strippers and drugs. We both know I'm aware of his coping mechanisms. I'll deal with that mess when I get back.

Resolved, I power down my phone, leaving it on the table. Vance will come over while I'm gone. He'll try to figure out where I went. He'll see my phone right away and realize that attempting to contact me is pointless.

I grab the burner phone Jett foisted on me and rise on shaking legs. Outside, I lock my front door, tuck my house key into the flowerpot on my porch, and make my way to the sleek black Mercedes sedan. It reminds me vaguely of a car my grandmother drove as a kid. But the warm fuzzy ends there.

As I approach, a tall stranger unfolds from the driver's seat and makes his way to me wordlessly, holding the back door open. I nod as I climb into the car. There's a partition between the driver and me. I hear him slide into the idling vehicle, but I can't see where he's taking me. I have no idea what's going on.

I must be crazy.

After a few turns, I lose track of where we're going. North, I think. We're on the highway now. The car is no longer starting and stopping with the traffic. So now this stranger behind the wheel is simply whisking me with no impediments toward my doom.

I swallow and peer out the window, into the night. Nothing. I see nothing but fields. Nothing is familiar. Nothing to use as a landmark to tell people where to find me if I'm in danger. I don't think Jett would hurt me.

But I've been wrong about him before.

I turn the phone he gave me over in my hands. It's not too late. I could still call him and tell him I've changed my mind.

But why? Vance needs his cash, and we have no new prospects.

That's not the only reason, the seditious part of my brain whispers.

If I'm being completely honest, I've waited eight horrible years to set eyes—and anything else I could—on Jett Dean. If this is the only way I can have him, I'm willing to take my chances.

But when I glance down at the device, digital numbers flash the time at me. Nine forty-seven. I'm two minutes late to text him. I don't hurry to rectify my lapse. Instead, I set the device in my lap and wait.

I'm going to surrender to him; that's a given. And despite the fact I'm baiting the bull, I'm not going to make it easy.

Suddenly, the phone in my hand vibrates.

With a bracing breath, I answer. "Yes, Jett."

"You didn't text."

"You made it clear that I would be at your beck and call once I was under your roof and in your bed. Until then, I'm still my own woman. Fuck off."

He doesn't say anything for a long moment. "You know there are consequences for your defiance?"

Of course. I'm looking forward to it. "I'm in your car with your driver, on the way to your location so I can be your sex slave for the week. I'd say you've already won and that you shouldn't bother sweating the small stuff."

"That's not how I operate," he grates out, teeth obviously clenched.

He's on edge. Where I want him.

"It never has been." But learning a little give-and-take would be good for Jett. And it might be fun for me.

Or it would if I wasn't risking everything to be with him.

"Listen, princess—"

"Good-bye." I hang up. A smile curls my mouth because I know I'm playing with fire.

And I hope very much I'm going to enjoy getting burned.

The car exits the highway and veers right, traveling down a winding two-lane road that seemingly leads nowhere. I have to be patient. It's not as if I can ask the driver anything, much less plead for information.

At exactly ten, the sedan rolls to a smooth stop. The engine goes silent. The driver exits and shuts his door. I hear boots crunch the gravel outside. Then my door opens, and the driver holds out a broad hand.

With a nod, I take it. He assists me to my feet, then gestures me toward the house.

But it's not a house, really. It's a massive white French Country estate in the middle of nowhere with a breathtaking fountain, perfectly trimmed evergreens, and ornate wrought-iron front doors.

I turn to the driver. "What is this place?"

"*Ya ne govoryu po-angliyski*," he says with a shrug of his wide shoulders.

He's speaking Russian, I think. Not that I know the language, but I can only imagine he's telling me he doesn't speak English. Leave it to Jett to think of everything. Even if I'd managed to sucker this guy into talking, we'd run straight into a language barrier.

His ploy should probably scare me more, but he's always paid attention to detail, so I'm hardly surprised.

Just slightly terrified.

"I understand." I lay a soft hand on his forearm.

He nods and pulls away, casting a nervous glance back to the house.

Does he suspect Jett is watching?

He probably is.

I don't bother the driver again. This is between Jett and me.

My journey to the front door seems to last a thousand steps. Not because it's long, but because I take it slow. I want to make him wait. And suffer.

Like I did.

Finally, I push the grand front door open. The white marble floor gleams by the light of an elegant chandelier hanging from the barrel ceiling above. On an exquisite hall table to my right rests a glass of red wine, clearly for me. I pick it up and walk another few steps. I find a white wicker hamper with the lid open. An empty acrylic shoe storage box sits beside it.

He wants me to undress for him. Kneel for him. Suck his cock. Spread my legs. Surrender.

I sip my wine. He can wait.

His stare is all over me. I can feel it. Somewhere, somehow, he's watching. And he's impatient.

Ignoring the receptacles for my clothes, I wander through the house. It's devoid of humanity now, but it has life. I feel the echoes of happiness here. I can almost hear laughter. Once, someone lived a charmed existence under this roof. But not the current occupant. Not at this moment. Jett's brooding seethes through the silence.

He wants me naked—now.

There must be something wrong with me. I'm impatient to give in to him.

"Hi, Jett," I call, my voice echoing across the tile.

No reply.

But I'm not fooled. He's here. He simply won't speak to me until I've stripped myself bare for him. I know that instinctively.

I continue scoping the downstairs, winding past a staircase on the left, then into a beautiful white kitchen with hand-painted tile, a rough-hewn island, and dark rustic beams over-head. Through an arch, I find myself in a cozy family room with a massive stone hearth and simple furnishings, dressed up with colorful accents and an unassuming chandelier. I sink onto a footstool and look out the wall of glass to the backyard beyond.

The swimming pool shimmers. The sound of cicadas singing lulls me. The twinkling summer stars lure me outside.

Not even sure where I'm going or why, I walk out, leaving the door open as a clue for Jett. Not that he needs it; I still feel his eyes on me. But I want this last moment of freedom.

I know he'll snatch it quickly and trap me under him for the next seven days. That's a given. Stalling is both foolish and reck-less, but I can't stop. If this is all the rebellion he'll allow me while we're together, I'm taking it. I want him to understand I'm not without my devices.

By the pool, the breeze picks up and whips through my hair. I set my wine aside and pluck the elastic band from around my wrist, using it to wind my long hair on top of my head. Then I tread to the side of the crystal-blue water and start shedding my clothes—shoes, dress, bra, underwear. In a blink, it's all gone, and I'm bare.

I still don't know where Jett is, but his stare has intensified. There's no escape.

I drag in a deep breath and walk into the warm water. It envelops me like a soothing blanket. Shutting my eyes, I sigh.

"Are you incapable of following instructions?"

I start at the sound of Jett's voice. Suddenly, he's standing at the edge of the pool, mere feet away. How did he sneak up on me so quickly?

Never mind that. Will he give me another stitch to wear for the next seven days?

Turning, I cock my head at him to see he's still wearing the same designer suit. "Not at all."

"So you're merely choosing not to."

My smile is nothing short of mocking. "Something like that."

"You understand I'm going to make you regret that?"

Excitement flips in my belly. "I'm sure you'll try."

Jett doesn't merely smile at my snarky reply; he actually laughs like there's a joke—and it's on me. "Out of the water."

"Or?"

"I'll make you suffer."

Thrill rushes through me. It dips low. I feel my sex swell and my womb clench.

He won't actually hurt me. I know him well enough to know that. I've heard the whispers about who and what he is in bed.

"I already am. I'm giving up my work, my life, and my fiancé for a week. And I'm stuck with you."

He rubs his palms together like they burn. "I'm going to count to five. If I have to come in after you, I'll end our arrangement. You can go home. I'll take my forty million and disappear. Your call."

Damn it. I pushed him. I don't think too hard, but he clearly wants some show of obedience. He wants proof I'm still choosing to be here. And he wants to know this week won't be a constant tug-of-war. I can't promise that. But I also can't risk calling his bluff.

With a sigh, I wade back to the steps and slowly ascend. My shoulders break the surface of the pool, then my breasts, my hips, my thighs. Water clings and drips as I meet his gaze and make my way across the deck to him, one swaying step at a time.

Possessive hunger blazes in his dark eyes. He wants me. Just to fuck...or for something more? I can't tell, but it's obvious he craves every inch of skin he sees. He's not even trying to hide it.

Less than two feet from him, I bow my head. Mostly because I can't stand the triumph on his face...but I've also heard the expectations he has of his lovers. I've wondered so many times if the whispers are true.

"There were three parts of my command," he points out.

You will strip. And you will kneel. Then you will wait for me.

I shiver. "I remember."

"Are you cold?"

"No."

I can almost feel his smile. "You're finally naked. Part two now, please."

My head rebels against this, but something far lower flutters with thrill. What does that say about me?

"If I don't?" I ask.

"I won't keep fighting you. And I refuse to spend the next

seven days threatening you, Whitney. You agreed to my terms and you got in my car. If you can't comply with these exceedingly simple commands, I'll turn around and leave. I doubt our paths will cross again."

He's right. I haven't seen Jett Dean, except in tabloid rags, since that summer all the promise between us burned away in a fiery blaze of betrayal.

I nibble my bottom lip.

Tick-tock. In my head, I hear time ticking away. I said yes in the bar because my only other choice is far less palatable.

Now I just have to find the courage to surrender to the man I've considered both my first love and my enemy since sixteen.

I swallow, steel myself, then kneel at his feet. The hard concrete beneath my knees presses unforgivingly into my skin. I'm still dripping, and the hot wind blows. Nothing about this is comfortable. But I don't move as Jett scrutinizes me. I feel every second of his stare.

He grabs my left hand. "Take it off."

My engagement ring.

I nod. It's always been a bit tight. At times, I would have sworn the diamond-encrusted band wrapped around my finger was somehow strangling me.

"What will you do with it?"

"Keep it with your clothing for the next seven days. At the end of that time, if you want to return to him, slip it back on." He shrugs. "I won't stop you."

I don't entirely believe he'll let me off that easily. Or is that wishful thinking? "Then why not let me wear it? Wouldn't the reminder that you're temporarily screwing my fiancé out of his bride-to-be give you a thrill?"

"No." His black eyes flash as he snatches my clothes from the table and into his grip. "I said naked. I meant naked. That means *everything* goes."

I've asked myself a hundred times why Jett wants me for the next week. Certainly, if he was going to bail Vance out, the arrangement could have been done through lawyers, brokers, and bankers. Instead, he came to *me* with this indecent proposal. From the moment I read his note, I could only think of two possible reasons why he would contact me directly. First, he could be eager to humiliate me. I've known all along that he'd likely want to repay me for the ignominy he suffered that summer. I'm sure he's even thought a time or two that I'm partially to blame. The second—and much slimmer—possibility is that he's never forgotten me and he now wants all the pleasure stolen from him that summer.

Still, I don't hesitate another moment. I simply slide the rock off my finger. "Does that please you"—I hold it out to him —"Sir?"

In the middle of pocketing the jewelry with a scowl, Jett freezes. "Yes. You've heard the gossip, I take it."

"I have." I want to ask if it's true, but I don't.

He rests his palm on my crown and threads his fingers through my hair before closing them under the elastic band holding my loose bun in place, tugging until I meet his gaze. "Everything goes, Whitney."

"It's just a ponytail holder," I argue.

"It's in my way."

As if his words settle the matter, he plucks the round elastic band from my hair deftly but inexorably. The skeins come tumbling down past my shoulders, clinging to my back, and curling in at my waist.

As he pockets my elastic band, heat flares in his inky eyes. "Wait here. Don't move."

Command rings in his voice. I don't dare cross him, even when he pivots around, turning his back on me utterly, and stalks back inside the house once more.

My knees ache, and the wind grazes my damp nipples again. Still, I don't move, partly because I fear he'll leave if I do…and partly because I'm desperate to know what he'll do if I don't.

So I'm alone with the night and my thoughts. With my regrets and worries.

He's going to realize the truth quickly. Then what will you say? What defense can you possibly muster?

The voice in my head is right, but I don't have any answers except the obvious. Jett Dean will know very quickly that I never got over him.

On the one hand, I want the truth between us because I'm dying to know if the knowledge will make a difference. On the other hand, once he realizes…I'll be so vulnerable it's terrifying.

It only takes him a minute to reappear. My clothes are gone, but he's slung a fluffy white robe over one thick arm.

His eyes are full of approval. "Excellent. I half expected to find you'd disobeyed me and retreated to some other corner of the house."

"No."

He holds out his hand to me. I hate the way I tremble as I take it and he helps me to my feet. "Smart. Hold your arms out at your sides."

I do, and he slides the robe around me, then belts it at my waist. "Until nine o'clock next Saturday night, you will not wear anything I don't provide. Is that clear?"

"Yes."

Jett sends me a quelling stare. "You know what I am. Respond properly."

"Yes, Sir."

He pockets my elastic band, then tucks my hand in his. "Come with me."

I don't say a word as I trail behind him and into the house. He locks the French doors behind us and leads me through the interior, all the way back to the grand foyer. The hamper and the clear shoebox are still sitting, open and waiting. I see he's tossed the garments I came in on the hall table. My engagement ring sparkles in the shadows beside the heap of my clothes. Then he releases my hand, gestures to the receptacles, and steps back.

I have to be the one to tuck my clothes away. It's symbolic. I'm shedding all my outward skin for him and coming to him naked, both literally and figuratively. That's doubly true of my engagement ring.

"I'm waiting," he growls behind me.

I chose to be here. I took a chance.

There's no escape. And once I comply, there's no going back.

Sucking in a steadying breath, I reach for my clothes and toss them into the hamper, then I tuck my shoes into the box, putting the ring inside between them.

"Close them both," he insists.

He's mind-fucking me before he ever fucks me at all. He's making me give up my one barrier between us, to willingly tuck it out of my reach before he commences with debauching me.

It's agonizing. It's awful. It's dirty. And I love the way Jett's mind works.

I do exactly what he says, closing the hamper and settling the lid on the shoebox. Then I turn to him expectantly. "Done."

He gives my effort a cursory glance, then nods and grabs my hand again. "Do you understand?"

The significance of his gesture? Yes. What's to come? Not exactly. We'll have sex, I'm sure. Beyond that...I have no idea what he'll demand for his forty million dollars. But since the price is so steep, I'm sure he won't make anything about this week easy.

"Yes, Sir."

"Very good. Upstairs with you."

He leads me up a slightly curved staircase with an ornate wrought-iron railing. At the top, we reach the landing. His hand at the small of my back guides me to the end of the hall without a word.

My breath catches when I take in the room.

A massive bed dominates the space, topped with soft white cotton and gray velvet. Pillows of all shapes, sizes, and textures are propped against a mirrored headboard and take up half the mattress. Above, a chandelier that's a balance between light-refracting crystals and elemental iron hangs. It's anchored to a ceiling covered in mirrors, too. There are a pair of nightstands flanking the bed and a plush white chair in the corner. A shaggy gray throw rug warms up the milkwashed planks of the floor. There's a cheerful hearth opposite the bed. Open French doors overlook the backyard, blowing gauzy sheers in with the summery breeze.

It's all warm and sensual and so perfect for a romantic seduction.

Except the thick black leather restraints dangling from each corner of the bed.

I can't help it. When I see them, I gasp.

Beside me, Jett smiles and points to an open door tucked into a corner. "Use the restroom."

"I don't need to go." The protest slips out automatically. I'm not trying to be argumentative.

His face tightens as he closes in. "Go now. You won't have another chance to use it for a while."

Because I'll be restrained to his bed. Right.

With a nervous bob of my head, I hustle across the floor and duck inside, turning to shut the door behind me. As I do, I see Jett watching me with an unwavering stare until the second the door clicks shut between us.

Dear God, what am I doing?

I flip on the overhead lights and blink. I look flushed and aroused, pupils dilated, cheeks rosy. What will happen when he actually kisses me? Touches me? Fucks me?

I swallow. I can't come apart yet. I need to hold myself together until I understand what he's *really* after.

Then, I'll have to make another life-altering decision.

After I peek at my lipstick, I take care of business, flushing the toilet and washing my hands. Then I fluff my hair again and sigh. I'm nervous and I'm wasting time. I just need to face Jett. I need to give him whatever he wants and let the chips fall.

Otherwise, I'll be marrying Michael Crawley in three weeks. And I'll never see Jett again.

Bracing myself, I pull the door open and step into the bedroom for what I'm sure will either be the best or the worst night of my life.

CHAPTER THREE

Jett

When Whitney finally pads out of the bathroom and into the room I brightly lit, I clench my fists for two reasons. First, it stops me from tapping my thigh impatiently. Second, if I don't, I fear I'll grab her, kiss her, throw her on the bed…and forget about every plan I have.

Breathe. Stay calm, logical, and measured.

When I see the stare she cuts my way and the uncertainty in her hazel eyes, it's hard not to comfort her. It's almost impossible to feel nothing.

I have to try. Unemotional was the way she treated me last time I saw her—in court. I do nothing except give her my power if I reveal everything in an unguarded moment.

"Are you ready?"

She shrugs. "As I'll ever be."

Maybe, but she looks nervous. That should please me. After all,

I need the upper hand if I'm going to win my way. But there's that part of me that remembers the innocent girl I once kissed breathless, who so softly and sweetly offered me her innocence. That girl didn't seem capable of giving me a knife in the back, just her heart. The me then would have punched the me now for my plans.

But the me now is more practical.

"Excellent. Take off your robe and hand it to me." I hold my palm up between us.

She hesitates, seems to gather herself to unknot the belt around her small waist, then slides the robe off her shoulders.

I stop breathing as she exposes her naked body to me again. No, I didn't imagine how sexy she looked by the pool, under the moonlight. Her breasts, like the rest of her body, have matured. They are definitely more than a handful now, topped with dusky nipples I can't wait to slide my tongue across. She's built like an hourglass with a small waist that's exaggerated by the lingering shadows in the room. Her hips have widened. They're not a girl's now, but a woman's. She's got long, sleek thighs for someone so petite. But it's her pussy I can't stop staring at. Under the sparse dusting of downy, dark hair, it's puffy and pink.

I know where I'm going to expend most of my effort and energy tonight.

Finally, she drops the robe onto my palm. I toss it on the back of the nearby chair, then sit.

"Come here, Whitney." I point to the floor in front of me.

Wordlessly, she does. I'd think she was calm—except for the pulse beating wildly at her neck. When we're sharing breath and space, she stops.

I nod my approval. "Kneel."

She hesitates, then descends gracefully to her knees, looking up at me with big, beseeching eyes that threaten to turn me inside out.

I can't let her.

Instead, I fist a handful of hair at her crown and jerk her head back before inching forward in my seat, leaving her no doubt I mean to kiss her, rob her thoughts, obliterate her resistance.

Make her beg.

God, how many fantasies have I had about that?

"Jett?" Her voice shakes.

She's incredibly brave to put herself completely in the hands of a wealthy, powerful enemy for a week who has an unending hard-on and an ax to grind. I have to give her points for that. The question is, what am I going to do next? Punish her for the choice she made as a girl that ripped out my heart? Or forget revenge for one night and give in to every urge I've ever had to make her scream my name?

"Whitney."

"What am I doing here? What are you hoping to gain?"

She's always been insightful. Then again, she's smart, poised, assured as only someone raised with money and surrounded by a family full of sharks can be.

"I want what you promised me eight years ago. But since I can't have your virginity"—*or your heart*—"I'll settle for my pound of flesh."

Whitney opens her mouth to say something. I don't want to hear it. I'm done talking.

To silence her, I grab her face with one hand, thumb and fingers pressing in just above her jaw with the right pressure to force her to open for me.

Her lips part. Her pink tongue perches on her upper lip as

her eyes widen with uncertainty. My heart shudders. My skin is on fire. My cock aches.

God, everything about this woman turns me on.

It's my last thought before I swoop down, seize her mouth, and force her lips even farther apart with my own.

The moment our kiss connects, I jerk. She's like a jolt of pure electricity screaming fire through my body, especially when she stills against me…then suddenly softens with a little cry and throws her arms around my neck.

That's all the green light I need.

I release her jaw, clutch my greedy fingers around her nape, and deepen the kiss by sliding my tongue against hers. Fuck, I can't stop myself from inhaling her. She's every bit as delectable as I remember—but more. She's no longer cotton-candy sweet. Now, she's a complex flavor, like a perfectly balanced dessert, some combination of sugary and salty that lingers and makes me crave more.

I fall into her. I lose myself in her. And even though she's killing my good intentions and self-control, I let myself drown in her.

A groan slips free as I pull her up. She clambers onto my lap. I barely have to encourage her to get closer before she melts against me, angling her head to allow me even deeper into her hot, honeyed mouth.

I drop a palm to her hip and use it to drag her closer. With the corner of my brain still functioning, I realize she doesn't kiss like a woman who's been satisfied well and often by her fiancé. She kisses with the desperate hunger of someone lonely, who's been craving touch. I can use that against her, to make her putty in my hands. But I can also use that to pleasure and sate her, to make her sigh with the kind of bliss she's never known. I'll make it my mission to be her fucking best.

And if she still walks away at the end...well, I really will know what she values hasn't changed.

I'm distracted when her fingers find their way under my tie, to the buttons of my dress shirt beneath. She plucks them open and slides her fingers under the fabric, smoothing the tips over my skin. I start sweating. Then she eats at my lips and makes these seductive little sounds that spark an even hotter desire in my gut. She climbs all over my lap, changing positions, trying to get even closer. It's all I can do not to plaster her against me and forget about everything but the pleasure.

As much as I'm curious to see what Whitney would do and how far she would go if I gave her free rein tonight, I can't forfeit that kind of control. I need her under my hand, under my command, under my body.

When she tosses my necktie over my shoulder and attacks the rest of my shirt buttons, I grab her wrists to stay her. "Don't."

Her breathing is labored, her eyes wide and excited. "Jett..."

I shake my head coolly. But my expression is a lie. Inside, I'm thrilled that she's so unabashed and eager. That she's already begging.

"Who's in control?"

She swallows as a frown settles between her brows. Resignation follows.

Her downshift is a kick to the solar plexus. I hate that I put that expression there.

But I have a plan. I need to see it through.

"You," she finally murmurs.

"That's right. I want you on the bed. Flat. Legs spread."

A wariness I don't precisely understand crosses her face. If she was ready and willing to jump on me mere moments ago, why is she hesitating now? Do the restraints scare her? Or do I?

Finally, she collects herself and nods before crawling off my lap, chin held high. Then she climbs on the bed on all fours and rolls to her back, meeting my stare with challenge in her eyes. She settles her feet a few inches apart.

That won't do.

But damn if she doesn't look absolutely beautiful spread across this sumptuous bed all sleek and rosy-cheeked and ripe for fucking.

Never taking my stare from her, I rise to my feet, standing tall, and slowly tear away my tie. My coat follows, then my half-buttoned shirt. I shrug it off my shoulders and stand over her, naked from the waist up.

She might want me to think she's ambivalent or even reluctant to be here. She might try to act as if she's rebellious, hostile, or indifferent. But the way her hungry stare gnaws at me makes a liar out of her. So does her wet pussy.

"What are you going to do?" she asks.

Her voice still shakes...but I don't think that trembling note is powered by fear now.

"Whatever I want. It's my forty million dollars."

The second the words are out of my mouth, Whitney stiffens. Shit, I fucked up. She might be a lot of things, but she isn't a whore. She'd never do anything purely for money. The question is, did she come with me strictly to help Vance? Or because somewhere deep down she wanted to?

That's what I need to figure out. That will tell me how to proceed for the rest of the week.

Her face closes up. "Don't let the money fool you, Jett. You always did whatever you wanted, regardless of anyone else's feelings."

That bullshit insult is an argument starter. She's baiting me, and I refuse to fall into the trap. "I'm not here to talk, Whitney."

"You're here to fuck me." She spits the words like I ought to be ashamed of myself.

"I am." I have to know what's left between us before I burn this bridge for good. "And I think you're here to fuck me, too. Find out what you missed out on all those years ago."

She doesn't answer right away. "Think what you want. You always do."

"I'm done talking." In fact, I'm over this cat-and-mouse game altogether. She's naked, spread across my bed, and open to me. Why are we even talking before I've stripped away her barriers? Once I've made her beg and plead for orgasm, then we'll see what she really wants.

I cup one of her ankles and reposition her leg toward the corner of the bed, then I bend to retrieve the cuff. She's gasping when I buckle her in, sliding my fingers underneath to ensure she still has adequate blood flow.

When I'm satisfied, I reach for her other foot.

She jerks it out of my grasp, biting her lip, "Jett..."

I shake my head. "You've heard the rumors about me. I've given you plenty of proof they're true. So don't act surprised. I won't hurt you, but I want you completely open to me. You agreed to submit to my every whim this week. I'm waiting."

This is normally where I would give my partner a safe word, but Whitney would only use it to escape her mental discomfort. I won't put her in physical peril enough to need to speak at all except a gasping, screaming plea.

In fact, I look forward to it.

"Do you understand?"

"Yes...Sir."

"That's right. Now give me your foot." I hold out my hand. In the other, I've already gathered the cuff.

Whitney stares at me. I sense her fear. And I smell her desire. She's confused and she doesn't understand her reaction.

I simply smile.

Slowly, she slides her free leg in my direction, then places her dainty instep in my palm.

Without any haste at all, I buckle her in and step back. And I stare at the banquet of female spread out before me. My mouth waters.

Since it's wiser for me to keep my pants on—at least for now —I shuck my shoes, then crawl onto the bed, hovering over her. I study her delicate face.

I remember when I thought I'd be the luckiest bastard in the world if I could just call her mine. It's been eight years, two continents, and too many meaningless fucks later. Goddamn it if I don't still think that having her, even just for the week, will make me a lucky bastard.

Whitney looks nervous. "Are you leaving my hands free?"

"For now." Unless she gives me a reason not to.

When she nods, it takes everything inside me not to give in to my urge to soothe and reassure her. Instead, I dip my head and take her mouth in a demanding kiss. Fuck if I don't have the urge to stay at her soft, bee stung lips and feast. There's something so delectable about them. The top bow tempts. The bottom pout lures. How can I not want her?

But there's more—a lot more—I haven't touched in what seems like forever.

"These breasts. Hmm…" The words slip out. I'm so busy staring at her swells and the dark nipples tipping them that I don't even realize I've spoken.

"I've changed since I was sixteen."

"For the better," I murmur as I open my lips to her neck and taste her skin.

She tips her head back and offers me her vulnerable throat. Absently wondering if she understands the unconscious trust she's giving me, I skim my mouth down her flesh, kissing the pounding pulse point at her neck, tonguing the swells of her breasts, and nipping my way to her hard, tempting crests.

I remember her being sensitive…but it was a long time ago, and I was the first man to touch them. Thankfully, when I catch one of her nipples between my thumb and finger and pull, her body tightens. Her breathing stutters.

Fuck, she's still incredibly responsive to my touch. I shouldn't let that arouse me more, but I gorge on the visual feast of her arching and sucking in a sharp breath as sensation hits her. Need flares through me unchecked.

Again, I pluck at her tender peak, gratified by the way she grips the bedding and stares up at me like she wants to control her body…and she can't.

"Do you want me to suck your nipples?"

I pinch her hard tip again, rolling and thumbing it without mercy. She swallows and presses her lips together. "Do what you want. You're going to anyway."

"Answer me." When she doesn't, I plant my knees on either side of her hips and take both nipples in my grip, manipulating them simultaneously. "I can do this all night, Whitney, until you're willing to beg me for relief. If you force me to, how much mercy do you think I'll have?"

She tosses her head back and closes her eyes as if she's trying to shove me out of her reality. But we both know I won't let her.

"None," she pants.

"That's right. Last time I'll ask. Do you want me to suck them?"

"No matter what I say, you'll undo me."

The crying catch in her voice flips more than my libido. "Yes, so you're only prolonging the inevitable."

"I hate you."

That hurts, but I hate myself far more for not being able to fall out of love with her.

Whitney is still pushing, testing. What is she after?

"So you've said." I tug and caress the tips. They harden more as she flushes and writhes in unconscious offering. "But that doesn't change anything, so why not take what you want from me?"

I release her and sit back on my heels, watching and waiting.

Seconds later, her eyes flash open. They're even more dilated than before. A little whimper escapes from her throat. Jesus, how long before I get inside her? How long before I feel—at least for a few precious minutes—like she's *mine*?

"Suck my nipples," she finally gasps. "Hard."

"Please?" I taunt.

She nods. "Please."

"Sir?"

She sighs, then jolts when I pinch the sensitive tips again, this time with more bite. "Please suck my nipples hard, Sir."

"I know that wasn't easy for you, so I'm inclined to comply. This time. But next time you want something, the begging will have to be much sweeter."

"You're a bast—Oh!"

Whitney stops berating me when I suck one of her sweet berry nipples past my lips and take it deep. I slide my tongue over the crest, swirl around it, nip gently, then draw it to the roof of my mouth and pull without mercy.

The sounds she makes are both desperate and animal. When I release the tip into the waiting vise of my fingers, I capture the other orally, alternately soothing and torturing it, too.

She squirms and twists, gasping and fisting the sheets. Unconsciously, she parts her knees wider like she burns for me alone. That sends my desire rocketing.

Fuck, she's going to my head.

"Princess..." I murmur against her glistening nipple before switching back to the first and giving it another suckle and jerk. "More?"

"Yes."

"Am I still a bastard?" I scrape the edge of her nipple with my teeth.

Her gasp sharpens. "Yes."

"Do you want me to give you an orgasm?"

Whitney's eyes slide shut as she thrashes under me, her voice and neck straining. "Yes. Please."

"Sir?"

"Yes, Sir." Even through clenched teeth, she sounds breathy. "Please give me an orgasm."

"Better," I praise, but I don't make any move to grant her wish, just keep at her nipples.

I'm enjoying my power over her, I confess. Not simply because I'm tormenting her—though that's part of it—but because she's so close to admitting she wants me, too.

I've fucking fantasized about this more times than I can count.

"Will you?" she pants.

"Probably. Eventually." I shrug. "We'll see."

Her keening cry of demand is music to my ears. As I curl my tongue around her nipples again, one after the other, I let the agonized sound crawl into my brain and fill the space between my ears so I can replay it over and over.

"Jett..." she whines. "Don't do this."

"Do what?"

"Deny me." She lifts herself enough to stare at me, eyes soft and pleading. "Deny us."

Her reply makes my heart stop. I feel my resolve wavering.

I'm so close to stripping her bare. Not physically. Getting her naked was easy. But emotionally, in the way I need her most? Yes.

God knows I'm ridiculously hard for her. But it's more—far more. I'm fast coming to a fork in the road. What I choose next may dictate my entire future.

Revenge or Whitney?

She reaches for me, pressing her palm between my legs. I have to bite back a groan. But it gets ten times worse when she curls her fingers over my aching ridge.

Why the hell didn't I take my pants off?

"Don't play games," she implores.

"We're already playing, princess." Brow raised, I grab her wrist and tug it away. "Right now, I have the power. The more you insist, the less likely I am to give in to you."

"Because you're vindictive?"

If I'm being honest? Because I'm susceptible. Because the minute I hear her scream for me, I'll probably rush to get inside her—heedless of the consequences—and meld myself with her. Because when she's near me, I have to fight for every ounce of my control.

Because I know if I don't have my head screwed on straight, my brain won't be the organ making my decisions.

"Think what you want. I only care what you do. Put your hands on the mattress, palms flat. Now."

She scowls. "Who are you? Not the Jett I used to know."

It's a valid question I'd rather avoid answering. "Ah, guilt. Sadly for you, it's a trite, ineffective response. Surrender, Whitney."

"No."

"Then we're both wasting our time. I'll call Valentin. He'll drive you home. Our deal will be null and void." It takes Herculean effort to back off the bed and stare at her, naked, restrained, and aroused, knowing our lust—and probably more—is mutual.

I can't force her to give herself to me; I know that. Just like I know I'm probably wasting my time. But Whitney is the single biggest regret of my life. Giving up now is the last thing I want. She's leaving me little choice.

Because she's moved on.

Biting back a sigh of defeat, I turn away.

"Wait." She grapples to her knees and grabs my arms. "Don't go."

As much as I'd like to sprawl her across the bed once more, urge her flat on her back, and tunnel inside her, I can't—at least not yet. "Your pride has no place in our bed."

"And yours does?"

"No." If I want to keep her, I not only have to meet her halfway, I have to give her the kind of reassurance she needs. "If you haven't figured it out, you're here because I want you more than forty million dollars. You're here because you haunt me. Because there hasn't been a day gone by that I haven't ached for you. Did you need to hear that?"

She blinks as if my blunt honesty startles her. "Oh."

"And unless you've completely changed, I know you too well to believe you came here simply for the money."

"I didn't." Her whisper is so soft I can barely hear it.

"Did you come to fight me?"

She shakes her head. "I fight you because you terrify me."

That deflates what's left of my righteous anger. "I said I'd never hurt you and I meant it."

"That's not what I'm afraid of." She lets out a trembling breath.

Now I understand. Whether she likes it or not, she never purged me from her heart. "Be honest. Why did you come?"

Whitney softly blushes. "I think you know."

I finally do. And I'm so fucking relieved.

Fighting a smile, I climb on the bed again, forcing her to her back and hovering over her as she lies bare and vulnerable. "I won't lie to you. I plan to exploit your feelings."

"I know."

And *that's* why she's terrified. But it's a two-way street. Maybe she hasn't figured that out yet, but I doubt it will take her long to realize that no matter how many years have passed, how far I've traveled, or how many hookups I've used to forget her—it was all futile.

"I understand."

"And?"

"Let's try this again. Do you want me to kiss you?"

"Yes."

"Do you want me to touch you?"

"Yes."

"Do you want me to give you an orgasm?"

An emphatic nod accompanies her response. "Yes."

"Are you going to surrender your body and will to me?" When she hesitates, I press. "Lie to me if you want. But don't lie to yourself. If you don't give in now, won't you spend the rest of your life wondering what if?"

Her eyes slide shut, as if she can't quite face the answer. She looks like she's fighting tears. "Yes."

Finally, she's being really, truly honest.

"Then offer me your mouth."

She closes her eyes, curls her arms around my neck, and lifts her face to me.

I've waited nearly three thousand empty days—and nights—for this. If my life depended on resisting her invitation, I'd be utterly doomed.

With a rush of breath, I bend and slant my mouth over hers, losing myself in the sweet spice of her kiss, in the whispered promise of what might be between us.

When I finally back away long moments later, my heart pounds. My breaths are unsteady. "Good. Offer me your nipples."

It takes her a minute to puzzle out my meaning. Impatience nearly rubs me raw before she finally cups her breasts and lifts them to me.

"That's it. Who do those belong to?"

"You."

"Yes." I fall to my elbows like a man kneeling at the altar of her nipples and take a stiff one in my mouth again, sucking, laving, tasting, tonguing, and tugging until Whitney claws at me, urgent for more.

With a final lingering lick, I back away from the hard, glossy crests. "Now offer me your pussy."

Her breath catches. She bites her lip as she meets my desperate stare—then flares her knees wider and raises her hips to me.

Oh, thank god, yes.

I can't even pretend to be removed or restrained. I drag my lips down her body without any teasing or finesse, with one imperative in mind.

To get her on my tongue.

Quickly, I wriggle down until I wedge my shoulders between her spread legs and lie on my belly, inches away from the succulent nirvana. She's swollen and rosy and pouting. When I part her with my thumbs and my gaze devours her most secret flesh, it's as if I've opened a whole new world. Yes, I've seen a woman's pussy before—lots of them. But *this* is the one I've craved for too many years.

My nostrils flare. I bite back a groan of need at her hard red clit silently begging me.

"Jett?"

"Do you tingle?"

"Yes."

"Do you ache?"

"Yes. I want you so much I'm cramping and throbbing. Please..."

If she's switched tactics and decided to use my own weakness against me, she couldn't have played her hand any better.

"Fuck." I grip her thighs and lift her to my hungry mouth, needing to worship her.

It seems like I've waited millions of barren minutes, but I'm finally pressing my greedy mouth against her pussy and dragging my tongue through her folds. Then I suck in her clit, drawing on her, pulling and working her stiff bud until she moans.

The second her spicy-sweet flavor coats my relentless tongue and registers in my brain, all my grand plans to toy with her half the night, then make her pant and scratch her way through a savage blow job before I ramp her up again—only to refuse her relief until she begs me to fuck her however I like—all fall away.

Now I only want her to surrender to the pleasure I give her... and the possibilities of our future.

"Come for me, princess." I swipe my way through her furrow again, drowning in her taste, desperate for her. "Come."

Under me, she grips my hair until my scalp tingles, gyrating and mewling, thighs parting more, cunt turning sweeter. "Jett…"

"Do it." I suck on her clit, tongue working the stone-hard tip. "Give in."

"Jett," she gasps, the sound rising another octave as her spine twists and her head falls back.

I glance up at the mirror above. The beautiful agony on her face undoes me. "Goddamn it, you're mine."

Relentlessly, methodically, I dismantle her with my touch. I'm never going to get enough of her. Ever. Hell, I'm still half-dressed, and I feel dangerously close to coming undone.

Digging my fingers into her, I press her even more tightly against my mouth and work a pair of fingers into her fist-tight sheath, already tightening and clamping around my digits.

"Jett!"

I barely have a moment to relish the heady broken cry of her surrender before her entire body jolts and shudders. Then she's clutching, clasping, and breaking around me. Her nipples peak. Hips to cheeks, her body flushes a splashing rosy red. Her lips part, and her eyes flash open.

Our gazes meet in the overhead mirror.

I've got her. We both know it.

I ride her to the end of her orgasm, until she's struggling to recover her breath and her body turns limp, until she sighs sweetly and reaches for me.

I can't wait another second to claim her.

Goddamn it, I hope she's the last woman I have sex with for the rest of my life.

I crawl up her sated body, taking advantage of her spread legs to fit my hips between them. With one hand, I cup her nape and fit our mouths together, reveling in the fact that her kiss no longer holds fight, just sweet, open acceptance. I work my free hand between us, make quick work of my zipper, then get my cock free just enough to align my crest to her still-pulsing opening.

Her eyes flutter open. Worry crosses her face. "Jett."

I grit my teeth. I've waited eight years to be inside her, but I can tell she needs to say something. "What, princess?"

"Gently." She swallows. "Please."

Everything—both the anger and the passion—is so hot between us. And all this time, she's fought back. Now she's asking me for mercy. Why? If I wasn't so rabid to be inside her, I might be able to apply two brain cells toward finding the answer. But I can't.

"All right, I will. For you."

"Thank you." She smooths her hands up my arms, then cups my shoulders as she spreads her legs wider in silent invitation.

Jesus, how am I supposed to maintain any self-control?

I'm still trying to figure that out when I sink the head of my cock inside her.

And I run into resistance.

Whitney isn't merely tight, she's... I freeze. No. That's not possible. There's no way.

"Jett?"

"You're not..." But she seemingly is. "Still a...virgin?"

Slowly, she bites her lips. Then she nods.

Holy shit.

And yet, she came here to spend a week with me, knowing full well I intended to fuck her?

That small, problem-solving corner of my brain is working overtime to figure out if that means what I desperately want it to. The rest of me has shoved off all mental protective gear.

I'm dying to be her first.

If I play this right, will I be her only?

At that notion, my heart thuds and thumps. Waiting doesn't feel like an option. Sure, we could talk, but I don't want to give her any reason—or opportunity—to get away.

"Oh, princess." I nudge inside her, incrementally working my way through her slick clasp until I lunge deep into her with one softly insistent thrust. Then I rock my hips forward, pressing as far into her as I can. "Now you're mine."

Finally.

If she has any objection, I don't want to hear it in this moment. At least this once, I want the fuck of my fantasies, where I'm deep inside her, bareback, for the first time, and she's with me, thrust for thrust, cry for cry, all the way to the scratching, hoarse-throated, cataclysmic end.

She lets out a soft, shuddering breath, her eyes sliding half shut.

"Right?" I prompt as I withdraw from her so slowly I groan the question.

"Yes," she breathes.

"Tell me who you belong to."

She doesn't hesitate. "You, Jett."

"That's right." I glide back in and set up a rhythm I suspect will unravel her restraint. "How long have you belonged to me?"

Her lashes flutter open. I see tears swimming there. "Always."

That's it. With one trembling admission, there's no denying she still owns my heart, too.

I dreamed up this scheme to indulge my every desperate desire, to show her what she was missing, to purge her from my system once and for all.

She's felled me instead. Now, my only hope is to fight to keep her.

"And I'm yours." I press inside her again, deeper, deeper, where she's so fucking sweet. Where I want to live. Where no man has been.

"Jett..."

I hear the pleading in her voice. My thrusts pick up speed, and she rewards me with a gasp. Her fingers curl around my shoulders. Her thighs do the same to my hips, as if she can hold me against her and keep me here forever.

I sink deeper into Whitney. Not literally, since I'm already as deep into her as I can be. But figuratively, viscerally, emotionally. And I drown. If she's how I'm going to die, I'll go gratefully and willingly, ending my time on earth a happy man.

I grip her hip with one hand and grab a fistful of her hair with the other, forcing her to look right into my eyes. "I never stopped loving you."

The tears spill over. "I never stopped, either."

Oh, fuck. That sends my heart careening.

I bang into her again, each stroke faster and more insistent than the last. "You really love me?"

Whitney hesitates, then she nods and lets out a low moan full of need and pain.

"Answer me," I bark. "Say it."

"I love you," she cries out, holding me tighter, pressing kisses across my shoulder and into my neck.

That's all I needed to hear. "I love you, too."

And I'm never letting her go. I don't give two fucks who she's engaged to, she's marrying me. And I hope like hell she's not on birth control because I'm going to do my level best to get a ring on her finger and a baby in her belly this week.

She's never getting away again.

"Oh, princess." I shuttle into her faster, faster. My lungs work like a bellows.

"Jett!" she screams seconds before her pussy grips me like a vise, her body jerks, and a low groan tears from her throat.

I keep pace, doing my best to prolong her pleasure, but I can't hold out anymore, not physically. Orgasm is going to run me over, ruin me, and it will be the most delicious end ever.

But I can't resist emotionally, either. Whitney has my heart; she always has. I've been lying to myself about that for far too long.

As she grips me tighter, the wave crests over me, too. I'm suspended in a pleasure unlike anything I've ever felt. Lights flash behind my eyes. There's a buzzing in my brain. Every part of me from top to toe pings electric. I clutch Whitney and let go, pouring every bit of myself into her.

There's no denying it now; I'm hers forever.

And there's no going back.

Clinging and kissing, we come down together, hearts racing, breaths harsh. As if by some unspoken understanding, our gazes connect.

We both know everything has changed.

"Did that really just happen?" she whispers. "Did you tell me you love me?"

A little grin flits at my mouth. Honestly, I haven't smiled much in years, and it feels good. "Yeah. As we were having sex."

"And it's true?"

"One-hundred percent."

Her lips curl up, brightening her expression. "Wow."

"Wow."

"So that's what all the fuss is about?"

"You could say that." Honestly, what we shared was so extra, it was news to me, too. "You waited for me?"

"To have sex?" She nods. "I had opportunities. There was always someone I tried to date or some flirty dude at a party.

But I never wanted any of them. No one made me feel like you."

"No one has ever made me feel like you, either." When I'm with Whitney, I'm centered. I'm myself. I'm whole. I never got married or serious with another woman because I couldn't replicate the feeling I had when I was with her. "How were you going to marry some guy you'd never slept with? And didn't love?"

She grimaces. "It was a business deal. You know Vance needs money. My fiancé needs plausible cover because he's in love with someone he can't have. He doesn't have any more interest in me than I have in him."

As far as I'm concerned, he's her former fiancé, but I'll get to that. "So he never touched you?"

"Except to give me a peck for some engagement photos, no."

Then I won't have to kill him. Good.

Reluctantly, I pull free of Whitney's body. When she winces and shifts, I'm instantly concerned. "You okay, princess? Sore?"

"A little, but I'm fine."

That's a relief because I'm going to want her again soon.

For now, I lie back and nestle her body against mine. She rests her head on my chest as if curling up against me is the most natural thing in the world. I caress my way down her back with a light stroke.

I sigh. We may be in love, but that doesn't make the road in front of us easy. Eventually, I'll have to be unflinchingly honest.

But first, it's time to talk about the elephant in the room. "What about your brother?"

We can't let him stand between us.

She nibbles on her bottom lip for a long minute. "Being here with you has made me realize I can't sacrifice my future for him. He has to stop being impulsive and getting himself into stupid situations. And if he doesn't, I have to stop bailing him out. He regrets everything eventually, but by then…it's usually too late. I think that's especially true of you."

I have mixed feelings about that. I'll deal with those later. "Tell me how he got in his current financial situation."

How much does she know?

"A few months ago in Vegas, he was drunk, and some asshole—he won't tell me who—dared him to bet a stupid amount of money on a hand of poker. It just happened to coincide with the value of his company. I think it was a setup. But like an idiot, Vance did it. And he lost. I was crushed because I went to school to help save and grow this company. Now it's… gone." She looks so distressed that I soothe her with a caress.

"Has he signed it over to this guy yet?"

"He refused to. I told him that's not the way the world works, that he needs to grow up and face his consequences. His answer was to call Michael, someone we've known personally and professionally for a few years. Vance begged him for a bailout. Michael agreed if I would marry him. Not that anyone asked me." She shakes her head. "I've had cold feet from day one. I've wracked my brain to figure out how I can help my brother without sacrificing my future. Then the courier knocked on my door with your note."

"And you met me in the bar."

Her face softens as she nods. "Not for the money. I couldn't not see you. I had to know…"

"If there was anything left between us? I needed to know, too." And it's time to come clean. "That's why I created a failsafe plan…or so I thought."

She props her chin on my chest with a frown. "What plan?"

"I'm the, um…asshole who got Vance drunk in Vegas and encouraged him to bet the value of his business. I knew he'd lose. For me, it was a win-win. Either I'd get back the company I lost or—more importantly—I could use the debt as leverage to see you again. So I'd finally know if I was still as much in love with you as I suspected. If so, I planned to forgive Vance's debt if you'd marry me."

Whitney gapes. "Why go to all that trouble? Why not just reach out and talk to me?"

"And risk rejection? My fragile male ego…" I roll my eyes at my foolishness. I'm usually so fearless, especially in business, but knowing Whitney would likely rebuff me terrified me. "I thought you'd tell me to go fuck myself. My negotiations with Vance seemed to be going great—until he suddenly stopped responding to my calls. Then I heard whispers that he'd arranged your marriage to someone else for money. So I came straight to you."

"And you sent me the note?"

I nod. "One way or another, I was going to get my hands on you, princess."

She giggles. "I'd say you got a lot more on me than your hands."

"Thank god. My sanity couldn't stand not touching you anymore." I tuck a strand of dark hair behind her ear. "I think I've always known you were it for me."

"You always have been for me." She caresses my chest. "I'm sorry I took my brother's side after that summer. He told me you gave him a few pointers on the app but that he'd actually written it. According to him, you only said you'd created it to impress me. I didn't believe him, but my dad pressured me to support Vance. If I didn't, he threatened to have you arrested for touching me. I had no reason to doubt him."

As she should have. Vance no doubt spilled my "transgression" to their father to use as leverage. The old man never liked me much and probably saw my lust as leverage to use against me.

"I get it. You were so young, and they didn't leave you much choice."

"I've spent a lot of time hoping I didn't hurt you too much." She bit her lip. "But I did."

There's no point in lying. Whitney crushed me. "You didn't mean to."

I see that now.

"I didn't," she rushes to agree. "Even the thought of it killed me. I suspected you hated me for my decision."

"I'll be honest. I tried."

"I know. After that summer, you flaunted all your hookups like you were trying to throw them in my face."

When I think back on the way I acted out after the rift between Vance and me, I'm ashamed. "I kept hoping like hell you would say or do something because I mattered to you."

"You did, and I was hurt."

Her quiet admission makes me feel like an ass. "I'm sorry. I wish I could take all that back. The whole rift seems stupid in hindsight. But I was young and dumb, too."

"What happens next, Jett?"

"What do you want?"

Whitney stretches up and plants a soft kiss on my lips. "I think you know. I want you. I want everything we should have had all along."

"I do, too." My heart starts pounding again for a totally different reason as I reach across the mattress and manage to fumble my way into the top drawer of the nightstand. I pull out an oblong box. "This is yours, no matter what happens between us."

She scrambles to sit up as she takes the box in hand. I'd

protest the loss of her warm skin against mine, but the view of her breasts is spectacular. And I want to see her face.

She lifts the lid and plucks up the letter inside. As she scans it, her lips slowly part until she's gaping. "You're giving me forty-nine percent of Vance's company? I don't understand."

"You've more than earned it. I know you've been trying to advise him for years. I know you're the reason the business has survived at all. He hasn't been a good financial steward, but he's occasionally listened to you. Now I'm giving you real power."

"How is this possible? You don't own—"

"I do. While Valentin drove you here, I called your brother again. It took some doing, but we finally hashed out a deal. So I own the company. Well, fifty-one percent as of now."

"What are you going to do with your part? And with Vance out of the organization, who will run it?"

"That depends on you. If you want the job, it's yours."

"Really?" Her hazel eyes widen. "You'd let me?"

"I can't think of anyone I'd trust more." I kiss her.

"Oh, my god. This is like a dream come true," she squeals. "I went to school for a position like this, so I could handle the responsibility and grow the organization. I mean, it's still relatively small, but it has so much potential and—"

"It absolutely does." Her enthusiasm makes me smile. "You've got some amazing tech developers on staff, too."

She nods. "I'm so excited about new products and updates we have in the works."

"So you're saying yes to the job?"

"Yes!"

"Excellent. I know you'll be great. And I'll be your supportive but silent partner."

Suddenly, her expression falls. "Is that all?"

I smile. "What do you think?"

Whitney looks nervous to jinx herself, but she draws up her courage. "You want to marry me."

"I do." Again, I reach into the drawer at my side and pluck out a smaller, plush square box. "And you want to marry me."

"You intend to ask me?"

Her hint of mischief makes me laugh as I sit up and pull her into my lap with a long, sweet kiss. Then I open the box to reveal a simple, elegant engagement ring that looked like it belonged on her finger the moment I saw it earlier this evening.

"I love you, Whitney. We've both made mistakes and wish we could take back some things we said and did, but all roads led us back to each other. I can't imagine the journey ahead with anyone but you. Will you do me the honor of marrying me?"

"Yes!" As I slip the ring on her finger, she cuddles closer and kisses my face. "I love you, too. Oh, my god, now we're official!"

Her excitement makes me laugh. I haven't felt this light in years. "We are."

"Why do I get the feeling this may be one of the last times you ask rather than demand anything of me?" She grins.

"You know me well."

"Yes, Sir." She presses her lips to mine once more.

From there, I take over, already hard for her again. I'm so aroused by the idea of making love to Whitney when she's wearing nothing but my engagement ring, I can't wait to get inside her.

Rolling her onto her back, I follow her to the mattress, fasten my mouth over hers, then ease inside her swollen, sweltering pussy with a groan.

Beneath me, she gasps and digs her nails into my shoulders. "Jett!"

"Yes, princess. Want more?"

"Yes. God, yes…" She wraps her legs around me. "But fair warning… I might need help with my job."

She wants to talk about work now? "If you need sex to do it right, I'm your man."

Whitney curls her arms around my neck and rocks with me. "I just might. But then I'll need time off. Unless we start being safer, we're going to have some babies."

Ah, she's figured out the other part of my plan—and she seems blessedly happy with it. "I sure hope so. I want you pregnant now."

"Me, too."

After we share bodies, passion, and our love, we fall into a heap, arms around each other. I cup Whitney's still-rosy cheek. "You happy?"

"Since you've made my every dream come true? Yes, Sir."

EPILOGUE

Sunshine Coast Bed-and-Breakfast, Maui
A month later…

Whitney

Dreams really do come true! Jett has found nearly every moment of every day to prove that to me. He's worshipped me. He's kept every promise. And he's made me fall even more in love with him.

Finally—after a lot of rushed planning and tricky arrangements—we're standing on the beach at the most beautiful bed-and-breakfast in Maui, just about to say "I do."

"Are you ready?" my brother asks, looking surprisingly dapper in a pale blue suit.

"Beyond. Thanks for being here and walking me down the aisle."

"I wouldn't have missed this for the world. I just want you to be happy." He kisses my temple and offers me his arm, then he escorts me toward the palms swaying gently in the sunset and my waiting groom.

I'm about to burst with joy.

For the last month, my brother has been a lot different—quiet and contemplative. He started seeing a therapist. He admitted he's had a drinking problem since college. He started apologizing to me a lot for things he's done over the years. And he's doing his best to mend fences with Jett. My husband-to-be, bless him, has been receptive. Guarded, yes. That's Jett, and Vance burned him horribly once. But they're working it out. Jett reached out with an olive branch—and offered to let Vance stay on as head of development. My brother reciprocated by inviting Jett to join an upcoming fantasy football league. It's progress. That's all I can ask for now.

The inn's owner, Keeley Reed, sings me down the aisle with her lilting, melodic voice. The gentle music carries on the breeze as my bare feet pad over the white runner, flanked by tiki torches leading me under a trio of arches seemingly braided out of twigs and bright pink flowers. At the end, we stop under a tall white awning framed by soft, draped swaths of white gauze. In front of an altar adorned by a floral garland stands the officiant.

And Jett, waiting for me.

He looks so handsome in tan pants, a billowy white shirt, and a navy jacket. As I approach, his smile turns brilliant. He has eyes only for me. Which is perfect because my heart is only for him.

Vance gives me away. Jett sticks out his hand. My heart threatens to turn over with love.

My brother shakes it, then pulls my fiancé in for a bro hug. "There's no one I trust more than you to make my sister happy."

There are a hundred caustic things Jett could say, but he

doesn't. "I love Whitney. I always have. Thank you for your blessing."

With a final nod, Vance makes his way to my side of the small crowd, consisting mostly of friends and a few cousins, and sits next to my mom. Jett's side of the aisle is filled with his father and new stepmom, Iris. The woman's daughter, Calla, recently married Jett's older brother, Quint. They announced last night that they're expecting a baby in the spring. His sister Ivy came with her husband Derrick. The younger sister, Lacey, is a wild child. I don't know if she'll ever settle down. It will take quite a man to tame her.

"Dearly beloved…" the officiant begins the ceremony.

My heart takes flight while Jett and I look into each other's eyes. The sun dips down the vivid, cloudless sky toward the horizon as we commit our lives together. Then Jett slips a wedding band on my finger, and I slide one on his. We seal our bond with a lingering kiss.

Finally, we're man and wife.

"Are you happy, Mrs. Dean?" my husband asks as we make our way down the aisle, toward our reception. He's all smiles.

If he's happy now, just wait. I'm going to give him the best wedding present ever.

I send him a glance so full of love and joy. I never imagined my life could be so sweet. "I am. How about you…Daddy?"

As we reach the threshold to the inn, he stops in his tracks and searches my face. "Are you saying…"

"I'm pregnant. I found out this morning."

He embraces me with a hearty laugh. "Well, that's one thing I can cross off my honeymoon honey-do list."

"You were making it your mission to knock me up?"

"Hell yeah." He kisses me. "I've missed out on eight years of being with you. I need to accelerate the timetable to start this family. Besides, you're going to be hot all round and pregnant."

I beam a smile at him. "You always seem to think I'm hot."

"Because you are. But it's more. You're smart. You're funny and understanding. And you're my other half. I love you, princess."

"If you had told me that afternoon you summoned me to the hotel bar that we'd wind up deliriously in love, married, and pregnant within a month, I would have called you crazy."

"I'm sure. But I arranged everything because I hoped all those things would happen." He swallows. "I would have done anything to be with you."

"I know." I cup his beloved face. "So instead of calling you my enemy that day, I guess I should have called you a genius."

"Oh, I like that," he kids. "A visionary genius, even. Maybe add brilliant to that, too."

I laugh. "Now you're laying it on thick. I don't need to inflate your ego any more."

He leans in for a long, slow kiss. "It's not my ego you're inflating, wife."

When he rocks into me, I giggle. "I can tell."

My husband takes my hand and leads me inside, facing me in all sincerity. "Can I do anything to make you happier? Nothing is more important to me."

When Jett looks at me like he could blissfully stare at me forever as he brushes a gentle thumb over my lower lip, I melt. "Why?"

"You've made me ecstatic every day since you came back into my life. I'm going to make you happy for the next seventy years."

"That's a deal I can get behind. I love you, too."

Then we seal our forever with a kiss.

Want another bad boy who seduces a stranger into becoming his? Meet Maxon Reed.

I hired her to distract my enemy. Now I'm determined to have her for my own.

MORE THAN WANT YOU
More Than Words, Book 1
by Shayla Black
(available in eBook, print, and audio)

I'm Maxon Reed—real estate mogul, shark, asshole. If a deal isn't high profile and big money, I pass. Now that I've found the property of a lifetime, I'm jumping. But one tenacious bastard stands between me and success—my brother. I'll need one hell of a devious ploy to distract cynical Griff. Then fate drops a luscious redhead in my lap who's just his type.

Sassy Keeley Kent accepts my challenge to learn how to become Griff's perfect girlfriend. But somewhere between the makeover and the witty conversation, I'm having trouble resisting her. The quirky dreamer is everything I usually don't tolerate. But she's beyond charming. I more than want her; I'm desperate to own her. I'm not even sure how drastic I'm willing to get to make her mine—but I'm about to find out.

EXCERPT

"Look, Keeley. I like you. And I want you. I'm not good at

talking or relationships or letting people know me. I'm good in bed. Can that be enough for tonight?"

I find myself holding my breath. If she says no, I have no fucking idea what I'm going to do. After a handful of probing questions, I already feel oddly raw. I rub at a sore spot along my breastbone.

"Yes. Sorry. I have a terrible tendency to be nosy. You're interesting…and I really am not a fan of sleeping with strangers. But I think I know who you are, Maxon… Damn it. What's your last name?" She gives an embarrassed little laugh. "Oh, that sounds brilliant."

Her joke totally lightens the mood. I need that. "Reed."

"Well, Maxon Reed, are you going to stand there all night or kiss me in the moonlight?"

The second I get the green light, my tolerance for banter flies out the window. I become a hunter who's just settled on his prey of choice, and I'm looking forward to fully sating my hunger.

I don't bother with words. Instead, I take the bottle from her hands and set it in the sand beside us. Then I fuse my stare to hers and tilt her head where I can most effectively devour her. Her eyes flash with something. Excitement, yes. Apprehension. That surprises me but no denying what I see. And hope… Maybe she's not the only one feeling unexpected things.

Then she parts those bee-stung lips again, and all my thoughts dissolve.

I lower my head and kiss her with a groan.

Fuck if her lips aren't every bit as soft as I imagined. She opens to me, presses against me, wrapping her arms around my neck like she needs to touch me every bit as much as I'm dying to have her bare against me. I'm sizzling, my senses reeling. I'm actually dizzy the longer I kiss her, but I urge her lips apart with my own and plunge inside.

I'm lost.

She's so sweet. Not like a Snickers, which I love. Her flavor is more refined, and the pleasure I get from her is like savoring a good red wine paired with a lush dark chocolate. Then she kisses me back with a sensual sway of her tongue and an indrawn breath that lets me know I'm getting to her, too.

I'm drowning.

My hands are suddenly in her hair, tugging until she gives me full access to every part of her mouth. I go in even deeper as if I'm trying to own her all at once. I haven't had the sort of drought she has, but I can't imagine another five minutes without being inside her, taking full possession of her. It's chemical. It's electric. I don't know how the fuck to describe it because I've never felt anything quite like this.

Suddenly, she breaks away from my kiss, nipping at my lips like a kitten, before tilting her head back completely. Her lips aren't on mine anymore.

I'm dying.

Not kissing her is unacceptable. Then…I see the arch of her delicate throat. She's exposed one of the most vulnerable parts of herself to me. Her ivory flesh glows in the moonlight. Even in the pale gleam, I see the flush staining her skin. I hear the catch of her breathy inhalations. I feel the hard beads of her nipples against my chest. How can I absorb her all at once, experience every facet of her in a single moment? I can't, but I'm damn impatient to try.

"Maxon?" She sounds shaky, uncertain.

I rush to set her at ease. "Why are you so fucking beautiful?"

"If you think I am, I'm glad. Are you going to touch me now?"

She sounds breathless and anxious. Does she imagine for a second that I might say no?

Are you craving a nail-biting, alpha-male seduces good-girl story? Meet One-Mile and Brea.

He's ruthless. She's off-limits. But he's just met his one weakness… Now nothing will stop him from making her his.

WICKED AS SIN
One-Mile and Brea, Part One
Wicked & Devoted, Book 1
by Shayla Black
(available in eBook, print, and audio)

Pierce "One-Mile" Walker has always kept his heart under wraps and his head behind his sniper's scope. Nothing about buttoned-up Brea Bell should appeal to him. But after a single glance at the pretty preacher's daughter, he doesn't care that his past is less than shiny, that he gets paid to end lives…or that she's his teammate's woman. He'll do whatever it takes to steal her heart.

Brea has always been a dutiful daughter and a good girl… until she meets the dangerous warrior. He's everything she shouldn't want, especially after her best friend introduces her to his fellow operative as his girlfriend—to protect her from Pierce. But he's a forbidden temptation she's finding impossible to resist.

Then fate strikes, forcing Brea to beg Pierce to help solve a crisis. But his skills come at a price. When her innocent flirtations run headlong into his obsession, they cross the line into a passion so fiery she can't say no. Soon, his past rears its head and a vendetta calls his name in a mission gone horribly wrong.

Will he survive to fight his way back to the woman who claimed his soul?

EXCERPT

Finally, he had her cornered. He intended to tear down every last damn obstacle between him and Brea Bell.

Right now.

For months, she'd succumbed to fears, buried her head in the sand, even lied. He'd tried to be understanding and patient. He'd put her first, backed away, given her space, been the good guy.

Fuck that. Today, she would see the real him.

One-Mile Walker slammed the door of his truck and turned all his focus on the modest white cottage with its vintage blue door. As he marched up the long concrete driveway, his heart pounded. He had a nasty idea how Brea's father would respond when he explained why he'd come. The man would slam the door in his face; no maybe about that. After all, he was the bad boy from a broken home who had defiled Reverend Bell's perfect daughter with unholy glee.

But One-Mile refused to let Brea go again. He'd make her father listen…somehow. Since punching the guy in the face was out of the question, he'd have to quell his brute-force instinct to fight dirty and instead employ polish, tact, and charm—all the qualities he possessed zero of.

Fuck. This was going to be a shit show.

Still, One-Mile refused to give up. He'd known uphill battles his whole life. What was one more?

Through the front window, he spotted the soft doe eyes that had haunted him since last summer. Though Brea was talking to an elderly couple, the moment she saw him approach her porch, her amber eyes went wide with shock.

Determination gripped One-Mile and squeezed his chest. By damned, she was going to listen, too.

He wasn't leaving without making her his.

As he mounted the first step toward her door, his cell phone rang. He would have ignored it if it hadn't been for two critical facts: His job often entailed saving the world as people knew it, and this particular chime he only heard when one of the men he respected most in this fucked-up world needed him during the grimmest of emergencies.

Of all the lousy timing…

He yanked the device from his pocket. "Walker here. Colonel?"

"Yeah."

Colonel Caleb Edgington was a retired, highly decorated military officer and a tough son of a bitch. One thing he wasn't prone to was drama, so that single foreboding syllable told One-Mile that whatever had prompted this call was dire.

He didn't bother with small talk, even though it had been months since they'd spoken, and he wondered how the man was enjoying both his fifties and his new wife, but they'd catch up later. Now, they had no time to waste.

"What can I do for you?" Since he owed Caleb a million times over, whatever the man needed One-Mile would make happen.

Caleb's sons might be his bosses these days…but as far as One-Mile was concerned, the jury was still out on that trio. Speaking of which, why wasn't Caleb calling those badasses?

One-Mile could only think of one answer. It was hardly comforting.

"Or should I just ask who I need to kill?"

A feminine gasp sent his gaze jerking to Brea, who now stood in the doorway, her rosy bow of a mouth gaping open in a perfect little O. She'd heard that. *Goddamn it to hell.* Yeah, she knew perfectly well what he was. But he'd managed to shock her repeatedly over the last six months.

"I'm not sure yet." Caleb sounded cautious in his ear. "I'm going to text you an address. Can you meet me there in fifteen minutes?"

For months, he'd been anticipating this exact moment with Brea. "Any chance it can wait an hour?"

"No. Every moment is critical."

Since Caleb would never say such things lightly, One-Mile didn't see that he had an option. "On my way."

He ended the call and pocketed the phone as he climbed onto the porch and gave Brea his full attention. He had so little time with her, but he'd damn sure get his point across before he went.

She stepped outside and shut the door behind her, swallowing nervously as she cast a furtive glance over her shoulder, through the big picture window. Was she hoping her father didn't see them?

"Pierce." Her whisper sounded closer to a hiss. "What are you doing here?"

He hated when anyone else used his given name, but Brea could call him whatever the hell she wanted as long as she let him in her life.

He peered down at her, considering how to answer. He'd had grand plans to lay his cards out on the table and do whatever he had to—talk, coax, hustle, schmooze—until she and her father both came around to his way of thinking. Now he only had time to cut to the chase. "You know what I want, pretty girl. I'm here for you. And when I come back, I won't take no for an answer."

LET'S GET TO KNOW EACH OTHER!

ABOUT ME:

Shayla Black is the *New York Times* and *USA Today* bestselling author of roughly eighty novels. For twenty years, she's written contemporary, erotic, paranormal, and historical romances via traditional, independent, foreign, and audio publishers. Her books have sold millions of copies and been published in a dozen languages.

Raised an only child, Shayla occupied herself with lots of daydreaming, much to the chagrin of her teachers. In college, she found her love for reading and realized that she could have a career publishing the stories spinning in her imagination. Though she graduated with a degree in Marketing/Advertising and embarked on a stint in corporate America to pay the bills, she abandoned all that to be with her characters full-time.

Shayla currently lives in North Texas with her wonderfully supportive husband and daughter, as well as two spoiled tabbies. In her "free" time, she enjoys reality TV, reading, and listening to an eclectic blend of music.

Tell me more about YOU by connecting with me via the links below.

Text Alerts

To receive sale and new release alerts to your phone, text SHAYLA to 24587.

Website http://shaylablack.com

Reading order, Book Boyfriend sorter, FAQs, excerpts, audio clips, and more!

VIP Reader Newsletter http://shayla.link/nwsltr
Exclusive content, new release alerts, cover reveals, free books!
Facebook Book Beauties Chat Group http://shayla.link/FBChat
Interact with me! Wine Wednesday LIVE video weekly. Fun, community, and chatter.
Facebook Author Page http://shayla.link/FBPage
News, teasers, announcements, weekly romance release lists...
BookBub http://shayla.link/BookBub
Be the first to learn about my sales!
Instagram https://instagram.com/ShaylaBlack/
See what I'm up to in pictures!
Goodreads http://shayla.link/goodreads
Keep track of your reads and mark my next book TBR so you don't forget!
Pinterest http://shayla.link/Pinterest
Juicy teasers and other fun about your fave Shayla Black books!
YouTube http://shayla.link/youtube
Book trailers, videos, and more coming...

If you enjoyed this book, please review/recommend it. That means the world to me!

OTHER BOOKS BY SHAYLA BLACK

CONTEMPORARY ROMANCE

MORE THAN WORDS

More Than Want You

More Than Need You

More Than Love You

More Than Crave You

More Than Tempt You

More Than Pleasure You (novella)

Coming Soon:

More Than Dare You (July 28, 2020)

More Than Protect You (novella) (TBD)

WICKED & DEVOTED

Wicked As Sin

Wicked Ever After

THE WICKED LOVERS (Complete Series)

Wicked Ties

Decadent

Delicious

Surrender to Me

Belong to Me

Wicked to Love (novella)

Mine to Hold

Wicked All the Way (novella)

Ours to Love

Wicked All Night (novella)

Forever Wicked (novella)

Theirs to Cherish

His to Take

Pure Wicked (novella)

Wicked for You

Falling in Deeper

Dirty Wicked (novella)

A Very Wicked Christmas (short)

Holding on Tighter

THE DEVOTED LOVERS (Complete Series)

Devoted to Pleasure

Devoted to Wicked (novella)

Devoted to Love

THE PERFECT GENTLEMEN (Complete Series)
(by Shayla Black and Lexi Blake)

Scandal Never Sleeps

Seduction in Session

Big Easy Temptation

Smoke and Sin

At the Pleasure of the President

MASTERS OF MÉNAGE
(by Shayla Black and Lexi Blake)

Their Virgin Captive

Their Virgin's Secret

Their Virgin Concubine

Their Virgin Princess

Their Virgin Hostage

Their Virgin Secretary

Their Virgin Mistress

Coming Soon:

Their Virgin Bride (TBD)

DOMS OF HER LIFE

(by Shayla Black, Jenna Jacob, and Isabella LaPearl)

Raine Falling Collection (Complete)

One Dom To Love

The Young And The Submissive

The Bold and The Dominant

The Edge of Dominance

Heavenly Rising Collection

The Choice

The Chase

Coming Soon:

The Commitment (Late 2020/Early 2021)

FORBIDDEN CONFESSIONS (Sexy Shorts)

Seducing the Innocent

Seducing the Bride

Seducing the Stranger

Seducing the Enemy